Blue Murder at the Pink Parrot

BLUE MURDER AT THE PINK PARROT

RUTH RAMSDEN

A Cutting Edge Press Paperback

Published in 2012 by Cutting Edge Press

www.CuttingEdgePress.co.uk

Printed and bound by CPI Group (UK) Ltd, Croydon, CR0 4YY

TPB ISBN: 978-1-908122-24-7
E-PUB ISBN: 978-1-908122-25-4

Dedication

For My Mother & MacTeague
She Knows

And for Mark
My Love & Inspiration

XIII

DEATH

This card signifies radical change, an end to something.
The death of an old way, the birth of the new.
It can also indicate death in the physical sense,
transformation and loss.

CHAPTER ONE

The round mirror propped on my dressing table has the Goat of Mendes etched into its surface. Baphomet The Beast, a simple fertility symbol, has always had a bad press from hysterical Christians. Or from Hammer Horror movies, when Charles Gray in a white frock summons him up near the end to steal the show in a puff of smoke. The mirror was a present from my minder, a biker who could probably scare seven shades of shit out of Satan. The latest talent show pop tart recently claimed she liked nothing better than snorting her way through bags of coke while staring at herself in a mirror. It must be nice to like yourself that much. But then, you'd have to be a complete imbecile, like the clothes horse in question. And I, of course, have much better things to do.

My morning-after face stared into the glass. Baby blues, crazed with carmine, shadowed with burnt umber. Skin, flake white and Indian yellow. Titian red hair in loose coils past bare shoulders. The eyes were glazed, the rest was impasto. I moved back. Everything else seemed present and correct – arms, legs, bosom all in flesh tint. A fine, fulsome figure liberally decorated with piercings and tattoos, an end-of-season line in middle aged Goth horror. Not that I go in for the terrible music and funeral couture associated with the adolescent un-dead. I'm far too much of a hippy. A shower of white powder on the glass dotted my queasy reflection. I stared at it for a moment, listening to the prickly hum in my head. Then I leaned forward and licked it off, the wet smear across the surface blurring the image while the chemicals numbed my gums. So much for pop culture.

Weak sunlight dribbled through the closed curtains. Empty wraps littered various surfaces. There was a half full bottle of flat champagne and something anonymous and sticky on the nightstand. Clothes were strewn across the floor, one of my best tarot decks lay in a haphazard Celtic cross by the end of the bed. My left nipple had lipstick smeared around it and there was a large bruise on my right thigh. I can see into the future, sometimes, but I doubt I'll ever know what the hell happened last night. I sighed and began a complicated attempt to dress.

For the record I am a twice divorced single white female and I own a small house overlooking the sea in the once fashionable Sussex resort of Dean's Bay. Long past its prime, the town now staggers towards its pebbled beaches in drunken architectural confusion, spewing up a tatty pier and neglected lidos amongst the belligerent shrieking of amusement arcades and seagulls. The town itself has no real centre. It trails aimlessly away from the rotten stump of a Norman castle on the West cliff and eventually runs out of steam in a scattering of pensionable, post war bungalows near a bowling green and a carpet warehouse. But where I perch, here on the East cliff, among antiques shops and some half-arsed optimism, normal service hasn't been resumed for quite some time and it's quiet and slightly bohemian. I live with far too many books and a careful collection of cheap furniture. And I don't really need too much else but the view.

I was trained as an artist, in case you're pondering the earlier rather OTT metaphors. Abstract figure work. Carefully glazed compositions in mixed media poured with gut-wrenching honesty from the tenderest depths of my soul onto pale, fresh linen. Attaching myself to a cross would be simpler, even with that whole last nail problem. Obviously I don't sell too well. Despite training at St Martin's, a fascination for actual painting ruled me out of the Brit Art boom that took off around me. My soul continues to bleed in my spare time, while the bitterness of my artistic rejection is channelled into something more visceral and lucrative.

I am a professional dominatrix with a side order of the occult. I offer tarot readings, palmistry, spells on the waxing and waning moon and a path to spiritual fulfilment through discipline. It's certainly more profitable than painting and a guilty pleasure rather than a dirty chore. Sex isn't on the menu but gentlemen callers (and very occasionally ladies – I'm not bi-curious, I'm bi-satisfied) can receive pain and humiliation at my hands for a suitable consideration. Normally between £80 and £150 an hour. You takes your choice and you pays your money. It sorts out the bills and the satisfying smack of leather on flesh makes those long winter evenings just fly by. It's true, I tend to afford temptation and indulgence a little more than most but then I plan to be re-incarnated as a cat and live the high life, guilt free, at someone else's expense.

Before I could make any attempt at gathering my wits and setting the karma right this particular morning, the telephone next to my bed burst into life, an irritating and persistent squeak that reminded me I needed to change the ring tone. Still struggling into clothes, I picked it up.

"Hello?" This was going to be difficult. Consonant, vowel, consonant, consonant, vowel. A strange sediment had settled over my soft palate.

"Hello. Yes. Could I speak to, er, JJ? JJ Franklin?" The voice on the end of the phone sounded crisply portentous. I sighed and closed my eyes. People often have difficulty with my name as I only use my initials. It's a short, sad story. There isn't anything precious about it, I just couldn't bear the shrieks of hilarity that would accompany every introduction. I wasn't about to enlighten the caller.

"Yes. Speaking."

"Ah, I'm sorry to bother you, *Miss* Franklin, is it? I'm Detective Constable Stevens, with the Sussex police. It's concerning a Mr. Ben Hammond. Do you know Mr. Hammond?"

Synapses twitched. Painfully. *Ben?*

"Er … yes." I said, cautiously.

"Could we come and speak to you about Mr. Hammond?"

"Yes. Of course. Er …is there anything the matter? I mean, is Ben in trouble?" I sat down heavily on the bed. The wreckage of the previous night began to dance around me as the sprinkle on my tongue gave me a little prod. I found I was clutching the duvet to my chest like a startled spinster. There were few things I wanted to be reminded of less this morning than Ben Hammond.

"I'm afraid Mr Hammond is dead, Miss Franklin …"

The policeman carried on speaking and I ostensibly carried on listening, listening to the sudden pounding in my head and the ringing in my ears. I was conscious of the weight of the telephone in my hand and I felt very hot.

"Er …sorry?" I said.

"Can we have your address, Miss Franklin, we need to come and speak to you." I gave it to them and was told the mass and majesty of the law would be arriving in an hour. I vaguely heard the clatter of the telephone as I hung up, thought about it for all of about two seconds, then bolted for the toilet.

After I'd finished throwing up, I sat on the bathroom floor for a while, letting the cool of the uneven lino assist my composure. Barfing before breakfast is a great way to wake you up but it doesn't do very much for your lady poise. Breathing deeply and slowly, I leaned against the wall and tried to scrape together some sensible recollection. The night's revels closed in on me in a series of pantomime crime scenes, becoming more and more debauched and less and less coherent. And through it all, a recurring leit motif, I could see Ben's silly pouting face as he stalked around my living room in distended purple panties and fishnet stockings with little silver bows on them.

Let me be clear, Ben Hammond was not a client. He could have been a lover. He could have been a friend. He could have been many things to many people but as long as I wasn't the victim of some massive practical joke, all that seemed to have ended and it didn't seem quite real.

We had met the previous week in one of the many new bars springing up along the seafront, replacing derelict kiss-me-quick tat with upmarket alcoholism. The clientele are offered sofas and café tables, the continental suavity of their table umbrellas and Tapas menus marred by hooting traffic and late night brawls. Big boned and good looking, Ben had thick, dark hair and dark, heavy lidded eyes that sparkled wickedly. He ran his own successful publishing company and seemed intelligent and eloquent. We had hit it off and made a date.

Was I too eager? Or just incautious? Surely no-one can buy cocktails with that much reckless ostentation, no-one can be that charming, without there being something amiss in the sincerity department. I sat clutching caffeine and toast, waiting for the county's finest and remembered the moment when it all went wrong...

"I'd say you're pretty kinky." We were sitting in my living room, having a quick drink (or so I thought), prior to tackling the milles feuilles at a French restaurant I'd been circling hopefully. He leaned towards me along the sofa and raised his eyebrows, "Are you kinky then?" He was certainly an attractive man but I'd felt my heart sink a little. Something about this easy assumption felt oppressive, even if he was right.

"Oh, yes." I said lightly.

"What are you into then?"

"How long have you got?" I smiled a little wearily and began to pour myself another glass of champagne (a nice Ruinart. If anyone's foolish enough to ask my poison, I really don't come in that cheap). I had no intention of revealing my super-hero alter ego on this slight acquaintance, although I began to wonder if my cape was showing.

"What do you think of trannies?" he asked. I laughed again.

"I was married to one." I said truthfully, although I tried not to think of my last husband's rather tiresome femme persona. And, to be fair to Tom, his predilection for false eyelashes and sturdy corsetry had been the least of our problems.

Ben looked at me steadily for a moment, resting his hands rather quaintly on his knees. I noticed how small and slender his fingers were.

"Hang on a second," he said, "I've got to get something from the car."

Ten minutes later and slightly out of breath, his eyes shining with excitement and anticipation, he asked:

"Well? What do you think?"

"Very nice."

What could I say? Ben liked to stuff what passed for his reproductive equipment into women's knickers. And not Winter Cotton mummy's keks, but lacy thongs and those strips of satin masquerading as underwear that aren't even designed to cover the female pudenda, never mind protect it from the Great British Weather. Bras and basques and stockings, too, all of this he dragged into my living room crammed into an airline hold-all the size and weight of a baby elephant. I've got nothing against the transgendered community, a broad and largely harmless church, but Ben quickly unveiled himself as a needy, panty-wearing sissy boy, displaying the full range of pouting, cringing, mincing mannerisms – with a distressing compulsion to masturbate continuously. You know that moment, don't you? Every woman knows it, when the ideal solution is a cheery goodnight, a little air kiss and the swiftest exit possible but you're stuck waaay past the point where that's feasible. Guh.

Conversation had dwindled. Like many hard working, driven men who crave submission to powerful women, it had to be entirely on his terms. And I realised sadly, as he paraded round in stilettos and stockings, that Ben was literally nothing more than a narcissistic wanker. The hope of intriguing romantic entanglement died once again as Ben explained, his eyes half closed, blissfully self satisfied, the details of his rape fantasies.

I indulged him for several hours in ways I prefer not to think about.

We parted just before ten that evening and he pressed his mobile phone number on to me with the furtive, grateful look of a double agent who has found a safe house. With a fake smile, I waved him into the night time drizzle.

Anger.

Then rage.

He'd obviously played me and I'd fallen for it. Dirty, cheap, nasty. And my own stupid fault. The terrible sense of déjà vu as he waved his pert little bottom in front of me. I should have told him then and there "OK Benny boy, you've had five hours of my time. Pull your knickers up and give me the cash." But I didn't and the joke was on me. Ha, fucking ha. At least my clients don't expect sex.

I fled the house with its debris of empty bottles and suspended disbelief and found my way into town and the lager-soaked oblivion of a night club, somewhat appropriately called 'Festers'. There, I'd bumped into an old girlfriend and, away from the crush, on a pair of slightly sticky sofas, I'd given her an increasingly drunken blow-by-blow account of the evening.

"And do you know what pisses me off most?" I howled above some shrieking teens and the dance floor noise upstairs. Gina was laughing, rocking and clapping her hands like an excited toddler. Beautiful, vain, childish and devious, she and I were poles apart. She had all the sinister prettiness of a porcelain doll: button nose, bee stung lips and lush lashes. Her chronic short-sightedness made her frail blue eyes strangely vacant and as mesmerising as a snake's. Kissing her was like eating white chocolate drenched in Sambuca. She's more of a sex addict than I'll ever be, which is saying something. I lose count of how many current boyfriends or girlfriends she has. As she doesn't seem to be able to distinguish between sex and sentiment: she picks up fiancés the way most people pick up junk mail. Sixteen engagements at the last count, you'd think her reputation would be a warning to all shipping but she still lures sailors onto the rocks with mind-numbing regularity. I'd been flavour of the month for about six weeks a few Summers back. She was like a tornado, a whirlwind of devotion, emotion and lust and I had to detach her gently. She got over it in exactly three days. Gina's so full on, I'm one of only a select group of former paramours who still speaks to her. I like to believe I've taught her some life lessons but that's probably wishful thinking. We still treat ourselves to one another occasionally – there's nothing wrong with having a sweet tooth – probably because I'm one of her few exes who actually understands the term 'fuck buddy'. For a genuine nymphomaniac, she's surprisingly vanilla. She's also one of the few women I know who takes Viagra.

"What pisses me off … he has smaller feet than me, and smaller hands and better fucking legs!"

She clapped her hands and laughed again,

"Is he rich?"

"Oh yes. Loaded. Would you believe he actually drives an Aston Martin?" I knew this because he had shown it to me with pride, a crouching silver monster with big wheels and cream upholstery. He had pressed the key fob to release the central locking with the flourish of a man challenging his rival to a duel and then given me a guided tour of the sound system and Sat. Nav. Who says men don't understand women?

"Go get him then."

"Bugger off! Why do men have this tragic compulsion to stuff their knackers into tiny lingerie. They look sad enough on me – it looks gross on him."

"For a small consideration – "

"For a large consideration."

"Well for a *large* consideration then."

But I wasn't going to argue the point. I didn't want to explain to Gina how I'd harboured some momentary excitement and how I'd allowed it to carry me through a morning of optimistic house cleaning. Yes. It had been *that* sad. Only for Ben to find me a useful stooge. I was spared revealing the depth of my hubris as Gina swept her long blonde hair back from her face and gave me an Uma Thurman look.

"I'm going to powder my nose." She said waving her tiny handbag in front of me, "Coming?" Oh, dear. Oh, deary dear…

Things got worse after that. Well no, actually, they got better first, a lot better. This is the problem with drugs. They may eventually drive you insane but they make you happy first. Whom the Gods seek to destroy…they first give ganja. Not that madness mattered to me as I began to start a riot with the night, dancing, laughing, loving it and reacquainting myself with Gina's gorgeous anatomy in the pine fresh confines of the ladies lavatory. There was more intake and uptake of various kinds, chemical, herbal and distilled. Stable recollection began to break down. By the time the fresh air greeted us in wasted, orgasmic triumph I had literally taken leave of my senses.

The rest of the night was a jumble. The mnemonic equivalent of listening to Stockhausen in a tractor factory. Crashes, honks and squeaks, inexplicable silences and occasional moments of clarity. I seemed to have gone to a party. I remember the thump of music and a confusion of faces. A woman in a red dress. Her nails scarlet as her fingers made an elaborate show of opening a cellophane bag and pouring the contents on to a table. *My* fingers leaving sweaty marks on the surface next to virgin snow as she performed an elegant slalom with her credit card.

Well. That had been the final straw. The chemicals hit the top of my skull with the careful subtlety of an elephant gun being discharged into a bucket of porridge. The last thing I remember was the first few bars of 'Firestarter' and someone saying "Shit." quite calmly.

The woman constable called herself 'Mandy' and wore a tidy uniform that was far too big for her. She was accompanied by a large sandy-haired detective with lugubrious eyes and a startling ginger moustache. In the cold light of day they looked reassuringly solid. I half listened to their introductions and solemn apologies as they carefully seated themselves. I faffed around for a bit making more tea, remembering with a little lurch, the illegal mess in the bedroom, hoping I looked as guilt-free as possible. With a little pre-amble to write down the formalities, they got down to business.

"I understand you saw Mr. Hammond last night, Miss Franklin?" The detective's basso profundo miraculously immerged with barely a tremble in the moustache. It was a good job I wasn't tripping or I'd have become fixated.

"Yes. Yes, I did. I met him a week or so ago and we agreed to meet last night. There was nothing to show, I mean, I don't know how...why?" That's right, Jay, gibber...

"It's too early to say for sure, Miss Franklin but it appears he died of a drugs overdose. Do you know if he took drugs?"

For some reason I was taken aback and must have shown it. The more I thought about it, the more stupid it seemed.

"No. Certainly not when he was here and he didn't mention anything like that. I'm quite surprised, actually."

"Why is that, Miss Franklin?"

God, how could I say? Ben had seemed, well, kinky for sure but he hadn't even joined me in more than a half glass of bubbly. While I'd been guzzling away, he'd smilingly demurred. I tried to explain,

"He wasn't even drinking. He was a big man but he was fit and healthy and he just seemed…well, straight, I suppose. But, honestly, I wouldn't really know." I petered out.

"I see." The moustache nodded and made a note.

At their bidding, I told them about the rest of our date. What we'd talked about and how he'd seemed, still trying to puzzle out how I could have missed Ben as a drug user. I glossed over some of the more grisly details of the evening's entertainment. I didn't see how it could matter and it didn't feel right somehow. I doubted very much that his panty wearing peccadillo was something he broadcast among his nearest and dearest.

"So he left you about ten?" Mandy smiled at me.

"Yes. Maybe a little before."

"What did you do then?" the moustache asked without looking up from his notes.

"Me?" that horrid lurch was back in my stomach, "Er – I went out." I thought again about the wreckage in my bedroom.

"Straight out?"

"Yes. I went into town. To a club – Festers, in the parade. I met a friend there, Gina Harrison." I gave them her address and phone number, "You said it was an overdose..?"

"Possibly," said the detective with rumbling detachment, "What time did you leave the nightclub?"

"Er…" I glanced from one to the other of them. The moustache looked up expectantly but it wasn't helpful. "I…I'm sorry I really can't remember. That's not much good is it?" I added, "I'd had quite a few drinks by then and I wasn't paying attention to the time. It was probably around two in the morning, the club kicks out round then." Mandy raised her eyebrows, "I'm sure Gina could tell you. We left together." The sandy haired detective let out his breath with a hiss like a deflating tyre.

"So then you came home?" he raised a sardonic eyebrow and I wondered if he was deliberately taking the piss.

"No. I went to a party. I think. No, well, I'm sure I did. I passed out." I felt myself blushing and began to get self righteously angry. I don't usually have to justify my occasional lapses to anyone but myself and as it's only me, I can always find suitable excuses. And I haven't blushed in a *very* long time. "I'm not too sure where it was. I'm not trying to be difficult," I glared at him unwisely, "I know it doesn't look very elegant..."

"I'm not here to judge what looks elegant, Miss Franklin," DI Moustache rumbled, becoming dangerously bland, "We're just trying to establish your movements last night."

"My movements? Why? I thought – "

"We are treating Ben Hammond's death as suspicious, Miss Franklin – "

"Oh."

" – and nothing you've told us so far alters that. You don't know where the party was?"

"No."

" So how did you get home?"

"Some bloke gave me a lift. I was half-asleep. I just staggered out, got in the car and he drove me home. I got back about six this morning." Mandy smiled again encouragingly but a kind of creeping guilt was rendering me less than poised. I think the shock was starting to sink in.

"Have you been in Mr. Hammond's car?" she asked, "He had a rather flash Aston Martin."

"Yes," I said, feeling on surer ground, "At least, I sat in the passenger seat while he pressed buttons and showed off all the gadgets. He seems – seemed – very proud of it. I'm not really into cars but it *was* impressive, I suppose."

"Well, it doesn't look too impressive now." The detective said in a rare show of partiality, "Someone's poured paint stripper all over it and smashed the windows. The seats are ripped and the keys are missing."

"Christ!" I just looked at the both of them, stunned. Mandy said from out of the depths of her collar:

"Do you know anyone who might have wished to hurt Mr. Hammond? Or vandalize his car?"

"Christ no! I've literally only met him twice! We talked about art and music, just getting to know you stuff, you know."

"I see." The moustache bristled, clearly unsatisfied. "As far as we know, Miss Franklin, you were the last person to see him alive – " I gawped, " –so anything you can tell us would be helpful."

They waited for me to fill the silence but I couldn't. Not with anything 'helpful'. I made noises about our small talk, his good taste, his intelligence and sanity, trying to knock down, in memoriam, the tower I'd rather selfishly erected to anger and humiliation. After they'd gone, vaguely threatening to return should anything else occur to them, I wondered how I'd misjudged him. Death levels all things to the utterly mundane, including our assessment of character. Was he sick? Suicidal? Careless? None of those seemed to fit the man who'd been so greedily relishing life's little treats the previous evening. 'Suspicious' hardly seemed the best word to cover the end of Ben Hammond. 'Startling' was only marginally better...

The ripe light of early autumn was starting to fade and I watched the big sky in silence for a while, hoping that someone might flip a switch and illuminate my little corner of it. But I just felt exhausted and confused so I retreated back to bed and managed to doze for a while, in spite of the persistent sizzling in my head. Soon I really wished I were awake again. Caught between day and night, I became trapped in a vivid courtroom drama, standing trial for a crime I couldn't quite recall. I couldn't breathe. I had no voice, I couldn't move. The verdict was in. Some of the jury avoided my eyes while some glared triumphantly, ecstatic that they had chosen my fate. The usher was dressed in scarlet. Scarlet nails, scarlet shoes ...The black cap was ready. An ominous murmur from the crowd grew until someone shouted "Hang the bitch!"

"Silence!" roared the Judge and banged his gavel repeatedly.

I sat up abruptly, among shadows. My heart was thumping but my head was astonishingly clear. Guilt assailed me again. What the hell had I done last night? As the dream shredded itself into silliness, I heard footsteps retreating firmly down the alley in front of my house. Maybe I'd been jolted awake by nothing more sinister than a knock on my front door.

I made my way downstairs in the dark, rubbing the cricks out of my neck and flung open the door. But my visitor, if there had been one, had vanished. I stared out at the breakers on the shore below and felt the freshening wind. Traces of the day trailed away along the horizon in bruised purples and angry black clouds blanked the stars into inky vacancy. Selene, my muse was waxing gibbous in the uneasy gloom and the lights of the town's small fishing fleet were starting to bob and twinkle. Autumn had been mellow but the mean wind reminded me that nothing lasts forever and Winter smelled very cold indeed. I shivered. Turning in the hall, I trod barefoot on something sharp enough to make me yelp. After cursing and hopping about inelegantly for a bit, I switched on the hall light. There, sprawled like a dead spider amongst the litter of takeaway leaflets, was a set of keys. The novelty key fob read 'Bad Motherfucker' in sticky cherry red. I recognized them, I knew the car keys belonged to an Aston Martin. They were Ben's. What. The. Fuck. I felt my scalp tingle. Next to them on the mat was a large brown envelope. There was no address but someone had drawn a small smiley face on the shiny surface in fine black marker pen.

Puzzled and alarmed I took these anonymous gifts back into my lounge. I placed the keys carefully on my coffee table, strangely shy of handling them and opened the envelope. Inside was a clear cellophane bag and I stared in shock at the contents. Glossy 4" X 6" photographs, about half a dozen of them, pin sharp, breathing guilt and excited corruption.

The pictures were full-colour graphic and not too well framed, they looked as though they'd been taken on the sly. Surprised, I recognised parts of the bar of a local fetish club called the Pink Parrot. But this looked way too extreme for public play. A private party? And a spy with a camera? I felt my heart beat faster, as I also recognized the leading player in these grisly little tableaux. All the photographs featured Paul Fuller, a notorious local villain and I could see they were not for public consumption. One saw him doubled over a flogging bench, leg spreaders opening him wide, blood running from the scourge marks on his legs and backside. A tall trannie whose face was largely hidden by a daft feather mask was grinning manically, holding Fuller's hair while shoving in a dildo that would have given the most acquiescent queen pause for thought. "Pig" was written in lipstick across Fuller's forehead. Another pose had him on his knees, gagged, his genitals made grotesquely large and purple by a tortuous binding. Then... a sweaty spit roast and he was on his knees again, sucking on a strap on while the trannie penetrated him, this time using the ample gift nature had provided.

The general public, raised on the harmless silliness of John Inman and Larry Grayson, used to think of homosexuality as effeminate. Well, you couldn't get any more *manly* than this heavily muscled, cheaply tattooed sprawl of hairy, glistening flesh. This didn't look, in the fetish scene mantra, 'safe, sane and consensual'. This looked like torture. But Fuller's grinning compliance, not to mention his all too obvious arousal was a study in gluttony. Ronnie and Reggie Kray were both gay, one out of the closet, one in, so the love that dare not speak its name could still be hissed through gritted teeth into pillows by East End hard men, as long as they were hard enough. But even so, just calling Ronnie Kray "a fat old poof" still counted as famous last words for George Cornell and this looked like material for dangerous blackmail.

I shuffled the prints, trying to slow my breathing down. Still and all, who the hell would be stupid enough to try blackmailing Paul Fuller? His name was enough to stop any conversation stone dead and his appearance on any scene enough to make most people regret leaving the house. If a fraction of the horror stories were true then he was ruthless as well as artful, with a single minded devotion to his own best interests. He forgot nothing, forgave nobody. Like a small, angry dog, his tenacity in pursuing grievances was legendary. Short men had to fight twice as hard to prevail and after decades of swift, decisive violence there was no-one left to taunt him.

Fuller was floating trailer trash, brought up on a barge, where the effluent from the Medway washed up shopping trolleys and dead cars on the mudflats of Chatham. His family were from a long line of Romany horse traders who'd dealt in motors, drugs and weapons. Their son had surpassed their wildest expectations. He prospered ostensibly through his real estate businesses while the authorities tried in vain to bring him to book. Pictured outside various courtrooms, after yet another inexplicable acquittal, he always looked like he was starring in a burlesque production of Guys and Dolls. Sharply suited with far too much gold jewellery, his mirthless shark's grin, grey ponytail and purple-tinted glasses gave him a kind of ominous jauntiness. I was sure few people imagined his leisure activities involved giving talks to the W.I.

But this wasn't leisure. This was serious. Serious shit. And I was in it.

I sat in the gloom for a while, one glowing table lamp illuminating Ben's keys but very little else. I put the photographs away, right away, in the drawer of my desk where they lay in the dark like a nasty secret. Several times my hand hovered over the telephone, impelled to do the right thing and call the Police. And several times the nasty secret in the drawer whispered obscenities in the shadows. Was Ben somehow involved with Fuller? Maybe Fuller had actually killed him. But why? And why the hell should any of it involve *me*?

Aware the moon was waxing and things were only likely to get worse, I unwrapped my main tarot deck and laid out a quick three spread. This deck is darkly erotic with Beardsley style illustrations – tangled bodies, soft kisses, shining leather, hard eyes. They are a powerful fetish and I designed them myself. Although I practice many of the arcane arts, I'm actually not that superstitious. I don't need to be. But it's useful sometimes to get a little help making decisions and I find it strangely calming. One, two, three. "As I do will, it shall be done". On my left, the Ten of Swords, more eviscerating and terminal than 'Death'. At the centre, The Moon, blowing madness, spells and confusion at me. And on my right, twinkling with celestial serenity was The Star. Hope. I made a decision and picked up the phone.

I

THE MAGICIAN

This indicates great skill and slight of hand,
perhaps revelations to come and positive ideas.
The Magician can also be a man of charisma and magnetism.

CHAPTER TWO

The Pink Parrot isn't a London Fetish Club, but what it lacks in cache, it makes up for in suburban enthusiasm. It opens its doors to pervs on Friday and Saturday and doubles as a regular bar for the rest of the week, occasionally hosting lap-dancing parties for bored commuters. Rather oddly sited on a hill between an impoverished branch of Marks and Spencer and a 24 hour locksmith, it faces the world with all the grimy allure of a working men's club. But the drinks are cheap and the people are friendly. Although Tony, the owner, is vivaciously gay, his appalling sense of style sadly lets the side down and there is more sleaze than chic about the Parrot. It wasn't his style I was interested in tonight though. I planned to ask a few discreet questions about his booking policies.

OK, in the end, I hadn't bothered the police. The less rootling around in my drawers they did the better. That was going to be plan B. Instead, I'd called Gina. She is always happy to party, being virtually indestructible. She might also be able to help me fill in some of last night's blanks and help me wipe away the creeping illusion that I might somehow be responsible for...

"Remind me why I'm here again?" she said as we arranged ourselves at the bar , "I mean, I sort of understand the drinking bit but it's really not your fault if Bendy Boy took a drugs overdose." Gina looked edible, as usual, in a tiny pink vest top and sarcastic red hot pants. She'd pulled her blonde mane up into two high, swinging pigtails and she wore white, sixth form knee socks. I regarded her with a mixture of jealousy and naked lust. Thankfully the Parrot doesn't have a strict dress code. To be honest, these days I can't really be bothered pouring myself into the kind of expensive latex or leather outfits that are cunningly styled to be bloody uncomfortable. Instead I'd decided on a corseted Mistress Strict in tailored pinstripes. We looked like a his-and-hers lesbian couple and I wanted to have fun cultivating the illusion.

Tonight offered, of all things, a live jazz line-up and the Parrot's eclectic clientele were milling around looking a little baffled. A shame, because the band were good. Still, it was early yet. Opposite the bar, under a fitfully turning glitter ball, the Pink Parrot boasts a small dance floor and bottom lit boudoir décor that consists of plastic pot plants and randomly scattered wipe-clean sofas. There is also a dungeon area discreetly located behind the fronds for those wishing to get their rocks off slightly less conventionally. Upstairs, in a sea of cream shagpile, there are chillout areas and private booths.

"I know it's not my fault," I said, still feeling slightly unconvinced. It seemed odd to talk about Ben in a bar over drinks, reducing him to a tale told by an idiot, signifying nothing. "It's a shock. Look, I was angry with him and now I feel awful. Ill-wishing is never a good thing." I looked at her uncertainly, "I feel guilty…"

"Why?" Gina sipped her red wine. "You didn't kill him, did you?"

"What did I do last night, Gina?" I asked tentatively. She looked at me, aghast for a moment and then burst out laughing.

"Don't be stupid, babe!" she said, "We had a great time at Festers and you were wasted. Look," she took my hand, still giggling, "the only way you could have hurt anyone last night was if you'd fallen on them!"

The music changed abruptly to something more up tempo and complex, as if the band had suddenly lost the will to live and decided to go out on a high. I watched the saxophonist on centre stage with increasing fascination. He was shaven-headed with a goatee beard, neatly trimmed, and had broad, powerful shoulders. I noticed those especially. He looked like Satan's emissary, complete with all the good tunes. He was wearing leather jeans but was otherwise stripped to the waist, showing the riot of colourful tattoos on his shoulders and forearms. I noticed he wasn't wearing any shoes or socks either. Even though he was obviously older than his band mates he looked infinitely more stylish, with round mirror shades perched on the very end of his nose. The piece finished with a wild, exhilarating flourish and I wondered if I should break ranks and show my appreciation through the smattering of catcalls and belching. An unidentified villain in a clump of PVC Goths yelled, "Play Baker Street!"

The sax man favoured this rude mechanical with a look of magnificent disgust and I began to speculate about whether he was wearing anything *under* the leather jeans. Further rude fantasy was curtailed as familiar forms loomed up.

Several of the usual suspects were assembling in a raucous huddle around the bar. And the usual suspects in this case would certainly have drawn the eye at any regular venue. The eye would then probably scurry quickly away and resolutely feign an interest in something else, glancing back occasionally to rubberneck. Like many transvestites and transsexuals, it is unfortunate that a large proportion of the frock and cock club resembled disconcertingly dressed bricklayers. That's a little harsh. I suppose that after the last ex-husband, I'm suffering a little from gender-issue fatigue. As a woman with a lifelong dieting habit, I appreciate the difference a good self image can make, but I'll never become the woman of my dreams and I started out the right sex. In a sense, we are all victims of society's idolisation of feminine beauty and most of us are just travelling hopefully, gender happy or not. Which, of course, goes no way at all to explain how the hell Peter Stringfellow gets laid.

Nikki and her partner Jane were setting out their stall for the night, accompanied by their lodger, Lois. All the girls were post-op transsexuals whose transition had been accomplished with varying degrees of success. Nikki herself was in her sixties and looked precisely, and coincidentally, like a retired builder, now bizarrely resplendent in a floral halter-neck and pink sling backs. Her partner, Jane, was a stocky girl with unfortunate receding blonde hair and a square, earnest face. She enjoyed distressing me with girlish confidences. Mostly about her explorations with a vibrator. The pair had settled into a comfortable, semi-detached Darby and Joan existence that belied the years of struggle it had taken to achieve it. Apart from her colourful name, Lois could best be described as a ginger drama queen with a lisp. Small and wiry, she was easily the prettiest but her temperament usually made her too caustic to be likable. I had seen her screaming insults and purple with rage as well as weeping uncontrollably. But I knew myself that offers of sympathy or friendship would be dourly rebuffed. Life in the confusing emotional ghetto of the trans community can be hard but Lois would have tried the patience of Buddha.

As I finished the introductions, she had already finished her first drink and was looking peevishly over her second, enveloped in her habitual ectoplasm of cigarette smoke. As I explained to Gina, I knew the girls from various alternative clubs and parties but principally from a regular house party hosted by Nikki. It was known locally as '47', after her house number and I attended this first in my guise of supportive wife, while my ex-husband paraded his mid-life crisis around in a mini skirt and a blonde wig.

There is nothing lewd or risqué about the parties at 47. They are just friendly social gatherings that Nikki and Jane had started in order to give local T-girls a comfortable haven to swap gossip en femme and discuss lifestyle problems and shoes. Nikki would potter from room to room in a Gingham housecoat and red mules, welcoming old friends, reassuring and introducing newcomers. Some came in DRAB – dressed as a boy – and changed upstairs in the bedrooms, others would announce themselves in splendid devil-may-care on the doorstep, lace, Taffeta, Chiffon, elbow length gloves and preposterous heels.

"So what's up?" Nikki asked, smudging her lipstick on a pint of Guinness. "You look a bit glum."

"A problem called Ben," Gina said, staring at the foam on Nikki's upper lip, "She's come out to 'forget'." She laughed again at the irony. I pulled a few faces at her. I didn't really want to spend the entire evening obsessing over Ben.

"Is he fit?" asked Jane, displaying her usual subtlety.

"Yeah, he's OK," I said, evasively. No-one could describe Ben as fit anymore. "He...er...looked good in stockings." Why the hell had I said that? It was the memory of fishnets again. Gina was about to speak and I shook my head.

"Would I know him?" asked Nikki, "Has he been to 47?"

"I don't know," I said truthfully. I threw in a few vague facts. It was amazing how little I actually knew about Ben.

"He was, is...that is, I don't know how much he dressed, actually," I finished rather lamely.

"What about TX?" said Jane.

"What's TX?" Gina asked. She was clearly enjoying herself.

"It's a club in London," I told her, "He didn't mention it." I said to

Jane. I've had many strange experiences at TX. It was a club mostly frequented by transvestites and their admirers and I was usually one of the few women present. It had been an odd sort of staging post on the way to much kinkier pleasures. I had once almost got into a serious fist fight there with one TV who had clearly resented the waft of actual lady hormones. She was a strange girl with glaring mental health issues who wore a strappy black dress over thick tights and dirty white plimsolls. She routinely carried a Gladstone bag that contained nothing more than a packet of Players cigarettes and a mobile phone. Bloodshed was averted when another T-girl, unrestrained by delicacy, sat on her and advised, "Oi! Avril! Fucking can it!" in a tone generally reserved for abusing football referees.

Ben might very well have liked to ponce around his living room enjoying the dirty frisson of frillies on his nads but the appeal for him lay in *forced* feminization. It was a pointless exercise unless he was being humiliated. I seriously doubted he had ever visited a trannie bar. Not that I'd proved a very good judge of his character so far. Nonetheless, I began to wonder whether he might have approached another Pro Domme. We had a few more drinks and chatted a little about life in general before a sudden interjection silenced everyone.

"Ben Hammond. Ha!"

Gina and I swivelled simultaneously to face Lois, poised as a pointer on her bar stool. She drained her drink and stubbed her cigarette out with a messy flourish.

"He was in here last night *tarting* it," she said. I felt a little swoop in my stomach. We both waited for her to continue but she looked as if something was amusing her and she needed to savour it fully. "I wouldn't worry about him," she said at last. Nikki was intrigued,

"How do you know him then, Lois?" she pronounced it 'Looey'. But 'Looey' began to gather up her cigarettes and her bag. She flapped her hands about as if she were shooing away flies.

"Whatever. I'll see you later. I've got a date." And with evident enjoyment at her exit line, she stalked a little unsteadily out of the bar.

"Well, I'm buggered," said Jane.

"Not as much as she hopes to be." Nikki grimaced in distaste and gave her attention to another Guinness. I turned to Gina,

"What the fuck was he doing here last night?" I hissed, "He told me…"

"Men do that." She said vaguely. But I had started thinking. This is not normally a good thing. I steered Gina over to one of the sofas during the swell of surprised applause that greeted a particularly gifted solo from the sax man and sat down, resolutely facing away from the stage.

"What was Ben doing here last night?" I demanded again, "And why was Lois looking so smug?" Grim possibilities opened up before me. No…surely not…

"She's weird," Gina crossed her legs firmly at a thin young man in Latex shorts who smiled wistfully at her and began to hover. "What kind of name is Lois? She doesn't look like a Lois. She looks more like a Doris, or a Mabel –" Gina seemed to be getting a little tipsy. Sadly, as is often the case, the hair of the dog was keeping me sober.

"Maybe Ben saw another Pro-Domme," I wondered out loud.
" – or a Wendy. A Pro-Domme?"

"Yes," I said, "a professional dominatrix."

"Oh, you mean like you?"

"Yes," I said, " only I was daft enough not to charge him." But Gina's rambling and a flash of imperial purple glimpsed through the crowd had given me an idea.

I left her chatting to some hopeful but misguided young man who was twisting himself into attractive poses and eyeing the hot pants with some reverence. My mission took me upstairs and through the growing stream of people that were seeking solace in a quieter atmosphere.

Madam Vixen stood by the small first floor bar, stirring a tall green drink and talking to a plastic coated nun. Her thick platinum blonde hair was teased into a spiky crown that framed flawless skin and huge Bambi eyes. She looked like every teenage boy's anime wet dream. Her cleavage preceded her by a good few seconds and a good few feet; it could have doubled as a drinks holder. She was awesome. The whole dynamic was almost always in fluid motion and tonight it was barely encased in a silky smooth purple latex catsuit, all elegantly balanced on Perspex platforms. Madam Vixen had definitely cornered the Goddess market. Our clientele very seldom overlapped. I tended to go in for schoolroom roleplay and corporal punishment. Madam Vixen had a lucrative line in maid training – she liked her house kept spotless – and most of her charges were sissyboy sluts, burley stockbrokers forced to dress inappropriately and debase themselves with polish and cream cleanser. If Ben had been partial to a bit of pay as you go, then this was the place to come. I dived straight in.

"Jay!" she said, flashing me an unconvincing smile, "Nice to see you again. How are you doing?"

"I'm fine", I said, wiggling my fingers at the girl behind the bar, "what are you drinking? I'll get you one in." A certain amount of respectful circling is always required between dominant ladies. It avoids bitchiness and facilitates the sharing of slaves amongst equals. Egalitarianism is alive and well in this ruling class.

"That's very generous," she said, "I'll have a Mojito." I looked at the list of cocktails and their prices above the optics and blanched. "Great," I said. "Can I pick your brains for a minute?"

"Sure."

"Have you ever come across a guy called Ben Hammond?"

Madam Vixen pushed juicy lips around her straw and green drink disappeared with an unladylike slurp. She nodded.

"Oh yes," she said, "I know him. He wanted to book a session but I wasn't that keen."

"Why not?"

"Well, in a sort of way he was rather nice. Very James Bond. Polite and a bit naughty, you know. But he got a bit too pushy in the end. I don't think he really understood that I wasn't going to have sex with him." She raised her eyebrows and sighed. "And I think from what he said that he had a few girls on the go. Messy. I don't know why he couldn't just spice up his fiancée a bit." I slumped a little against the bar. Super. I stared briefly at the shiny swell of Madam's bosom and wondered just what else I didn't know…

"Still," she said, "He obviously got in touch with you in the end then?"

"Er – what do you mean 'got in touch'?" I was going to have to hear it. In some ways it didn't really surprise me that Ben was engaged. A good few of my clients are married or generally busy elsewhere. But Ben was not a client. Or so I'd imagined.

"Oh, I thought – well, in the end he asked me if I knew anyone who would just let him dress and give him a bit of Corporal Punishment." She picked up the fresh drink and swirled the ice round, "And I mentioned your name. He wanted your telephone number…" I realised I was glaring at her as she went on, "…so I told him your website. I said I'd seen you in the Sail Bar." She added helpfully. The Sail Bar was where Ben and I had met. By chance? I now seriously doubted it.

"When was this?" I said through gritted teeth. Madam Vixen raised her Bambi eyes and thought for a moment.

"Maybe three weeks ago. I got the impression that he'd heard of you anyway, said he'd seen you around. There's not a problem is there?"

A problem? *A problem?* The sneaky fucker! The problem was that I had been comprehensively rolled. It was clear he had absolutely no intention of exploring any relationship other than the very intimate and committed one he already had with his dick. Not only had he sweet-talked me into an evening of cheap, no, actually, strike that, *free* sex, he had done so with colossal calculation. I was loath to speak ill of the dead but...

"Bastard!" I said.

"Who's a bastard?" a voice behind me said. I saw Madame Vixen's face light up before I turned. To my surprise, it was the sax man.

"Oh, just a man," she purred. I was astonished to see the Goddess float down to earth.

"Ben Hammond," I said bluntly. To add to my annoyance, I still found sax man slightly overwhelming, especially at close quarters. He'd put boots on now – emerald green Doc Martens – but he was still bare-chested. I stared at him, resentfully in thrall. He was such an odd mixture of broad strokes and fine touches. I guessed he was in his forties but determinedly vital. Without the shades, his eyes were striking – a blue so pale they were almost transparent, fringed with heavy black lashes. Oh dear.

"Oh, yes." He said. He looked at Madam Vixen, who had moved forward to drape herself, "Didn't he bug you for a while? I seem to remember him oiling around in here the other week playing the big spender. He was the one making dirty movies with Angel Falls, right?" He smiled. He had dimples and a slight gap in his front teeth. "What's he done now?"

Really? Dirty movies? I stared balefully at both of them. Rather belatedly, Madam Vixen seemed to realise that I was not a happy bunny. In fact I was as angry as a bunny can get without turning into a Rottweiler.

"I hope I haven't dumped an idiot on you?" she said, looking commendably concerned. Suddenly I felt very tired. I shook my head.

"Don't worry about it," I said, "It's not important." Indeed it wasn't. Or was it? Why should it be? In any event, I found I'd had quite enough of Ben Hammond for the second night running.

"Well, he certainly seems to be upsetting people," said the sax man, smiling again, "my name's Max." He added, as if someone had asked.

"Er...JJ, Jay." I said, "And this...well I guess you know who this is." I saw the dimples again as Madam Vixen thrust her best assets forward.

"Yes. I know who you are, bad girl," Max said. I began to back off. My predilection for interesting people always seems to lead to some kind of self-harming. I decided I'd better salvage what remained of my dignity and see if I could find Gina.

"Well," I said, "I'd better rescue my friend. I'll leave you to um..." Max looked mildly amused.

"Listen," he said, as I inched away, "I'm playing at Bar Bleu on Monday. Might see you there?"

"Er...yes." I said and fled. No, no, no, no, no...

I backed off towards the welcoming scrum of the chillout zone where arms and legs and other appendages were busy getting hot and bothered. I had no idea that Ben was such a player. A publisher and now a pornographer. I fervently hoped this had nothing to do with the photographs in the drawer of my desk. I wondered vaguely if his fiancée was in the loop. What other nasty surprises were there? I now had more unanswered questions than I'd set out with.

I couldn't see Gina anywhere so I parked myself and allowed a very pretty young boy called Will to remove my shoes and massage my feet. He was very dedicated and, in exchange for buying me a drink, he was permitted to lie on the floor, my personal footstool while I pressed my toes gently into his face. I closed my eyes while he sucked and licked and pushed his fingers into my insteps. Oh, yessss! Very nice. This was by far the best way of trying to forget why I was here. Feeling generous, I moved one foot down his torso and began to massage his crotch. Encouraged, Will pressed his thumbs harder into my soles. I felt my shoulders ease and began to plan much nicer ways of spending the rest of the evening. But I wasn't destined to hear the last of Ben. Sadly, my reverie was rudely interrupted by the thick, guttural tones of bonny Scotland.

"Hey, girlie!" I opened my eyes on to a familiar unpleasantness.

Boyd was a dour Glaswegian sadist with flat dark hair who displayed all the insouciance of a pipe wrench. His only concession to fetish wear this evening had been to cover his nipples and part of his beer belly with a grubby leather waistcoat. For all his gruesomeness, he managed to retain a small coterie of slaves and admirers, possibly more stunned by his barefaced cheek than any actual charm. On the other hand, some amongst this select group were actually less attractive than he was. A random assortment formed a small gaggle around him now. An embarrassed elderly trannie with torn stockings and a strange green wig, her Chinese boyfriend, who was a shuffling homage to Marilyn Manson and, of course, the inimitable Janice. She struck a pose next to Boyd now, half-naked, wearing only an SS officers' cap and a strap-on black dildo. Her black lipsticked mouth could occasionally twist into a smile revealing a dental pile-up of grotesque proportions. She normally saved this facial car crash for recipients of the accessory below the belt, a distinctly upsetting thought.

I favoured Boyd with a look he couldn't possibly mistake for deep joy.

"What's up?" I asked, "I'm busy." My footman acknowledged his duties by growling and delicately kissing my toes.

"I heard you asking about Ben Hammond. You know him? I've got a bone to pick with that wanker." Oh, Christ…

"Why?"

"He upset Janice." Janice was a poulterer's assistant whose neck-wringing duties must have made her difficult to offend.

"Oh dear." It was hard not to laugh. The dildo wobbled in agitation. "Why'd he piss you off, Janice?" I said. She made an unpleasant face,

"He spent most of last night bugging the crap out of me. He kept saying he wanted to take me to some party or something. He thought this was really funny, though fuck knows why." She went on, "He was an arsehole! I lent him the last of my cash for a taxi, then he pissed off with some other bird," her eyes bulged like dirty snowballs, "I had to walk home, three fucking miles at 3 o'clock in the morning."

"I want a word with the fucker," Boyd added, thrusting his chin in my direction.

"Look," I said, "He's pissed me off as well. For what it's worth, I don't think he's going to be bothering anyone else."

"Why?" Janice gloated, "What did you do to him?"

"Me? Nothing." I said rather loudly, "I just heard a rumour, that's all."

With relief, I noticed Gina at the top of the stairs and waved at her extravagantly. Although Boyd looked as if he was keen to carry on being argumentative, I retrieved my shoes and joined her.

"Who's that?" She asked, frowning at Janice.

"An idiot," I said, "I've got to have a word with Tony."

The evening was livening up and the Pink Parrot had abandoned any pretence of sophistication. With its live music line-up retired hurt and downing pints of Stella, it had reverted to its old staple of Hard House and Trance. I found Tony soaking up the atmosphere and a lager and lime at the end of the bar. We both briefly admired Gina as she started to dance with my erstwhile foot slave, the cat-like smile lifting the corners of her eyes suggesting that Will would soon be attending to daintier toes than mine.

"Can I ask you something?" I raised my voice above the din. I didn't know Tony that well but his presence was reassuringly familiar, like a dull and undemanding pet. A guinea pig, perhaps. He was small and beige with a character so oblique it often seemed he hadn't one at all. He leaned towards me enquiringly, his head nodding in time to the music. "Do you do private parties here?"

The nodding stopped. He raised his head fractionally and our eyes met. *Not* a guinea pig. Gina had borrowed a pen from somewhere and was writing her phone number on Will's bare chest.

"No." Tony said, "I can't afford to close the bar." We both knew he was lying. We watched as Will made a comical effort to reciprocate with the pen and was rewarded with a playful smack. The music moved up tempo. Boom, boom, boom.

"Why?" Tony took a mouthful of his drink and made a poor show of casual.

"It's my birthday," I lied.

After doing a brief tour through the bar, Gina and I retreated from the sweaty cacophony of the dance floor to the sweaty seclusion of the downstairs dungeon. This gloomy corner was festooned with chains and lit by plastic candles in large floor-standing holders: An Inquisition designed by Homebase. Despite its stylistic shortcomings, it did boast a fine selection of equipment to be tied to, spread over or hung from. The whole area was actually caged off, a permanent fixture, and participants could enter or leave through the cage door, the keys to which were held by the Dungeon Master or Mistress of the night. Voyeurs could ogle through the bars as long as they behaved. Gina and I ogled while an extremely pert young Goth girl, wearing naughty black pigtails and very little else, was being given a fairly serious caning, while Madam's assistant judiciously applied nipple clamps. Listening to her delightful squealing, I began to get a little warm.

"I've never got why you like this sort of thing," said Gina, looking bored. I raised my eyebrows, my smile broadening as a particularly solid blow was landed. The luscious girl's bottom was now very rosy indeed. "I don't understand," she said, shaking her head, "It just doesn't seem sexy."

The DM was a svelte woman I'd not seen before in a black PVC mini skirt. She was wearing huge platform thigh boots and a stern leather corset decorated with straps and buckles. Her dark hair was piled on top of her head and her face was a mask of concentration as she applied cream to the stinging red welts on her victim's bottom. Occasionally she caressed the sweet spot between the girl's legs. A vibrator was called for and passed across. The girl began to moan attractively. Gina had spotted Will again and started to fidget.

"Can we go?" she asked. "Have you had enough of this?"

"Yes. Sorry," I said. The evening hadn't exactly been a success in terms of laying Ben's ghost to rest. And I was none the wiser as to who could have sent me the keys and photographs. I wasn't surprised that Tony had lied about the party. Discretion would definitely be the better part of valour when dealing with Paul Fuller. And so what if Ben had been economical with the truth? It was hardly going to matter now. I gazed resolutely into the small crowd surrounding the cage as the girl's moaning intensified. It was there I spotted Stuart Crouch, his eyes fixed with vivid attention on the scene, his hands thrust deep into his pockets.

As I watched, he slowly turned his head and gazed directly at me. His expression was disturbing. I gained the impression that not only had he been aware that I was standing behind him at that moment but that he'd known precisely where I'd been all evening. Suddenly it seemed my trip to the Parrot in search of the sinister might not have been wasted after all.

It also occurred to me that this could actually be quite a dangerous game to play.

"You're right." I said, "Time to go."

THE FOOL

The beginning of a journey, a blank canvas, a fresh new start with no baggage. Be wary of taking false steps, looking foolish, or worse…

CHAPTER THREE

"And so he's dead." I said, "And that's not normally how I end my relationships."

"You're being flippant." Lucy looked at me patiently and sipped her coffee. Lucy Pellow is my agent. She takes care of what passes for my artistic output and she's a good friend. She's actually an accountant and, unusually for a species designed to operate in the twilight of accretions and ledgers, she's much more skilled than I am at dealing with galleries and publishers and people. Things I find difficult.

"Yes. I'm being flippant." I sighed. Lucy is soothing. Lucy is rational to the point of being banal. She's also more co-ordinated than I'll ever be. She wears half moon glasses on a chain and talks with a sixty-a-day growl. Her hair is the colour of her nicotine stained fingers and falls in no particular way from a side parting, resting on her shoulders like dirty curtains. She has remarkably bright eyes, though and her tasteful Autumnal separates are so unmemorable and suit her so well that even a predator like me cannot imagine her naked. This is definitely a good thing. We'd met after I'd responded to her small ad offering accounting services. As you can imagine, filling in my tax returns registers as a trauma similar to a fanny wax from Gok Wan and we'd bonded over coffee and mutual marriage disasters. Though I suspect she doesn't really approve of me, our friendship has remained firm through the chaos of my temperament for several productive years.

Though it was the middle of October, the weather was kind and we were sitting outside a café on a breezy Monday morning having Cappuccino and a Danish. It wasn't exactly New York, but the view was nicer and we had marginally less chance of getting mugged.

"What's really bothering you?" she asked. I thought about it with reluctance. If I was going to have a confidante, I couldn't think of anyone calmer or more sensible than Lucy so I told her about the keys and the photographs.

"You should tell the police," she said at once, "This hasn't got anything to do with you, has it?"

"No. It hasn't. But there's someone who wants to make it my business and I don't like being messed about with. I want to find out. I can't think who I can possibly have pissed off *so* much that they'd want to drop me in this kind of shit."

"What are you going to do?"

"I don't know. There seems to be an awful lot more going on with Ben than meets the eye. Maybe I'll find out. You know I'm not a helpless girlie. I'm not going to be made a victim here, Luce." Lucy smiled. I may have looked less than impressive with bits of pastry and sugar round my mouth but I meant it. I dusted away the patisserie.

"You know there's Bob's opening this week, don't you?" Lucy said.

"Bob? His opening?" I was having a comedy moment.

"Bob Carlton. You promised, remember?" Oh, God, that's right. I'd agreed to attend an exhibition by Bob 'The Balloon' Carlton. I sighed. A comedy moment indeed. I really didn't feel up to having to make polite comments about Bob's bizarre video installations.

"I've got a few more pressing things to deal with, Luce – " I began but Lucy put her coffee cup down with a clatter and wagged her finger at me,

"I know Bob's a bit of a pain," she said, "But one of his New York buyers is going to be there and I want you to meet him. This guy's got money burning holes in his pockets and we need to redistribute some of it in your direction." She pulled a face, "Just do happy, smiley for a couple of hours, Jay."

I put my hands up,

"OK. I'll be there. And I'll be nice," I added, as I could see Lucy was about to launch into one of her etiquette lectures, "But I *am* going to get to the bottom of this Ben Hammond thing."

"I still think you should go to the police." She said.

"Do you honestly think they'll believe me?" I asked her, "'But hofficer, someone put his keys and this pornography through my letter box' – they'll go rummaging everywhere and they're not going to be kind about my extra curricular activities, are they?" Lucy just raised an eyebrow,

"It's not illegal." She said tonelessly,

"No but I can't see them being very enlightened about it either. And, Christ…they'd be all over my clients like a rash. No. Fuck that." I finished my coffee, "I'm going to have a poke around."

"I still don't understand why you want to involve yourself in something that might be dangerous." I looked at the flavoursome sludge in the bottom of my coffee cup and dipped the spoon into it,

"I don't want to be involved, " I said, "I really don't but someone wants to involve *me*! I really don't like the idea that someone out there – " I made an expansive gesture, taking in the seafront, the bustle of the pedestrian arcade and a surprised looking woman with a small, hairy dog " – is trying to implicate me in all this. And anyway, I feel guilty about Ben. It's not often I meet a bloke I really like." I said, "I like some of my clients and some are a real pain but I don't fancy any of them."

This was all too true. My 'work' had started as a hobby. After my divorce, instead of getting a new haircut, meeting John Hannah and being knocked down by a car, I'd flung myself into ruthless indulgence, determined to sleep with as many people as nature and any remaining grace would allow. Kinky sex with willing partners, a polyamorous jumble of arms and legs and fun, had evolved into one to one tuition for a fee. I often worried that I could no longer give anything of myself, in spite of the desire. Sex and lust and passion were favourite accessories, like putting on perfume, stockings, shoes, adjusting my makeup, nothing really personal, nothing I couldn't buy again new. But I had been genuinely attracted to Ben and I thought he'd been genuinely attracted to me. Obviously I'm not the cracking judge of character I thought I was. And I don't like being used.

"Look," Lucy said, "There's nothing you can do about the fact that he's dead. And from what you've told me, he wasn't being exactly honest with *you*, was he? You don't owe him anything, Jay."

"No. No, maybe not, But there's something not right." I said determinedly. The little dun bird tipped its head sideways and one glittering eye peeped out from behind the curtain of hair.

"What do you mean?" she asked.

Well, for my sins, I know about drugs and drug users. My teens and twenties had been littered with king size Rizlas, wraps, baggies, spoons and rolled up banknotes. I'd smoked, ingested, snorted and, yes, injected all manner of things in pursuit of the good life my fucked up childhood had denied me and as we know, some of these habits have stayed with me. But I was as certain as I could be that Ben, for all his faults, had never indulged in anything more mood enhancing than post coital endorphins. For some sure reason I couldn't put my finger on, I just didn't believe it.

"I just don't think he used drugs at all," I said, "It really surprises me."

"People are often surprising," Lucy said indistinctly as she cupped her hands round the cigarette she was lighting in preparation for departure. The wind whipped the smoke away. She checked her watch. "I'm sure the police will get to the bottom of it. You should be careful you don't just make things worse."

"How can they be worse," I said, with a spectacular lack of foresight, "He's already dead."

"Well, you take care, anyway," Lucy said, gathering up her shopping and her handbag, "And don't forget – Wednesday afternoon, 2 o'clock, Bob's the word."

I walked home via an artist's supply shop, buying some brushes, filled with good intentions, even as I knew I'd probably spend the rest of the afternoon perving round the internet. I had no clear plan of action but I'd been intrigued by the notion that Ben had been making 'dirty movies', as Max called them. I thought about Max for a while with a certain amount of wistful regret. And I thought about the Pink Parrot and the furtive little soul in the dungeon on Saturday night. I thought about Stuart Crouch.

Stuart was a scene photographer and voyeuristic frequenter of clubs like the Parrot and I'd always found him slightly creepy. He'd wined me and dined me, presumably in the hope of sixty-nining me after I'd met him at a private party in the leafier suburbs of the town. The party itself was a woeful affair that displayed a leather clad mistress with a tendency to embonpoint, half-heartedly flogging a small clutch of unattractively willing slaves. She performed this procedure with one hand, whilst stuffing vol au vents into her face with the other. Inexplicably the gentlemen abasing themselves beneath the shower of flaky pastry were lapping it up. Stuart had been on hand to photograph the whole jolly jamboree for her website. We met several times after that and I'd managed to work my way, in a rather mercenary fashion, through the entire duck menu of the local Chinese restaurant before calling a halt to proceedings.

Small and Saturnine, Stuart is probably the most intensely repressed person I have ever met. He spoke about sex as if he were reading from a Haynes manual. For him, fellatio demonstrated the same eroticism as changing the spark plugs on a Hillman Imp. He had a fondness for combat trousers, firearms, foreplay involving knives and duct tape and, rather bizarrely for a man who was actually, rather than notionally tone deaf, Hollywood musicals of the forties and fifties. Things between us had not ended particularly well and I had no wish to renew his acquaintance. I remembered his hunched form in boots and army jacket as he stared at me, a cross between Hannibal Lecter and Elmer Fudd, and decided to put Stuart on the back burner for the moment.

I'd just sparked up a soothing J – just as an aid to creative thought, you understand – when a furious hammering on the front door made the whole house shake. I quickly stubbed out the offending article, made sure everything was legal and staggered to my feet. A tall woman dressed in elegant and striking drapes and ruffles stood on the step. She looked a refined and sophisticated greyhound of a thing with dangerous cheekbones and thin lips and her shiny, dark hair was cut in a short bob that remained commendably static in spite of the breezes swirling around my cliff top cottage. I stared at her dumbly.

"You're called Franklin?" she said, looking more than slightly put out.

"Yes." I suppose I didn't look too promising in me trackies and a sweatshirt. As you can see, I fall quite a long way short of the inimitable Miss Page when I'm off duty.

"Can I come in?" she said, "My name's Amanda." She kept looking me up and down and clenching her fists. She appeared to be grinding her teeth.

"Er…I suppose so." I was a little bewildered, "Will this take long? I'm working." I lied.

"No. This won't take long," she said grimly as she followed me into the living room. She stood amidst my cheerful clutter like a Regency sucrier on a sticky plastic table and took deliberate deep breaths. I started to get annoyed.

"I told you, I'm working. Look, I don't know who you are. Perhaps you could tell me what it is you want?"

"No. *Obviously* you don't know me. Amanda Dyson. Of *course* you don't know me."

I folded my arms, stood still and waited. If she'd hoped to intimidate me, she was going to have to try harder. I'm 5'8" in my stocking feet, rather nicely statuesque, if I say so myself (even if it's Rodin and not Giacometti) and Ms Dyson was seriously starting to get on my tits.

"If you don't tell me *now*, what you're doing here – " she held up a hand and closed her eyes tightly, all restoration and Royal Court Theatre. I'm afraid I snorted with laughter. She turned on me.

"Did you do it in here? I thought he had more taste," she looked me up and down, "In everything. Obviously I was wrong. Was it upstairs? Or maybe you fucked in his car?" The penny dropped, finally. Seeing my face she said:

"Yes, that's right. Ben Hammond was my fiancé. You were having an affair," she shook her head as I opened my mouth to speak, "Don't try and deny it. The police told me, my father's a barrister. You wrecked everything. I thought it would be some kind of tart but…Jesus!" she looked me up and down again, she was obviously having trouble with my slob-wear, "Jesus! Did you give him the drugs? You *look* like a junkie."

I am a woman who beats up men for a living. I can run for a taxi in 5" heels. I can endure the privations of the tightest corsetry for twelve hour stretches. I have sat on the chest of a 6'5" rugby prop forward and slapped his face until he cried (he was a *very* naughty boy). I really wasn't going to take shit from this uptight young lady, no matter how grey with sack cloth she was.

"In the first place, honey," I said, going on the attack, "Ben and I were *not* having an affair. I met him precisely *twice*. Maybe the police didn't tell you that. Maybe you should ask daddy again. In the second place, I had nothing *at all* to do with his death and in the third place…" I walked around her, opened the front door and stood beside it, "How dare you come into my home, stand here like some kind of minor royalty and insult me! You're going to fuck off now." Amanda favoured me with a look of complete disgust. Her eyes blazed at me but good breeding kept her under control.

"I know you had something to do with his death and I'm going to find out." she said, literally looking down her nose at me. That she had to tilt her head back to do this lessened the desired effect somewhat, "I'm going to find out and hold you personally responsible. I wanted you to know."

"Well, good luck with that," I said, still holding the door open, "Please don't bother calling again."

She drew herself up and pushed past me into the lane.

"I'm sorry for your loss!" I shouted after her, through a residue of Chanel No.5.

"Fuck you!" Her refined tones rang like a peal of bells as she swung stylishly up the alleyway. Obscenity sounds so much more obscene when it's trumpeted via Rodean, don't you think? I wasn't being entirely sarcastic in my condolences either. I'm not entirely insensitive and I realised that Amanda was definitely going to get the worst of it. She'd obviously skipped right past denial and alighted on anger as a way of dealing with her grief. It wasn't going to be easy for me to forget that her betrothed was dead either, not under such attack from all sides.

That Ben was playing away didn't surprise me at all. After all, men have been coveting their neighbours' oxen since Moses told them not to. I wondered how much more of this kind of thing Ben indulged in. Amanda looked just like the kind of trophy wife who'd be in for more than a few surprises when the shit hit the fan. I was fed up with surprises though.

I retrieved the joint from the bin and fired up my laptop. I found Angell Falls' website without any trouble. What's the internet for, if not trawling for porn? Adult Content – click 'yes I am 18', all completely child proof.

The pages I surfed through afforded ample scope to gaze in wonder at the diva's best assets. A fine figure of somethinghood, s/he was certainly supple. Her website contained a short, definitely apocryphal biography (I know for a fact that she's from Dagenham not Suriname), contact details for her professional services, the opportunity to purchase DVDs or video streams and galleries of professional photo shoots together with more informal pictures sent in by devoted admirers. None of the provocative contortions on display, with or without accessories, were very enlightening and I leafed disinterestedly through cock shots, cum shots, dildos, enemas, pearl necklaces, nipple clamps, doctors and nurses, wanking and spanking until I came across some more interesting pictures of Angell taken at various clubs. She liked to pose, imperious and smouldering, with exactly the same pout and posture at any venue, no matter what was going on around her.

And here I found the picture proof that Ben Hammond knew Angell Falls. It was taken outside a club, a group of trannies, grinning and waving, glasses raised, Angell at their still centre, were gathered round a silver Aston Martin. This wasn't the really interesting thing about it, though. After all, I already knew that Ben was working with Angell. I expelled some smoke with a sense of grisly recognition. There in the happy huddle of flashed out grins and red eye, was Lois, looking like a glum fairy with her fag and a glass of red wine. Even this wasn't a serious shock. I took another toke and groaned because there, unmistakably, unambiguously and unquestionably was my ex husband – Tamara a.k.a Tom O' Connell, modelling an unbecoming black satin kimono and fishnets. He was wearing a long, curly blonde wig and looked exactly like a hooker at a Christmas party.

This opened up all sorts of unpleasant possibilities. On a list of people who wouldn't be tragically moved if I fell flat on my face in a snow storm, Tom would be at the top. I couldn't see him being involved in killing anyone, that just revolted the intelligence, but being spiteful enough to drag me into someone else's mess? That would be a definite maybe. I felt tired and unsatisfactorily stoned. You know when the high just leaves you listless and ever so slightly paranoid?

I'm not always this bad, you know, not really. The problem is I tend to react badly to adverse stimuli and apart from the sheer pleasure of it (am I overstating that?), indulgence is also my coping strategy. First, avoid the problem, then if it doesn't go away, try viewing it through a toxic haze and hope it looks different. It's been the same for as long as I can remember and I know I'm not the only one underwriting chaos this way.

I recall the clear, still hours on the brink of a December morning and a voice shattering the calm with the impact of a ballista.

"You fucking whore! Bitch! You fuck …you…"

This tide of revelation washed around the blank faces of the houses in the leafy little neighbourhood of my childhood home and returned to sender with twitching curtains. He was a large, unshaven man with untidy grey hair and a shapeless overcoat. I watched the careful pantomime as, legs apart for maximum stability, he delicately placed a half consumed bottle of Scotch on the porch. He then began to kick the front door, forcefully. The sound shuddered through the house.

"You cunt! You fucking bitch! Open this fucking door! Come here ..."

Even though I was only eight I knew these were very rude words indeed. Peeping carefully out of my bedroom window, I could see his bald spot, getting redder as his apoplexy grew. The object of his attentions – our house, its contents – remained shuttered and dumb. My mother may have been peeping too, I didn't know but I continued to crouch in watchful silence as he raged, occasionally grabbing fistfuls of grass to throw ineffectually at the brickwork. I wasn't at all afraid, just curious. The man in the garden below wasn't my father. At least, he looked like my father. But his behaviour, this shabby, stumbling mannequin with its flapping coat caught in the roses, falling to its knees, lurching up, windmill arms, was so at odds with the man I knew that I felt strangely detached. In the end, hoarse and exhausted, he wound down like a clockwork toy. He was still sitting on the step muttering, the remains of his courage gone with the empty bottle, when police arrived to restore tranquillity for those who preferred their cornflakes unaccompanied by anguish and profanity.

Nearly three decades later I still wonder what had managed to rip his dignity to shreds *that* morning above all others. My parent's unhappy marriage was a study in tight lipped acrimony. Without the modern trend for emotive disclosure, or indeed 'closure', my childhood often floundered in the wasteland of my parents' marriage. Unengaged in any Trisha type chat about child rearing, I was as ignorant as they were that mum and dad were making a complete hash of things. The silences seemed endless and there were no brothers or sisters to lighten the mood, to pick on, to play with. As a bumpy childhood matured into neurotic adolescence, I began to see mummy and daddy as two human beings separate from any notion of family and the realisation dawned that they were a desperately unsuited couple. My father had been a career soldier sidelined by an injury he refused to discuss, and my mother was a late blooming flower child, discouraged into atrophy by his bitterness. I sat silently between them as they stared at each other across a widening chasm.

Characteristically, that December morning was never mentioned or discussed, it might never have happened, a tree falling in the forest, unobserved. Incidentally, it was my mother who gifted me my ridiculous names. Only a very select few know the awful truth of *them* and it's going to stay that way.

They divorced when I was eighteen. My father finally found the courage to end the torture by writing a dramatic exit from the safety of a Manchester hotel room, only to return, briefly, to awkward silence when he found he'd left the keys to his new flat on the hall table. Exit stage left – no, wait – stage right. By then I had devised my own escape strategies – sex, drugs, art, alcohol, probably in that order – unencumbered by applause or opprobrium from either of them. I like to think I created myself, springing fully formed, like Athena from the godhead. Even if that's not true and the drunk in the garden prefigured some kind of delinquency, my parents don't deserve the blame for horrors of my own devising, any more than they can take credit for the joys. Certainly neither of them are around any longer to comment on the stinking mess I seemed to have got myself into this time.

I stared dolefully at the silly tart in the blonde wig on the screen in front of me and rolled another joint. Hey, dad! If at first you don't succeed…Then I went to the pub for a drink and a scampi.

My local – The Dog and Duck – is literally a minute's walk from my front door and, thankfully, deeply unfashionable. It brims with tatty, 'witty' character; low, smoke-blackened beams, garlands of dusty hops and specious collections of Breweriana. There are cartoons of its most popular locals, fading tributes from drinkers long past, a Camra Award: Regional Finalist 1980; horse brasses, bizarre agricultural implements, comfortable alcoves and fusty upholstery. There is no juke box or fruit machine and the landlord is called Reg.

I sat in its yeasty comfort in the sour of the early afternoon, nursing a large glass of Merlot and studying the photo of my ex I'd printed from Angell's website. The implications behind the keys left on my mat were enormous. It was obvious that someone had been into Ben's flat and taken them. When? And for God's sake, why? Could the grinning idiot in this picture really be involved in something the police nicely referred to as 'suspicious'? I didn't really want to know the answers to these and other irritatingly pressing questions and I felt a little as if I'd been set a surprise school test without the benefit of any revision. My scampi arrived and I regarded it without favour. I squeezed lemon and made a concentrated mental effort. OK. Was there anything I could do about any of this? There seemed to be plenty of people who were annoyed with Ben, ranging from the slightly miffed to the downright outraged. Boyd, Janice, Miss Vixen, even the dashing sax man seemed to think he was rather tiresome. Best not be distracted by emerald green footwear. Then of course there were Lois's mysterious pronouncements, I'd forgotten about that.

I wasn't really concerned to play the detective on Ben's behalf, I just wanted to know who the hell had sent me those photographs and those keys? Presumably the 'why?' would make itself known. I remembered the flashed-out smiles and a silky kimono. Oh, God.

I was loath to get in touch with Tom after the way we had parted. But then I thought about my promised date at Bob The Balloon's 'event' and inspiration struck. Bob Carlton and Tom O'Connell had been close friends for years. If anyone knew what Tom was up to these days it would be Bob. I could kill two birds with one stone, make a few discreet enquiries and hopefully leave Tom none the wiser.

The buzz from the hash was beginning to wear off. A seagull landed on the flat roof extension of the junk shop opposite the pub. Tatty furniture spilled out on to the pavement. I could see the predatory form of the owner in the shadows at the back of the shop, waiting with the stillness of a trap door spider to rush out should anyone linger too long in front of a chest of drawers. The seagull tilted its head back, opened its ugly, yellow bill and began to shriek raucously at the sky. A silly, pointy bird, Laughing. And I knew exactly how it felt.

THE HIGH PRIESTESS

*This card cautions us to consult our inner wisdom before acting,
to listen to what is arcane within all of us. The high priestess
has much mystic knowledge that we can channel.*

CHAPTER FOUR

Angell Falls is not the easiest person in the world to get hold of. Although she likes to visit the seaside, she's not based in this rustic backwater. She lives in South London. I looked for quick contact details on her website but the mobile number listed went straight to voicemail. I phoned a few friends to try and get her address without much success until I finally got lucky with the information that, on Saturday at least, she had actually been staying at The Pier Hotel, just 500 yards down the front. I suppose this made sense if she had been involved with Ben somehow, but it was a coincidence of the sort that my moustachioed policeman would scratch his hairy knuckles over. A quick phone call confirmed that she hadn't checked out yet. I decided on a bracing walk to see if I could catch her in residence.

The Pier Hotel is one of the tallest buildings on the promenade. Although it's large, it's still remarkably restrained for what must once have been an extremely fashionable and expensive Victorian hotel. It's a turreted seven stories at its tallest, all slate pitches and Gothic arches with sinewy wrought iron balconies. Art Nouveau stained glass decorates its main entrance. The façade looks a little shabby these days but the reception area is still impressively plush despite the rather overwhelming mahogany panelling. Candle lights dabbed the walls with rich highlights and an absurdly elaborate metal lift cage offered guests a rattling alternative to the sweep of the stairs. I loitered purposefully and managed to catch the eye of a marvellously bosomed receptionist.

"I wonder if you could help me," I said, "I understand that a friend of mine, Angell Falls, is staying here. Could you tell me if she's, er, in at the moment?"

"Miss Falls hasn't checked out yet." The receptionist said, without batting an eyelid, although Angell must have been one of their more unusual guests, even if the bosom didn't realise *how* unusual.

"Could I possibly have her room number? I need to speak to her fairly urgently and she's not answering her mobile."

"I'm afraid I can't give out guest's room numbers." She said primly.

"Then can you phone her room for me and give her a message?" The bosom sighed and prodded some numbers into a switchboard behind the reception desk. "Can you tell her a friend of Ben Hammond's needs to speak to her."

I waited while the receptionist conducted her side of a murmured consultation with the matchless Miss Falls and then I was on my way up to room 17. As I've said, I don't know Angell that well, in fact I'm probably so far off her radar that she almost certainly won't know who the hell I am. For that matter she certainly won't know what the hell I'm doing here – I wasn't that sure either. Never mind. The more I thought about it, the more I needed to know about the photograph on her website. The spectre of Tom lurking in the crowd of extras had prompted all sorts of unpleasant thoughts.

Tom O' Connell in his masculine guise was deceptive. Short and slim, with a mop of curly black hair and an apologetic hunch, he was a smiling Mr. Average. A laugh, a weak joke, a polite enquiry about your journey, this blandly jaunty exterior clothed a surprisingly well-tended self-regard that occasionally bordered on the deranged. He could be mean, small-minded, jealous and childish, all the while believing quite genuinely in his own basic niceness. OK, I might be a bit biased here but trying to second guess his good nature had eventually worn me out, especially when his flashpoints were so random. He seemed to have all the attractive fire of the Celtic temperament with none of the creative flair. Who knows what commonplace resentments might have festered over the 18 months since our divorce?

On the other hand, *Tamara's* motives might be less clear cut. There's a strange kind of split personality involved in cross dressing. Made up and dressed, en femme, there's a certain excitement and compulsion, a freedom from normal constraints that sits uneasily alongside the frustration and repression of the usual nine to five. Deception and guilt drive a lot of transvestites barmy, especially those with unsuspecting wives and partners. And I was sure Tamara's new girlfriend had no idea what lurked in Tom's closet. Otherwise, he had the advantage over quite a few other TVs. He was 5'8" in his (fishnet) stocking feet and he had fine features. His thick dark curls and large Irish blue eyes meant that when made-up and dressed he was more than passably pretty.

We had met at a London club and I remember he looked ravishing in a short, tight skirt and knee high lace up boots. He wore a little off-the- shoulder top and a fabulous long black wig, a cascade of corkscrew curls that matched his colouring perfectly and put to shame some of the precariously balanced thatches sported by other party goers. Earrings dangled, a silver necklace glittered. Remembering Tamara, I was reminded of why I had fallen for Tom in the first place. His dress sense was discerning and he was just on the kinky side of femme – everything I thought I wanted in a boy/girl, man/woman thing; a convincing transvestite always seems like a gift if you're bisexual. But then I remembered that beauty is only skin deep. And covered in foundation and blusher and lipstick.

I thought again about the last time I'd actually spoken to him. Our divorce was in progress and he had all but moved out. Although it had not been a happy time for either of us, we had decided to be civil and more than several glasses of red wine had been consumed (a Cotes de Beaune, I seem to recall) in an effort to try and recapture some of the good old days. Sadly, our good intentions prompted a serious attack of boozy bad temper. He had accused me of having sex with one of his friends and had adopted some loud moral high ground, a tricky manoeuvre as he was already having an affair himself. It was still my fault though. Obviously. The evening had ended in ridiculous middle aged fisticuffs: the only time he ever hit me. I never let him into the house again. I put the rest of his clothes into bin bags along with his few remaining possessions and left them outside. He had taken them away without comment the following morning.

Could this have prompted him to some belated revenge involving car keys? Had he been involved in some after hours' fun at Ben's house and decided to get rid of them somewhere satisfactorily troublesome? It just didn't make sense. If someone had Ben's keys, even if they had vandalized his car, why not just leave them in Ben's house where they wouldn't excite any attention. There was one thing I knew about Tom, though. He had a passion that had bored me rigid for the makes, marques, capacity and performance of high end sports cars.

Angell answered the door so quickly I thought she must have been standing behind it. I'd forgotten how small she was. And slight. Out of fetishwear she looked, if it were possible, even more stunning in a white scoop-neck top and tight white jeans. Her blue-black hair was loosely piled on top of her head and secured with a black silk scarf. Her coffee and cream colouring and large, dark brown eyes were free of makeup and the little mole above the bow of her lips gave her face an impish look. She seemed like an actress stylishly 'resting', poised for her interview with Paris Match. Which of course she was, after a fashion. As long as the journal in question was Ass Driller Monthly.

"Who are you?" Angell looked puzzled but she let me in without waiting for an answer. The room was surprisingly small and very old-fashioned. Enormous windows overpowered with light and space a small clutter of dingy furniture. A single bed, a portable TV, a coffee table and a shiny, button back wing armchair. The wallpaper looked like it hadn't been changed since the old king died. That's Elvis, not George.

"You said it was to do with Ben?" Her voice was like a cello – deep, melodic and ever so slightly camp.

"Yes," I said, debating options, "I've been told he was working with you?"

Angell had perched herself on the bed, her arms straight by her sides with her palms flat on the mattress. She was swinging her legs like a little girl on a high chair. The look she gave me from under arched eyebrows was anything but childish.

"You came all the way up here to ask me that? Are you his girlfriend or something?" She didn't wait for a response, she probably didn't care. Instead she pointed to her suitcase, packed and ready by the door, "We were supposed to meet yesterday. I'm going home this evening. You can tell him I don't like being stood up."

"I'm sorry," I said, "I'm not his girlfriend."

"So what do you want?" She bounced to her feet and paced around me trying to impose the weight of her personality but she was far too short in her bare feet. "I'm only waiting for Danny to come and pick me up," she said, "Look, honey, I don't know how well you know him but he was *supposed* to be taking me out to dinner. It was a business thing. I've been sitting in this shitty hotel waiting for him to get his arse in gear since Saturday. A fucking phone call was the least I could have expected." Silent she might be sultry but Angell had a peevish way with words.

"Is that what you wanted to know? Because if so…"

I sat down on the button back chair, although Angell clearly expected me to leave.

"I've got to tell you," I said, "Ben's dead."

"What?!!"

"On Saturday night."

"Fuck!!" Angell backed off and sat heavily on the bed again. Unless she was a very good actress (and she wasn't) this was clearly the first she'd heard of it. "What happened?"

"Apparently he took a drugs overdose." There was a few seconds poisonous silence before she said:

"Bollocks! I don't believe it." I just looked at her. She was on her feet again, waving her hands about. For a model and a fetish icon she was puckishly animated. "He didn't take drugs. Not any. He didn't even drink that much. Christ! He even knew how many units he'd had in a week. 'I don't do that shit'" she mimicked, "Danny offered him some coke one time and he spent half an hour boring everyone with a health and safety lecture. "I'm an executive, I have to keep my head clear…" I pounced.

"So what was this business thing?" She made a dismissive gesture,

"It's my production company, we were going to discuss financing," she thought for a moment, a shadow crossing her face, "Are you sure it's drugs?" she said.

"Well that's what the police said." I told her.

"Shit." We both sat in silence for a while. Finally she narrowed her eyes at me.

"Who *are* you?" she asked again.

"I was his date," I said, "The night he died. I wasn't *with* him when he died," I said quickly as Angell opened her mouth to speak, "But this has dumped me right in it."

Angell pouted attractively. It might have been sympathy or it might have been force of habit. I said:

"I was hoping you might be able to help me out with

something." The pout turned into a scowl that was considerably less alluring.

"It's nothing to do with me." She picked up her mobile phone and flipped it open, "Where the fuck is Danny? The sooner I leave this dump the better."

"I'm sorry," I said, still not moving, "But can you just look at this picture?" I fumbled in my jacket pocket and unfolded the print of the picture from her website. Angell looked as if she definitely wanted me to leave now but I remained obstinate. "I just need to know who these people are. I won't bother you any more, it's just this."

"Christ, you don't want much do you," she said. But she stared briefly at the photo, "That was taken in the Summer at Dazzlers. I remember because Ben bought drinks for everyone and I think he regretted it."

"Do you know anyone in that picture?"

She shrugged,

"I meet a lot of people." She looked again and vaguely stabbed a long red polished nail at a couple of the figures,

"I know her," she said, "And that's Marissa, I know *her*," the finger tapped at Lois's scowling reflection. Then it hovered over the kimono, "Not sure about her," she said, "Look, I see a lot of these people at lots of places, I don't really remember who they all are."

I smiled at her and put the picture back into my pocket.

"Well, thanks anyway," I said getting to my feet, "I'm sorry to just barge in here and grill you like this – "

"I know you!" Angell said suddenly, "I've seen you at the Pink Parrot. Weren't you at Torture Garden last month as well?"

"Er, no," I said, "Thanks for your time. I'd better let you get on." Angell sat back on the bed cross-legged. She looked almost pixie-like, making even a single bed look large. A coil of hair escaped from her scarf and bounced across her cheek. She brushed it away.

"Thanks for the heads up." She said and smiled a practised smile.

"Did you ever take a ride in his car?" I asked, thinking about keys, my hand on the door knob. Angell shook her head and shrugged again as she began to punch numbers into her mobile. She liked shrugging.

"That monster? Why the hell would I?" she glared at her unresponsive phone, "I'm supposed to have my own fucking driver!"

I saw myself out and strolled slowly back towards home, wondering if I was any closer to finding out who had sent me the keys, and realizing I wasn't. I decided to try another tack. I took a short detour and popped into the canary yellow and gingham charm of one of the many sea-view cafés on the promenade below the West cliff. With a grainy coffee staining my teeth and a sticky bun under my fingers, I called Adam.

Let's not beat about the bush, Adam is a drug dealer. I have sometimes cause to purchase from him medicinal amounts of various substances and I try to do so as discretely as possible, always with the usual slight twinge of resentment at being the demand element in this particular chain of supply and demand. Having said all this, it could be a lot worse. Adam is actually perfectly respectable. He works in project management, pays his taxes, mows his lawn and holidays in Devon. Far more agreeable than some skulking low life on a street corner, or an ex-hippy so retarded by decades of potage that he can barely string two sentences together. From art school digs, where I justified my face-down-in-powder portrait of the artist as some kind of sophisticated Dada installation, to the bright, hard, super smashing hahahaha fuck fuck fuckity fuck ecstasy and coke-fuelled partying of my renaissance as a sex worker, (where I'd ceased to bother justifying anything at all), I'd known every kind of dealer. I was at least afforded a cup of tea on the patio when I visited Adam.

Adam himself is short and darkly balding with slim, rimless glasses perched on the very end of his nose. He is now in his mid-forties and has 'never married' as they say in the North, living instead with four noisy and extremely superior Siamese cats, irreverently named after the Marx brothers. I sipped Twinings Breakfast Blend and watched them stalking around the garden, their tails waving fluid semaphores at each other as they pounced in and out of the Rhododendron borders. I suspected Adam would remain in the closet forever. I wasn't about to mention it to him, though, he's a strange wee bunny.

"Here you go." He said, handing me a small bag containing various things. He sat down and smiled, staring enigmatically towards his tidily maintained garden and the antics of his cats. We both watched them for a while and listened to the tinkling of wind chimes hanging from a pergola twined with parched relics of Wisteria and Laburnum . A little breeze rippled through the evergreens and scattered a few leaves onto the patio. I put my cup down noisily in the saucer. You always got a saucer at Adam's. He favoured Wedgewood.

"Can I ask you about something?" I began, a little hesitantly. You never knew quite where you were with Adam and it was sometimes a little tricky judging his moods. He looked at me enquiringly.

"Sure."

"Did you ever come across a guy named Ben Hammond?"

"It is an ex-parrot, it has ceased to be." He said, smiling more broadly than I liked the look of.

"Ah."

"Yes, ah indeed. I understand he has gone to meet the choir invisible…"

"Yes," I said, "And I know rather more about that than I'd like to," I forestalled him as he opened his mouth to speak again, "I don't really want to go into it. How do *you* know anyway?"

"Stuff gets around." He said, being deliberately annoying.

"What I really want to know is, if he was in the market, you know?"

I took a moment to swallow some more tea, looking over the rim of the cup at him as he looked grimly amused.

"If you're asking me if I supplied him, then I certainly did not." He said, "But then I wouldn't necessarily know." This I didn't necessarily believe, "I only know about him from what happened with Paul Fuller."

I let my eyes roll heavenwards. It went without saying that Adam knew him. I was myself, at this very moment, on the end of a convoluted series of transactions initiated by Fuller. So there *was* a Ben connection...

"So how did Ben know him?" I asked, in spite of not really wanting to know.

"Bare Faced Cheek," Adam said.

"What?"

"It's the name of a film production company."

"Ah."

"They make porno movies. Lots of different sorts. Ben wanted a slice of several of his favourites – that's what I heard anyway. Bare Faced Cheek run a lot of small independent film companies – I don't know... "Tit Films" or "Pussy Films" – stuff like that. Ben took over some of them. Fancied himself an auteur."

"But surely taking over a film company – "

"It's not Hollywood, Jay," Adam looked amused, "It not even straight to DVD wank fodder, it's just a couple of blokes with cameras or whatever, filming someone getting stuffed. Edit, pay, download – that sort of thing. Fuller runs a whole load of websites."

"Oh." I said, a little disillusioned. Was this all Angell's 'production company' had amounted to?

"Paul owns Bare Faced Cheek, finances all these dirty little entrepreneurs and takes a big cut of the premiums. I wouldn't really know." He held up his hands in a rare show of skittishness,

"I don't want to either. But he was seriously pissed off when he found out your friend Ben was cherry- picking the good stuff."

"Like Angell Falls?" I asked, trying to sound casual. But Adam smiled a slow smile, inscrutable as his cats. He always looked as if he knew everything that was going on in the universe but didn't like to say. Either that or he was just more of a stoner than I thought.

"Trannies R Us," he said at last, "Yeah Angell's one of his. She's not easy to forget."

"So what did Fuller do?" I asked, moving swiftly on. But Adam shrugged.

"Warned him off." There was an awkward silence while we both did the maths. I changed the subject.

"How do you know all this?" I asked, "You don't look like you're a porn fan." Adam laughed, not very pleasantly and I began to wonder again about him.

"Well, you're right about that, " he said, finally, "It's not that Paul and I are chums, if you know what I mean. Definitely not." He pointed at me, "And definitely not business associates." I nodded. OK. Definitely. Not.

"But stuff gets around, you know." He said again and leaned back, placing right ankle on left knee. He was wearing pink socks. I sighed and put my cup back in its saucer with a civilized little chink. I looked straight at Adam.

"Look, do you think Paul Fuller might have …?" I let the sentence drift into the chiming breeze but he was already shaking his head. Slowly and emphatically. His eyes looked dangerous.

"No I *don't*," he said positively, "And I'd keep that to myself if I were you. All this hoo-hah happened months ago. Some time in June or July. As far as I know, the late Mr. Hammond had taken the good advice on offer and left well alone." I nodded slowly. The only problem with this was that I knew for a fact that he hadn't.

XVI

THE TOWER

A shocking truth is going to be revealed and throw beliefs into chaos.
False structures and ideas will come crashing down.
This may be painful but it is better to know the truth.

CHAPTER FIVE

I showered and changed, armed myself with a small amount of petty cash and went to Bar Bleu. I just wanted to drink, on my own, and I wanted to think. Bar Bleu is another of our seaside drinking holes that cultivate urbanity. Unfortunately, the English Channel has consistently censured continental taste from the English psyche and its leather sofas, glass tables and wi-fi access have been roundly abused by the locals who regularly cover it in lager vomit processed via the Indian takeaway next door. You want rice with that, sir? It was still early and I sat in relative peace and quiet in the ambient lighting, staring at a glass of house red and chewing over this latest intelligence. On the face of it, it seemed quite likely that Ben had met his end at the hands of Paul Fuller and his henchmen. Did he even *have* henchmen? Associates? *Friends?* If Ben was still in negotiations with Angell, it was fairly obvious that he hadn't taken the hint and backed off. But getting rid of him? With an overdose? Especially when he wasn't a known drug user. Why not just bust his kneecaps? And this didn't explain the keys on my doormat, or the photographs, which I presume Mr Fuller would be anxious to retrieve. It seemed the horrible truth of Ben's death was not going to be allowed to pass over hurriedly as something tragically incidental to my life – someone, presumably someone *I knew,* wanted to involve me. Christ!

"What's up?"

I looked up startled, realising I must have sworn out loud. Good grief! It was Max, the sax man, dramatic in purple shirt, plum coloured cords and his green DMs. He was wearing a black leather hat with a colourful bragg around the crown and carrying an instrument case. His sense of sartorial timing was frightening. I flapped my hands about like a Regency heroine,

"Oh, yes. Monday, I'd forgotten." I said, remembering.

"Oh." He did mock disappointment, "Well, I obviously made an impression here then."

"Sorry, I've got a lot on my mind... Well," I said, a bit unwisely and still a little flustered, "I'd better get you a drink then."

When I returned with a pint of lager and another glass of wine, he'd made himself comfortable on the sofa beside me and I realised I was probably going to have to talk to him.

"So what's up?" he said as I sat down next to him. He was twisting round to face me and I could see his slightly gap-toothed smile and the dangerous dimples. Despite the dire distractions. every fibre of my being was desperate to flirt with him – wiggle my bottom, cross my legs, shove my bosom in his face. Sensible brain cells reminded me that this was the sort of stupid behaviour that had got me into this situation in the first place. In another similar bar, not 100 yards down the front.

"It's something that's happened," I said, "Bad. Really bad. And I'm trying to decide what to do."

"I'm sorry to hear that. Anything I can do?" He looked so genuinely concerned that I felt myself falter. I'm not usually in the habit of giving my intimate all to strangers, even ones as lovely as Max, but, well... By the time I'd finished telling him, I felt a lot better and Max looked a lot worse. Most satisfying.

"You see", I said, warming to my theme and waving my wine glass at him, "It really looks like he might have been deliberately killed. I mean, I don't know why. And I don't know why someone would post me his car keys and these bloody horrible photographs. It's too much of a coincidence to be random so it must be someone I know." I thought about Tom and felt my eyes narrow.

"Not just that, though." Max said.

"What do you mean?"

"Think about it," he widened his eyes. Very affecting. "It has to be someone who knew that *you* were seeing *Ben* and you weren't exactly an item, were you? You said you'd seen him twice. That's hardly 'Love Story', is it? None of the people you mentioned knew that you were seeing him, did they?"

He was right. And I hadn't thought of it.

"Fuck." I said. The barman was busy attracting Max's attention.

"Look," he said, "I've got to go and get set up. Steve's here." He nodded at a slim, blonde man in a cable knit sweater unlocking a guitar case on the stage. "We'll talk in a while. Yes?"

"Yes." I said, "Sure."

I watched him go over and chat to his guitarist while I thought furiously. Ben and I had met in a bar. We had talked together without company. We had met the following week. I hadn't told anyone about our date. I just didn't think Man Meets Woman Shock was newsworthy at my time of life. And I was betting that Ben's domestic arrangements made it unlikely he'd spread my acquaintance far and wide. In fact, on my part, the only person who might have had a chance to know that I had met Ben, ante mortem as it were, was Gina. Gina is a sexy bi-sexual temptress with an erratic disposition and hair extensions. But for God's sake, she works in a chiropodists'! Now nothing made sense. I had to talk to Gina, urgently.

While Max started his set with something vaguely familiar and Cole Porter-ish, I slipped out of the bar and crouched over my mobile in a quiet doorway.

"Hi, Gina! How are you?"

"Hey, baby! I'm just freaked right now! I was just going to call you. I've just heard something really outrageous!"

"Outrageous?" Nothing was certain with Gina. Her grandmother's funeral had been 'outrageous'.

"God, I've had a day. I'll tell you. You know that friend of mine, Michael, the one with the Cairn terriers and the gay dad? He lives next to those friends of yours, you know, the whaddaya call-ums and he rang to tell me. Apparently one of them's gone missing! They had the police round and everything – oh yes – I gave you your alibi, hah-hah! They came round to see *me* this morning as well, they're a very suspicious bunch aren't they? "

"One of who's missing?" I had been vainly trying to interrupt this stream of consciousness by pulling faces at the phone and jumping around impotently.

"The trannies! All the girls together! Michael got the goss from one of them."

"Oh, God, Gina! Who the hell are you talking about?"

"Sorry, you know, that er, whatdayacallit, 47 club, from the Parrot. One of them. The one with the stupid name and the lisp. She's gone, disappeared. Left all her stuff behind. No-one's seen her since Saturday. Since she left *us* in fact!"

"You mean Lois." I said flatly, "Lois has gone."

"Yes! That's her! Isn't that weird though? Well, I mean, Michael's going on and on about it. He thinks something's happened, he said she'd never just go, she was dug in there like a tick…"

'Weird' didn't even remotely cover it. Years of occasionally spectacular recreational drug use had prepared me superbly for the paranoia that began to seep like black ink into my soul.

"Jay?"

"Yes. Sorry. You're right, it *is* weird." I tried to think, "Sorry about the thing with the cops. Thanks for talking to them. Did they want to know what you'd been doing the rest of the night?" I added, a trifle mendaciously, "I can't remember anything much after leaving the club." Gina laughed.

"I'm not surprised, babe, you were wasted. But you got me horny, girl. I spent the rest of the night abusing Keith. Strangely enough they didn't seem very interested in that!" Keith was one of Gina's current boyfriends, "Where did *you* go?"

"I ended up at a party." I said. I felt relieved and puzzled at the same time. She couldn't have been at Ben's house ruining his chances of becoming a Rotarian if she'd been getting all sweaty and breathless with Keith. If she was telling the truth. Oh, Christ Jay, why wouldn't she?? Stop this *now*! Gina was speaking and I had to ask her to repeat herself.

"I said 'That must have been the car you got into.' You know – party bound?"

My jaw dropped and lolled about unattractively for a bit. My mind was a complete blank. Nada, nix, zip, zilch. A chemically-induced black hole that any amount of matter could have tumbled into.

"Car?" I said finally.

"Yes. There were some guys outside the club, I think they were going to this party and you went with them. You were dancing around and singing. Don't you remember?"

"No." I said. In my youth, when drunkenness and stoned dolce vita led me on with no fear of an endless future, my recall, when completely toasted, had been perfect. Every pratfall, every slurred syllable and silly laugh was etched with clarity into my consciousness for humiliating dissection the following morning. Even through a hangover.

I can clearly remember the pre college pub-crawl, fuelled by acid and home-grown that left wreckage in its wake. The happy travellers were the contents of five cars, a caravan which descended onto the quiet country pubs of Sussex with all the subtlety of a crashing air bus. The hostile stares of the locals were wasted on the wasted public brawl we had become. People shouting, laughing, rolling joints, spilling beer, falling over. I was obsessing, acid fashion, on my idée fixee of the night – my desire for a dry Martini. A demand I repeated like a fairground automaton until the clatter of the words made my brain ache…

As vivid as the mental cringe that accompanies it, a temp not particularly perdu, the bedroom of my childhood: pink-rosed and still strewn with the relics of smaller enthusiasms; pictures of horses, pottery pigs, Teddy bears. I was chopping coke on the bathroom mirror. One of my associates, unused to the big bang of the white stuff, began to vomit copiously. I beat a babbling path downstairs to enquire of my mother for a bucket, convinced the request was not at all unusual. It was the only time she ever said anything to me about my drug use. As I hopped from foot to foot, clutching the bucket, her face twitched and she said, "You should just see how your eyes look." The peals of laughter I was unable to control at this radical concept turned her to stone…

Even the impressive mixture of coke, ecstasy and speed that had me *starting* the evening lying on my back in the ladies lavatory, a human chicane, is picked out in Technicolor. The hideous pink of the tiles, the cities I was building from the Artex swirls on the ceiling, manically telling anyone who came near me to "Fuck off!" when they were rash enough to try and step over me…

But my brain seemed to have lately developed an alarming tendency to skip any bits it couldn't be bothered with. Like a tired secretary hoping to get the sack and move on to a less predictable and more fulfilling job.

"Jay?"

"No. Sorry. It's OK." I said, "The news about Lois. And, fuck

I don't know." I felt cross at being under such assault, "Thanks for letting me know. I suppose I'll have to talk to Nikki and Jane."

We exchanged farewells and I hung up. I didn't know which was the most irritating – the news of Lois or my total memory loss at some possibly crucial juncture. In the day's excitements I'd managed to forget all about the guilt. Now it was back – an undefined horror buried somewhere in the void of my recollection; now I was aware of the dark, I wondered if there was a monster lurking there. All bets were off again. I stared at the diminished change in my purse and reminded myself not to buy drinks for strangers when I could feel an awful lot better just buying them for myself. Then I told myself not to be so bloody melodramatic about everything and went back to Bar Bleu.

"You know what I see is the problem?" I said some time later, inhaling deeply, pulling the sweet, foul smoke as far into my lungs as possible and holding it, holding it. There was a pause. Exhale.

Max had finished off the evening with a beautiful, wistful rendition of 'Laura'. He skated around the melody with smooth and gentle skill, never losing his timing or direction. I'd watched hungrily as he swayed through the beauty of it, his eyes closed, his powerful, flat fingers stroking the keys, and just for my personal damnation, he smiled at me as he finished. Bar Bleu's clientele were slightly more appreciative than the Pink Parrot's had been and he got a good round of applause at the end of his efforts. I'd made my mind up that I wasn't going to weaken when it came to Max. I knew instinctively that I couldn't just have fun with him. The penalty for involvement would likely be another painful emotional shambles and I hadn't sorted out the last one yet. But I *did* want to talk to him. I'd decided Max the sax was going to be the lucky recipient of my growing paranoia.

"Mmmm?"

"The problem is the problem …" I said. Max was now reclining, renaissance Romanesque on my sofa amidst the cushions, looking relaxed in his purple haze, eyes half closed. I passed him the joint. "The problem is who the hell would care?" I said expansively, "Who??"

Max and I had talked again after the gig and had a few more drinks. He had recently moved to the area from London and was acquainting himself with the rude bohemian counter-culture that thrived by the seedy seaside. He was a thrice- divorced, currently single professional jazz musician and he was irritatingly articulate and witty. His soft voice belied a hardness and an unexpected introspection that sometimes seemed rude. He listened as if he was watching and he occasionally spoke as if he'd leapt on to a train of thought which he only brought to your attention halfway through the journey. It made him an entertaining and difficult conversationalist. Unexpected was a good word for Max. Where you would expect him to lounge he was tight and quick, where you expected tension he was unaccountably relaxed. There was the call of the wild about him, yet he seemed tired of the wilderness. Then, of course there were the dimples …

"These two people might not be connected. Lois, Ben," He said on a breath of fragrant smoke, "You don't know they are."

"True." I thought about the word 'true' for a while as Miles Davis joined us ethereally, doubtless to the annoyance of my neighbour, whose tolerance for my taste in elaborate modern jazz had been ground paper thin. "How do you know Miss Vixen?" I asked at the end of a complicated train of thought.

"Oh, you know," he said vaguely, "We met at The Parrot." I remembered Gina's pronouncements on Lois's name with a smile – "She looks more like a Doris, or a Mabel –"

"You know her real name's Wendy, don't you?" I said, only slightly vindictively.

Max burst out laughing and I joined in. It was the kind of

joyful, infectious, cathartic laughter that a few puffs and a sudden shared consciousness can create. It took some while to die down.

"I feel like we just had sex." He said at last, his eyes full of bliss. I didn't know what to say to that but found myself nodding and smiling back. Damn it to hell!

Max stayed the night. On my sofa. We spent an enjoyable few hours slicing and dicing music, art, literature, celebrity and porn into a foul stew of increasingly hilarious and shattered conversation. It was lovely to be free of my recent worries and I even forgot to beware of the dimples. But the herbal essence had eventually taken its toll and Max had fallen asleep. By the time morning announced itself in drizzle and some disconsolate squawking from damp seagulls, he had gone and I found a hastily scribbled note with his mobile phone number on it and 'call me' written with several exclamation marks.

In spite of other fairly pressing matters scratching at my consciousness, not to mention warm recollections of the sax man, I spent the morning tarting myself up for a client. After all, there are bills to be paid and memory loss on the scale I was currently running doesn't come cheap.

Ken is almost literally money for old rope: a rubber fetishist who enjoys total enclosure and restraint. My entire workload with Ken consists of zipping him into several layers of tight latex with certain admonishments, then tying him up on the floor of my dungeon come spare bedroom. Thus cocooned, with his breathing tubes in place and an alarm to hand, Ken can spend a couple of happy hours enjoying his inner space while I get on with some housework. I would check up on him every so often, but other than a heartfelt hug afterwards he's no trouble at all.

I have ceased to be even vaguely surprised how people press their hot buttons. After all, I've got a few odd ones of my own, not for dissection here. Most folk outside the scene assume the fetish community are a bunch of unattractive sexual deviants with personality disorders and an urge to dress like teenagers at a Halloween party. They are, of course, largely correct in this assumption. Where the subsequent conjecture goes awry is in believing that there is actually anything wrong with this. Despite all the fantasies that range from the grotesque to the plain hilarious, consensual is the watchword of all this well-lubricated enjoyment. Of course there are weirdoes in every group of enthusiasts. But the anoraks obsessing over trains and planes, twitching in bus shelters and plotting in the eaves to take Middle Earth with Orcs and trolls never have the extra topping of tut-tut-tut to deal with that sex hobbyists do. The truth is that nothing could be simpler or more satisfying than a pastime with a really primitive imperative. Ask Ken. The stars in his eyes as I help him up after his rubberised sojourn will carry him home in dreamland to the best orgasm he'll have until the next time he visits me.

While Ken wiled away his time upstairs, I spent my spare time this morning sitting like a vulcanized Goddess in latex corsetry, staring at Fuller's photographs and being amazed again by their savagery. I thought about Tom. As our marriage had dwindled into routine hostility, boredom had eventually fertilized his desertion to postures new with a feckless, curly haired dwarf who wore putty coloured slacks and Hush Puppies. God help us all, she's actually older than me! Still, he had embarked on a hopeful voyage of discovery along more conventional lines and seemed happy. Perhaps I couldn't abandon the bizarre for the mundane, perhaps he grew up and I didn't but I thought Tom had cast aside his female alter ego, along with some other interesting fetishes, to get on with life unsullied by the years of guilt his provincial conscience had lumbered him with. Some of his guilty secrets remained with me, though. As did a large collection of make-up and two very bad wigs. And, of course, there was the proof on Angell's website that he not only knew Ben but that going straight hadn't been entirely successful. But *this*? I turned the pictures over and studied the back. The photo paper itself was marked Ilfochrome RA4 Super Glossy. I sniffed tentatively at one corner and the pungent odour of developer, stop baths and fix prodded my memory cells. I'd done a little photography at Art College and these prints were actually enlargements taken from a colour negative, rather than printed on photo paper from a DCIM file. So, they'd been taken with a good old fashioned SLR on good old fashioned film, not with a digital camera. It occurred to me that they really weren't the sort of happy snaps you'd want to trust to a 24 hour photo booth and that colour processing is definitely no straightforward matter: unless you're a photographer.

Which brought me right back to Stuart Crouch. I'd wondered before if Stuart might know someone who could have taken the photographs, now my Spidey-sense and deepening paranoia made me sure he'd taken them himself. Yup, great, here's another ex who's less than happy. Was I going to have to trawl through my entire back catalogue?

I remembered a dazzlingly bright February morning. An unexpected cheeky wink and a smile from the weather, after winter had thrown in chill reminders in the shape of frosts, freezing drizzle and snow. I was standing in the front room of the flat trying to get hoops of varying size through numerous piercings, encumbered by nail extensions the length of raptor's claws, reducing my ears to red flaps in the process. My soon-to-be mother-in-law offered fluttering hands in febrile and irritating assistance and my soon-to- be husband swore and swore and swore in the bedroom as his bootlace broke for the second time.

And the bride wore black. She did. Black velvet, black lace, a black top hat. It was only intended as a sartorial middle digit to convention, not an omen, although both my marriages, first Alec, then Tom, could have been better served by my dress sense.

Weddings are a wonderful opportunity to blow enormous sums on a big party made memorable by effusive and schmaltzy goodwill, and guests throwing up in pub car parks. This is what should happen if they are done properly. Both my big days, by this yard stick, could be judged a roaring success. Fade to credits. Welling soundtrack. Unfortunately, the needle is ripped from 'Lara's Theme' after only a few bars and real life intercedes again. I discovered, to my dismay, that relationships are about people, not ideas. I realised I had compromised for the sake of an idea. The idea that marriage is wonderful. Just that. And for the sake of expediency I'd managed to involve two other people, apparently willing participants, in a romantic fantasy, regardless of our suitability.

Alec was a bearded, long-haired hippy with light blue eyes and a wretched roll-your-own cough that announced him half a mile away. He loved smoking dope, progressive rock music and gardening. A happy combination in the Summer when he could baffle our elderly neighbours with Vanilla Fudge and King Crimson, while he pottered in a haze around the exquisite garden he'd carefully nurtured. We managed quite a few years of cheerful co-operation before the vehicle came to a gentle and barely noticed halt. We had become siblings without realising, a brotherly, sisterly comradeship that shared many things but delivered our marriage into retirement while we were still in our 20s. The outcome was divorce and a rebound into another marriage which I regretted shamefully, even as the registrar smiled benignly at me in front of my friends – none of my few remaining family could be bothered to attend, perhaps less an indication of their lack of commitment, than their convictions about mine – while I wore a posh frock and a smile twitching with nerves. Beside me, facing this dispenser of stupidity, Tom, the closet psychopath.

A girlfriend once said to me "Marriage is an institution. Who wants to live in an institution?" A little unfair, perhaps, as she was a shaven headed dyke who'd pierced her own labia with a darning needle. But I doubt that I'll be institutionalised by that kind of madness again, even in the unlikely event I find a suitable candidate for treatment. Stuart certainly wasn't it. Had he seriously thought he was?

I checked on Ken, poured some scalding hot coffee and dialled Stuart's mobile. The phone rang for a long time before he picked it up.

"Hi, it's me." I said a little too cheerfully.

"Hello, Jay. What do you want?" Not promising.

"I'm sorry to disturb you Stu. I was hoping I could pop round. I need to talk to you about something."

"Talk to me about what?"

"It's difficult on the phone," I said, picking up the photographs, "It won't take long, I promise. Can I come over in about an hour?" There was a very long pause and I could hear him breathing, eventually he sighed and said,

"I'm busy right now. You can come over after six." The line went dead. Not a happy chappy. Oh, well. I remembered the last time I'd seen him. It had been a smiley day, all wave borne white horses, fluffy clouds and shining sea and in the midst of it all, in the beer garden of my local, Stuart had been a small tragedy under a bad haircut. It astonishes me now that I'd ever considered the compromise of his unspecified affections for some small change in the way of companionship. I'd made the right decision, but he didn't see it that way.

"Why did you lead me on like that?" he said when I told him we were through. He looked as if I'd struck him across the face. "Why didn't you say 'Fuck off Stu' if you didn't want me?"

"I'm sorry. It's not you, it's me," I'd said falling back on the old staple, "I don't know what I want. Neither do you. It would have been shit."

"You don't know that. We haven't tried." He had been persistent but I didn't dare reveal the awful truth: the more I'd got to know him, the less attractive he'd become. It turned out that still waters didn't run deep, they didn't actually run at all. In the end, to my horror, he'd broken down and wept into his lager, seizing a large blue handkerchief and blowing his nose with embarrassing gusto, while other punters fixed me with judgmental hostility. I hadn't realised how raw his emotions could be when they were allowed to escape the confines of fortress Stu. That had been a little over six months ago and I wasn't at all sure of my reception now.

I sat for a few more moments looking at the photographs before putting them back in the cellophane bag, and then picked up the phone again. I decided that while I awaited my date with destiny and Stuart Crouch, I would pay a visit to 47 Southwood Road, where Lois had been Nikki and Jane's permanent and increasingly resented house guest. I wanted to try and set my mind at rest. She couldn't have had anything to do with Ben, could she, in spite of her presence at Dazzlers? He was surely far too rich a dish (or possibly too fastidious a diner) for the rasping, cheap and cheerless Lois. But the little imp on my shoulder reminded me of the smug expression at the centre of the Marlboro miasma, "I wouldn't worry about *him*…".

A time for withdrawal and thought, working through frustrations, looking for clarity. Perhaps someone can give enlightening advise; stay patient and things will become clear.

CHAPTER SIX

47 Southwood Road was a mid-terrace house lost in a line of many dingy terraces that hurried up the West cliff in tendrils of sturdy Victorian stucco and tile. 47 had seen its heyday come and go but clean net curtains brightened the windows and a large pot of Autumn crocus perched cheerfully on the step. It was clearly making the best of a bad job.

When I arrived, Nikki was cooking some kind of delicious smelling stew and it simmered fragrantly in the kitchen while she sat with me in the lounge sipping Liebfraumilch from a mug and shaking her head.

"I just can't think where she could have gone. It's surprising when I think about it, I don't know very much about her at all. Who her friends were, whether she had any family. She was always making up crap about herself and I just stopped listening."

I looked around at the mix and match of plain second hand furniture, brightened with colourful throws and scatter cushions, the framed family snapshots and knick-knacks crowding every available surface. Pride of place on the sideboard went to a large silver darts trophy that was filled with fresh fruit.

"How did she end up staying with you?" I asked.

"We advertised on the web. Jane wasn't working then and we were struggling with the mortgage. She was the only serious reply we had. Christ, that was three years ago and she's never done anything like this before. All her stuff's still here."

"I wanted to talk to her about something." I said truthfully. "I don't suppose she said who her date was on Saturday?" Nikki shook her head and shrugged.

"No. The police wanted to know about her friends and I couldn't tell them. She was going out a lot more on her own, mostly down the Prince Albert I think, but I don't know who she met." Nikki put her mug down with a thump. It had 'World's Greatest Dad' written on it in a gift of sad entreaty. "To be honest," she said, "We didn't really care. Anything that kept her out of our hair was a plus." She looked up, "Has this got something to do with Ben Hammond?"

I was a little taken aback,

"I'm not sure," I said, "I'm surprised you remember me mentioning him."

"Haven't you seen the news?" Nikki filled her mug again and gave me a hard look, "There was something about an inquest being adjourned and the police are asking for information. They said they were treating his death as suspicious. What happened?"

Oh Christ. It was, of course inevitable that the whole thing would become newsworthy. Dean's Bay wasn't a big place and Ben was a wealthy and handsome 'love rat' with an Aston Martin, a penchant for trannie porn and ladies' knickers. It was surprising a mini-series hadn't been commissioned. I sighed.

"I saw him the night he died." I said holding up my hands to forestall comment, "And some other things have happened that have been kind of personal. After Lois said she saw him I wanted to try to find out what she meant."

"Fuck knows what Lois ever meant. She drank too much, she took too many drugs and she was a pain in the arse. Like I said, she was always talking herself up. You remember that reality show, David To Davina? She claimed she was in that but they cut her out." I remembered the show. It had been a notorious depiction of the ultimate 'makeover'. An insult to the cause of the transgendered and a trial by humiliation for its eponymous hero/ine. "She said she'd been in an episode of The Bill," Nikki made a tired show of counting on her fingers, "Emmerdale, Casualty, Eurotrash, some Men and Motors rubbish and she was *always* auditioning for West End parts. Like I say, I just stopped listening. Mind you, " Nikki got to her feet and made her way towards the kitchen to check on her stew, "She was seriously chuffed with herself over something on Friday. She got in late. Crashing about in the kitchen, she woke me up. She was off her face on something. I told her to shut the fuck up but she just kept tapping her nose and laughing. I left her to it, stupid cow." She pulled a face and looked guilty. "Well, she *was* annoying." She said.

I thought about what I should do with this information.

"Could I have a look at her room?" Nikki raised her eyebrows at me,

"It is a serious personal problem isn't it?" she said but before I could answer she added, "Don't worry, love, I'm not really interested. Knock yourself out. The police have been over it. I don't think they found anything. At least they never said."

She disappeared into the kitchen and I made my way up the stairs wondering what the hell it was *I* was hoping to find. Lois's chain smoking and intemperance combined with her frequent rancid outbursts against the world in general had marginalised her to the Regency striped dominion of Nikki and Jane's spare bedroom. It was a very small room indeed, cramped by a wardrobe large enough to sleep in. An empty ashtray sat on her bed but the room was otherwise tight-lipped. I backed off and opened the wardrobe, the doors caught on the edge of the bed and I had virtually to step inside it to look at her clothes. It seemed quite possible I might be swallowed up by this massive piece of furniture and chucked out after digestion amidst snow and fauns and Turkish delight. But there were only clothes, the faint odour of tobacco, rich wood and polish. I leafed through the hangers, pushing my hands into pockets, feeling progressively more and more intrusive and stupid. Many of her things had a thin, second-hand feel to them and Lois seemed to keep tickets and receipts in profusion, some of them crumbling to dust in the linings. I'd just reached the edge of my tolerance for pointless nosiness when an apparently empty jacket yielded a strange lump. Delving further into the pocket I found a small tear. I wriggled my fingers in further and from amongst the crumbs in the jacket lining I drew out a card. It was a Sam Spade moment. Not as illuminating as a book of matches from the Kit Kat Club might have been, but it was interesting nonetheless. It was a pink glossy business card with a white crescent moon in one corner. There was no other printing on it but someone had written the number 124 across the card and underlined it several times. I'd no idea what it meant but I slipped it into my back pocket and left any other secrets in Lois's closet to the cast of Narnia and the stale fag smoke.

I still had a little time to kill before seeing Stuart so I decided to visit Lois's local pub where I thought I would at least be guaranteed something palatable to drink. This proved to be an unwise assumption. The glass of Vin Degoutant I sipped in the tepid confines of the Prince Albert was foul enough to etch a cracaleur into my tooth enamel. The Prince Albert is a large premises on a dusty street corner a few hundred yards down the hill from number 47. Just to give you the general idea, it is situated next to an undertaker. It has a large flat screen TV silently displaying the obscure footballing efforts of some European super league and fruit machines that occasionally burp into life whether they're fed or not. It has a juke box playing a dismal loop of Neil Diamond hits and a pool table with grey duct tape covering a tear in the baize. The tables are large, the seating is roomy and comfortable but despite its obvious efforts to be entertaining it seems to have been infected by the mortuary gloom of its neighbour. Everything seems dingy and slightly shabby, a cold, glum edifice with too much nicotine staining. A similar thing could have been said of its landlord as he loomed over me with a three-day growth and a superfluous smile.

"How's the wine?"

"Fine. Very nice." I lied.

"Don't touch it myself. The wife chooses it, she likes a glass or two with a meal." Ah, the joys of fine dining...

"It's been all go here." He went on. I looked around. The only other inhabitant of the bar was a young man in a lifeless beige sweater feeding crisps to a pair of small dogs.

"Really?" I said. I suppose I didn't sound convinced.

"Yes," he said, "Had the bloody police here earlier." He looked reluctant to go back to his stewarding duties and I realised rather belatedly that he was trying to flirt with me.

"What were they after?" I tried not to look disingenuous.

"There's a bunch of trannies up the road," he leaned further across the bar and I realised he'd been eating pickled onions, "Transvestites. Bloody stupid lot. One's gone a.w.o.l. Probably turn up dead in a field." He looked satisfied with this assertion and waited for my reaction. I feigned impressed shock mingled with distaste. Although I didn't have to peddle the distaste – I was looking at a potato- faced yokel flogging rancid wine.

"Yes," he nodded, "She used to come in here poncing around, upsetting people. I had to warn her once or twice. Too much sauce." Whether he was referring to Lois's cheek or her alcohol consumption wasn't clear.

"Upsetting people," I said, "That's bad." I looked at the young man and his dogs. They had finished the crisps and were looking disconsolately at each other. The landlord noticed my gaze and misinterpreted it.

"He's not one of them." He said in a stage whisper, "But he did have a row with her. The *victim*," he pronounced the word as if it had a 'k' in it, "The night she disappeared. I told the police that." Dog boy looked up and found us both staring at him.

"Michael!" The landlord was suddenly smiling, hale and hearty, "This young lady was just admiring your boys!" I was momentarily alarmed by this claim until I realised he meant the man's dogs. Sensing attention, they began to tail-wag experimentally. Looking at the expectant trio, I also realised that this must be Gina's friend, Michael. The one with the gay dad. Feigning a sudden enthusiastic interest in all things canine, I managed to escape the clutches of the awful landlord and make Michael's formal acquaintance.

"I think you know a friend of mine," I said as his hairy companions bounced around my shins vying for attention in the hope of more crisps, "Gina Harrison."

Michael looked like a young man hag-ridden into premature middle age. His baggy sweater was accompanied by matching slacks and limp suede shoes that looked like slippers. I knew this outer shell would conceal neat woolly socks and an abomination of Y-fronts. These things would probably be Christmas gifts from his mother. His thinning brown hair was parted in the middle and he wore a glum expression. When I mentioned Gina's name, however, his face lit up and he became practically animated.

"Gina's great!" he said, "Beautiful woman. How do you know her? Is she a good friend?"

"Yes, I've known her ages," I said, "We go back a long way. She's mentioned you a few times."

Michael smiled bashfully. It was an astonishingly sweet smile and it made him suddenly younger and very nearly attractive. I felt rather mean, ploughing straight in with my interrogation.

"The landlord was saying you saw Lois before she disappeared." I said, rather bluntly. "I'm sorry. I've just come from number 47. I knew Lois a bit. It must be quieter since she's gone?" He may have been surprised but he didn't show it. He raised his eyebrows at me and smiled.

"So you're not after me for my body then?" he said, then laughed as I started to protest, "Don't worry. Quieter is right. Yeah, I live next door to her and her pals. Nikki and Jane are alright, no problem at all. Lois was a pain in the arse. Sit down." He offered.

"Thanks." I said.

"We had a bit of a set to in here on Saturday night. It was about these two," he said, indicating the furry pair beneath the table, "Said they were getting into her back garden, which was bollocks and I told her so. God, it's not even her bloody house."

"What did she say?" I asked. Michael suddenly flung his hands up dramatically and adopted a screeching falsetto.

"I shall thoo you for twesspath!" I burst out laughing and Michael joined in. "Let me get you a drink," he said, "It's nice to meet friends of Gina. Don't touch the wine," he added sotto voce, "It's fucking awful."

Suddenly I could see why Gina liked Michael, despite all the unpromising camouflage. He was a humanist. We chatted some more, this time over a beer, and he seemed happy to share his opinions of his neighbours with me. I began to feel a little sorry for Lois. No-one, not even those that passed for her nearest and dearest, had many good words to say for her.

"No-one seemed to like her very much." I said, "Maybe she just found greener grass somewhere else."

"She didn't go out of her way to be likeable," Michael said evenly, "She used to come in here and get drunk and loud. Then she would hit on people. She didn't seem to know if she wanted men or women so she managed to piss off everyone. But I don't think she would just have upped and left. There really wasn't any reason for her to go."

'Dug in like a tic'. I thought. He leaned towards me,

"To be honest it wouldn't surprise me if someone had, you know…" he made a furtive, continental hand gesture, tilting his palm this way and that, "I could cheerfully have smacked her one. Like Saturday. I was having a quiet drink in here on my own and over she came and started howling on about 'my filthy dogs'," he looked briefly gloomy again, "She quite enjoyed baiting me in public. It was a row she started and kept up single-handed. Once she had a bee in her bonnet she never let things go. She would have bitched away all night if she hadn't had someone with her."

"Oh yes?" I perked up, "Who was she with?"

"Well, when she wasn't bugging me every time she got a drink, she was deep in flirty conversation with some woman. Well, I think it was a woman. Could have been another trannie, I suppose. I couldn't see properly from where I was sitting." I felt a rising excitement, "Thinking about it," Michael went on, "It could easily have been another TV. Lois sometimes hung out here with Nikki and Jane. She was sitting with her back to me in one of those pews," he turned in his seat and indicated some high backed settles in an alcove by one of the fruit machines, "All I could see was some long black hair and a red dress. Oh, yes and long red fingernails."

Life seemed to be turning into a huge practical joke being played out at my expense. My recollection flashed back with gloating uncertainty to scarlet fingernails and drugs and something else teasingly buried that shrank away every time I approached it. A red dress. Long red nails. Drugs. Unconsciousness. Total memory loss… I shook my head.

"You OK?" Michael looked at me quizzically.

"Yes." I said, "Fine. You didn't get a better look at her, I suppose?"

"No. I left before they did, why? Do you think you know her?"

"No," I said slowly, "I don't think so." I looked up at the clock above the bar. It was coming on 6 o'clock. "I ought to be going," I said and watched the glum shutters descend on Michael's expression again, "I've got someone I have to see." Ugh.

"Well, it's nice to meet you," Michael actually shook my hand as I stood up, "Give my love to Gina, won't you?"

"Thanks," I said, "I will. And it's nice to meet -" I indicated his canine companions.

"Ben and Jerry," he said and smiled.

THE HANGED MAN

A difficult, painful time when things don't seem to be working out. A situation seems to be stagnating but the trials experienced during this time will lead to a new perspective.

CHAPTER SEVEN

I felt tense. Alarmed and tense. I thought about going home and relaxing with the half ounce of Afghan Black I kept for emergencies. Collapsing into a much more eclectic frame of mind and listening to Miles or some of the terrible prog rock I kept especially for tense occasions. A lady in red. Common sense told me it was nothing more than addled coincidence but unfortunately my common sense has always been stunted by my lack of inhibitions and an overactive imagination. A song had started to run through my head. Thankfully it wasn't Chris De Burgh's gruesome homage. The earnest warblings of that mono-browed midget would definitely have driven me home to a soothing spliff. For some reason the rewind button was caught on Foxy Lady by Jimi Hendrix. Well, maybe this 'lady' was a repressed photographer in a wig. On the face of it, that sounded perfectly ludicrous but no more ludicrous than the engineers, accountants and security guards I knew sporting hair pieces and size twelve stilettos, and all of them necessarily repressed. Perhaps it *was* a woman. I didn't know but I wanted to find out. The thing that worried me like a hangnail was the conviction that I'd stood next to the bloody creature and I was too bonzoed to tell.

Stuart lived on the entire second floor of an unconverted Victorian town house that he had inherited from his great uncle.

It was a substantial piece of property but despite this good fortune he somehow contrived to be squatting there. His living arrangements were mixed with his studio and darkroom on the one floor and this would have been bohemian if anyone but Stuart had owned it. He never used the front door. The doorbell had been re-routed and his main entrance was via a rickety iron fire escape that health and safety had insisted on bolting to the side of the building. This seemed to give him an even less substantial foothold in the house. Ivy covered much of the front of the building, furnishing a sinister Gothic facade, an atmosphere enhanced by the single lighted window that that glowed through the rapid evening darkness. I wasn't exactly comfortable as my steps echoed coldly on the metal and I climbed towards the door.

Stuart let me in with a bob of the head and busied himself clattering around in his kitchen area, making breezy conversation. It didn't last for long. Polite exchanges over, there was nothing but awkward silence as we both sat and stared at one another from opposite sides of the room. His concessions to home comfort were rudimentary. Two tired sofas, frayed into cosy dilapidation, a wreck of bedding, TV on a packing crate, wires sprouting from the back like plant tendrils, connecting his satellite dish, his DVD player. The area was littered with newspapers, used takeaway cartons and empty beer bottles. This was all in sharp contrast to the studio area next door which was clean and organised. I wondered just how ingrained dividing up a life like this could become. And what the consequences might be.

"Well?" He said, looking at me steadily over a mug of politely brewed tea. His dark features were wary and slightly aggressive.

"I've been having some problems with photographs," I said and delved into my jacket pocket. I handed him the cellophane bag I'd brought with me. I watched as his eyebrows climbed his forehead. "- So, I was wondering if you knew anything about these. Maybe who took them? I can see they were taken at the Parrot. They're not digital. Anything you can tell me – "

"Where did you get these?"

I looked at him, trying to judge his expression. It was difficult, as always.

"They were posted through my letter box. Look, I think it may have something to with Ben Hammond's death. Did you see the news? Someone sent me his car keys as well." I paused and looked at him evenly, "Stu," I said.

But Stuart held up his hands and shook his head vigorously,

"Oh, no! Not guilty. Yeah, I heard about that. Are you mixed up in it?" I could see a faint smile playing about his lips as he handed me back the pictures. "Was Hammond into you as well?" *As well?* So Stuart *did* know Ben.

"I met him twice." I said wearily. Again, "Ben seems to have been into a lot of people. Do you know a TS called Lois?"

Stuart put down his tea and stood up ruffling his hair. He looked calculating for a moment, then awkward, then he smiled.

"Lois." He said, "I haven't seen that for a while. Brian as was. Hmmm…"

"Brian? Are you talking about Lois?" This was news to me and I boggled at him intelligently for a moment. He laughed. One of his short, humourless barks.

"Lois was a hospital porter called Brian. He had his op done in London on the NHS. He used to go clubbing in London. I met him at Antichrist." It sounded like an appointment with the damned, which wasn't actually that far from the truth. Antichrist was one of the capital's more Gothic alternative venues. I processed this information.

"How did you know Ben Hammond?" I asked. Stuart looked at me sideways as he walked towards his studio. He was thinking. A bad sign.

"Would you do something for me?" He said, rocking back on his heels and making an elaborate show of lacing his fingers together.

"Er ... what?" Watching him poised and expectant, I was being forcibly reminded of all the reasons I had discontinued our relationship. I had only been to his house on one other occasion and I was feeling distinctly out manoeuvred on foreign soil. Play nice, Jay.

"Can I take your photograph?" he said and I felt my heart plummet.

"Why?"

"I always wanted to get your tattoos," he said, "Just give me your skin," he laughed, "And I'll tell you about bendy Ben and Brian the lady boy."

This was a severely unattractive proposition but I'd had my tattoos photographed several times before for various fetish projects and I was used to the enthusiasm photographers displayed for my ink, if not for the actual canvas.

"It's OK," he said, "I'll even forgive you for being a bitch."

"Look, Stu," I began, "You know I didn't mean – "

"It's alright." He said, "Been and gone. Come on, fair's fair. I'll tell you what I know and we'll call it quits."

So, somewhat against my better judgement, I followed him into the studio and watched while he set up lights and reflectors. He led me to a white back drop at one end of the room, draped with gentle folds of heavy, ivory coloured cloth and took a light meter reading in front of my face

"Lois, as you call him, is a twat." Stuart said, "And a bit of a sneaky fuck at that." He brought over a rather elegant Regency dining chair, a carver with scrolled arms and pad feet and began arranging the cloth around it.

"What do you mean 'sneaky'?" I asked.

"Do you remember a TV documentary about ten, fifteen years ago. Sort of trannie sob story. It was bloody grim – "

"'David to Davina'?" I asked, remembering what Nikki had said. Stuart cackled,

"Yeah. That was it," he laughed a little more, shaking his head, "Twenty stone of camp saddo squealing "I want to look like Sophia Loren!" *I've* got more fucking chance. That, of course, was the joke," he looked at me evenly, "Anyway Brian – Lois, whatever, latched on to this Davina in the hope of grabbing a bit of limelight. Started dragging the poor bugger round the clubs, giving her makeovers, being her 'bestest friend'. Didn't work. I don't think Lois even had her fifteen minutes. She was too fucking gruesome even for car crash telly. She has this habit of latching on to anyone or anything she thinks might give her a free ride. She turned up at a shoot I did at a private fetish party in Mayfair, pretending to be one of the organisers. It was an invite only thing, you know. She managed to blag her way to a night of free booze and food and she made such a bloody nuisance of herself that they actually had to physically throw her out. Has she got something to do with Hammond as well? Come on," he added, "Get your kit off."

"I don't know," I said, "She's gone missing."

"Well, I wouldn't have thought Hammond would want to have anything much to do with her. She got pretty notorious on the scene in London." He shrugged.

I was slightly stunned by these revelations. I had assumed, like Nikki, that Lois was a fantasist giving it large. But it seemed, in this one respect at least, she had been telling the truth. I began to get undressed while I thought about it. Did this get me any further forward? Hardly. Although it did mean that Lois's mysterious pronouncements about Ben need not necessarily be taken with any seasoning. So where the hell had she gone?

I discarded my tee shirt and jeans, shoes and socks. The problem for my modesty, when displaying my tattoos in all their glory, is that I'm covered in them. My legs, back, feet, shoulders, two full sleeves, the lotus tattoo on my left breast has been the latest addition to the armour of ink that covers me. It is very colourful, much of it Japanese-style and the best quality. I have breaking waves and Carp, chrysanthemums and cherry blossom, a huge green dragon encircles my right leg, clasping his pearl on my hip, the lines are sinuous, the colours bright. Tattooed ladies are far too common these days to enjoy a place in a freak show but I've got no time for ink as a fashion accessory. Silly, chavvy girls with their tramp stamps and pouty starlets with Confucian homilies in shaky Franktur may have kept a lot of tattooists in the money but I take my body art seriously. There aren't many people with the coverage that I've got and even though I don't often notice my tattoos, I still get a lot of enjoyment from them when I do. Apart from anything else, girls, they're a great mask for cellulite. I stood in front of Stuart in my bra and knickers, feeling a little silly and apprehensive. But he looked encouragingly professional.

"They're really beautiful." He said appreciatively.

"Thanks." I said.

"Can you take the rest of it off? I can't really see properly in your undies." he raised his eyebrows, "You can cover your bits with this." He picked up a length of the same material that was draped around the chair and resolutely turned his back to me. I sighed. Well, I'd come this far and it wasn't as if he hadn't seen this lot already.

"OK," I said, a little reluctantly, "I suppose I owe you one."

When he turned round again I was resplendent on his dining chair throne, the material draped across my lap.

"So, do you know Fuller?" I asked, now determined to get my money's worth as Stuart began snapping happily away. He smirked,

"I did some work for him. A bit of still photography, you know the sort of thing. Can you move your shoulder to the right? That's lovely."

"What sort of thing?" I said

"Tits, pussy."

"Ben Hammond?" Stuart twisted his mouth and his eyes became hooded,

"I know he was planning some project or other, With Angell Falls. And I think there was another one. Christ, what was her name…Misty Licks! That's it!" He dropped his hands and stared at me with genuine amusement, "Where the fuck do they gets these names?" Where indeed? "There were supposed to be some juicy meetings," he went on, "to work out scenarios. More of an excuse for Hammond to wack off to a spot of buggery. I should think that's been postponed now."

"You didn't like him, did you?"

"No." Stuart said without rancour and I didn't pursue it. I was still thinking about Lois while Stuart pictured and posed me, muttering to himself. One of the disadvantages of being utterly odious is that people tend to disregard everything you say as if it's been poisoned by your personality. Perhaps Piers Morgan would find his wit and wisdom enshrined in public affection if he wasn't such a whining, self satisfied, self-publicist. Or maybe I'm being unfair. I doubt Piers Morgan would have his wit enshrined anywhere, just as it was hard to imagine anyone taking Lois seriously, regardless of her disposition.

Stuart was standing beside me, his camera slung round his neck, looking David Baily-ish.

"Can you just turn a little so I can see your back from round here?" He said. "That's it." I looked into the glum shadows of the living room as I heard the shutter click. But back to more pertinent stuff.

"So what about these photographs – hey!"

Stuart was quick. While my back was turned away from him, he had produced a length of rope from God knows where and slipped it in a double loop around the arm of the chair. He pulled the loose ends tight through the loop and in one swift movement, tied my left wrist to the chair arm.

"What are you doing?" I felt horror flood through me in an icy torrent. I tried to get up and turn but he pushed one knee between my legs and leaned against me determinedly with all of his stocky frame. Jesus Christ! I tried to grab him with my free hand and push him off.

"You bastard! Get off me!" I kept thinking 'no-one knows I'm here', a panicky, pointless jingle. I could smell stale cigarette smoke on his sweater. I could feel his stubble on my shoulder as he pushed me down.

"Shut up!" he said and grabbed my right wrist in a frightening hold, pushing his thumb expertly into the joint and numbing my fingers. I yelled.

"Shut up!" he repeated, dragging another coil of rope from the leg pocket of his combat trousers. In no time, my other arm was securely tied to the chair. He stood up, pulling the covering off my lap and throwing it to one side. I saw his face. The photographer in his clean and tidy studio was gone and a disturbing regression to the uncertain squatter that lived in the leaf litter next door had taken place.

"What are you going to do?" I said evenly. It always surprises me how calm I can be in a situation that calls for acute panic. Chronic unpleasantness is much more nerve racking. I suppose my grim childhood bequeathed me the fatalism to deal with unexpected bouts of violence. My father's occasionally hands-on approach to child- rearing made dealing with this kind of dread second nature. I stared at Stuart coldly. He looked feral.

"You'll see." He said and opened a pine trunk on the other side of the studio. The contents soon became apparent. Rope, large quantities of rope. He pulled out a length, threw it across the floor to measure it, then doubled it up.

"I thought a breast harness might be nice to start." He said.

I made a decision. I wasn't going to say another word. In matters of kinky sexual exploration, I am a top, a dominant. I might like chocolate and sparkly jewellery, I might like romance and candle lit smiles, I might even occasionally wave my hands about in loveable girly confusion, but not in this situation. He might be able to do what he liked but I was not going to submit to him or give him the satisfaction of a response.

Stuart passed the doubled up rope over my ribs and around the back of the chair, catching it in a hitch. Then he brought each single rope end over my shoulders and crossed them between my breasts, taking them under again to the back of the chair, securing them before he brought them forward and over the top of my breasts, twice, expertly pulling them tight each time. It wasn't a solace that I knew how these manoeuvres worked as I'd practised them myself on willing partners. Shibari, Japanese ropework, is an art and Stuart was very good at it. He stood back and inspected his handiwork.

"Lovely." He said, "Puppies' noses." He reached down and ran his fingers with horrible fondness over each of my breasts, feeling how tight he'd squeezed them with the rope. From somewhere at the bottom of a deep well I found the strength to remain stony-faced. He straightened up and smiled. I watched his mirthless smirk freeze into a grimace.

"What I don't understand," he said, backing off and taking a photograph, "Is why the fuck you would screw a cunt like Ben Hammond?" Ho-hum. Light dawned. "I mean, a panty wearing sissy boy? A knicker-sniffing saddo poncing about in tights?" he took another picture.

"I'll tell you what Ben Hammond was," he added, picking up his tripod and planting it at the other side of the studio opposite my chair, "He was an *admirer*." He began to set up his camera on the tripod, adjusting the height and angle. 'Admirer' is a term used by T-girls everywhere to describe men who like to socialise with, but more especially, have sex with transvestites. It's a way straight men can go at it hammer and tongs without feeling terribly gay.

"Except, of course, little Benjy didn't have the balls. He just liked to watch. So he wanted his own little production line. He wanted to pay people to act out his fantasies and then make money from them. A pretty expensive way of wanking, I'd say."

What about you, Stu? I thought, you like to watch, don't you?

"What's the matter?" he asked, "Cat got your tongue? Well, just for your information, *I* took those photographs. Yes, that's right. You know how it is – a fool and his money…And I'm sure you'd agree it would be a serious fucking tragedy for you if Mr. Fuller got to know about them. Yes? No? Never mind. I'm going to get some beer and a curry. This is going to be fun. I'm glad you dropped round this evening." Stuart was fiddling with a small digital remote. The camera on the tripod opposite me beeped a willing response and the shutter clicked.

"This takes a photograph automatically every two minutes," he said, "Enjoy. Back soon." I watched him skip out of the studio, gather up his jacket and leave. My heart sank as I heard a bolt being rammed home.

Fuck! Fuck! Fuck! Fuck! My chest was firmly bound to the back of the chair and my wrists were firmly bound to the arms. I sat for a moment while the camera clicked thinking of all the terrible things I would like to do to Mr. Crouch. Strangely, I wasn't in the least bit frightened. Perhaps I should have been but the thought of Stuart attached by his genitals via some *big* crocodile clips to a small generator was far more motivating than fear. I tried experimentally twisting and turning and pulling but he really was good with rope and it had just the right thickness and bite to remain firm. *Click*. Great. Another shot of me in idiotic extremis. I gave up with pulling. I tried standing up. But of course the chair came with me and I ended up a crippled, furniture carrying hunchback. *Click*. I sat down again, heavily. I stopped testing the rope and tried testing the chair, holding on to the arms and pushing outwards. But I couldn't get my shoulders behind the effort as they were held firmly to the chair back and the chair was sturdy. Damn Hepplewhite! Damn Chippendale! *Click*. My only free limbs were my legs. Now, for a– er – Rubenesque – 37-year-old I am astonishingly supple. An old party favourite, after the requisite cocktail consumption, had been to tangle my legs round the back of my neck. This trick is not as useful as it sounds and I stopped doing it, drunk or sober, after someone took a photograph and I realised how silly it looked. I wriggled around in the chair. All I needed to do was raise one foot high enough to push against the opposite chair arm. So I tried, twisting myself, holding on for dear life and getting as much of my weight behind it as I could. I listened to the camera click and whirr on this grotesque image as I pushed and just when I thought it was going to be pointless ... *CRACK*. The arm splintered then gave way and I took a relieved delight in pulling the stupid thing apart. Once I had one arm free, it was relatively easy to escape, untie my wrists and find the ends of the harness and loosen them. Then just to relieve my feelings and the general tension of the last few days, I smashed the chair to pieces while the shutter carried on snapping. The set of photographs Stuart had engineered would probably have made quite a good art installation but they weren't going anywhere near the light of day. I retrieved my clothes and dressed hastily, grabbing the camera as its final click captured my absence for posterity.

The door to the fire escape was bolted on the outside, so I hurried down the main stairs, through dark and echoing emptiness to the front door. It was locked and dead-bolted and I rattled it uselessly for a few moments. A quick tour of the ground floor revealed that the back door was actually boarded up along with the back windows and the sash windows at the front were nailed shut. There was no furniture, no tools, not even anything I could usefully use to club Stuart to death with on his return. This was ridiculous. What was I going to do? Hide? I turned on the light in the front room, hoping to find any small thing I could break a window with and stopped dead. The dusty candle lights around the walls unpleasantly exposed peeling blue wall paper. There were bare floorboards and patches of crumbling plaster. The dust rose in a soft sparkle at my hurried entrance and there, amidst neglect and the dour smell of rising damp, I saw an entire wall had been given over to a photo gallery. Christ! Who said that printed media was dead? Glossy 5 x 8 pictures pinned in a celebratory panorama, documenting a life. *Mine.* I recognised shopping trips, meetings, friends, visits to clubs, clients, paparazzi like shots of my living room, my bedroom, the depth of focus on the zoom blurring everything but me and anyone I was with. I saw Ben, Lucy, Max. I felt physically sick. And angry, very, very angry. Mentally, I detached Stuart's genitals from the generator and wired them up to the National Grid. But standing in front of this wall of obsessive journalism, I was suddenly inspired. It was stupid I hadn't thought of it before. I punched a number into my mobile phone and prayed that Stuart would take his time with the vindaloo.

"Hello, Treacle, what's up?" A loud, deep voice boomed into my ear.

"Gripper!" I said gratefully, "I need your help really, really badly. Now!"

If you are a woman leading a remotely alternative lifestyle,

Gripper is a useful person to know. 6'5" tall and seventeen stone, he's a biker with a mandatory cocaine habit and an aggressive personality disorder. Sectioned on more than one occasion, he is none the less loyal, albeit occasionally extremely violent. He has a lot of very bad 'old school' tattoos, a full beard and a piratical gap-toothed grin. Shaven-headed, except for a ridiculous 'Que' plait which falls from the top of his head to his waist, he has no time for Zen teachings, preferring at all times the strategy of chaos. He and his brethren regularly gorge themselves on bouts of alcohol fuelled knife-play in the kind of pub where the landlord wearily asks if you couldn't take your efforts at mutilation into the car park as he's run out of bleach. Gripper is my safe call, my minder and an excellent solution to Stuart.

While I waited in the dark, I took down all the photos from the wall. My life was coming home with *me*. I paced nervously back and forth, my footsteps echoing on the bare boards of the hollow house, thinking with relish of all the genuinely painful tortures Gripper might devise for Stuart at my bidding. After what seemed like an age of watching at the window in dingy silence, I heard the loud throb of a powerful engine cut through the darkness. I stared out pointlessly through the grime. It shut off abruptly and my mobile phone rang. In the same instant, the headlights of Stuart's car swung into the drive in front of the house. I could hear my heart pounding.

"He's here!" I hissed into the phone.

"Yeah, I can see him." Said Gripper. The car door slammed and I heard the crunch of footsteps on gravel.

"He'll go up the fire escape." I said desperately.

"Sorted." Said Gripper and rang off.

Clutching my picture collection, I made an unwise, fitness-exposing dash back up the stairs. Not a happy task for my less than toned physique, but I arrived, only slightly out of breath, back in the cheerless tattiness of Stuart's living room just as he opened the door. He stood and stared at me, his hands full of carrier bags, the smell of warm curry invading the room. The tableau lasted for only a moment before the door was barged fully open and he was sent sprawling forward as Gripper emerged through the entrance behind him. Stuart dropped his carrier bags with a chink of beer bottles and regained his balance, spinning round to face the denim clad mountain.

"Who the fuck are you? This is my house. What the fuck do you think you're doing?"

Gripper ignored him.

"You alright, love?" he asked me enormously from the doorway.

"I think so." I said and held out my find, "This perv's being photographing me!"

Stuart looked venomously in my direction and said,

"Those are mine. You've got no right taking them. And that's my camera!" he added, pointing to the Nikon still slung round my neck.

"Fuck off." Said Gripper, evenly walking into the room and slamming the door behind him. The gentle patter of plaster falling from the ceiling punctuated the brief silence.

"No! You fuck off!" Stuart was actually either very brave or very stupid and we were all going to find out which. I knew he had boasted about his martial arts training and now he turned and balanced on the balls of his feet, trying to look Oriental and dangerous. Gripper cocked his head to one side like a Millwall supporter with a spilt pint. In the event, the contest was over as soon as Stuart moved. A steel toe capped motorcycle boot with a seventeen stone pile driver behind it was aimed accurately at his crotch and dropped him like a bag of damp laundry – a victory for Western common sense. Gripper pulled Stuart's head up with a massive hand through a fistful of hair and dragged him like a doll, making unpleasant mewling sounds, to where I sat on the arm of a sofa. He lay at my feet, doubled up and groaning.

Gripper stood over him and looked down with all the subtle tenderness of a bulldozer.

"If you *ever* bother this lady again, I'm going to fucking kill you. Understand?" Stuart made a sound that may have been recognized by a rutting moose but may or may not have been comprehension. Gripper stood heavily on his hand. *"Understand?"*

"Yes!" Stuart nodded furiously. Gripper loomed over him and maintained his ascendancy by stepping down casually on to Stuart's other hand. He was now pinned to the floor by two size twelve Grinders.

"Why did you take photos of Paul Fuller?" I asked him. I felt surprisingly remorse free as he wallowed on the floor beneath me.

"Hammond paid me. I take what I can get," he said through gritted teeth, "Look, will you tell this bastard to – aaaah!" Gripper rocked heavily onto his toes, his hands thrust nonchalantly into his pockets.

"Why?" I said

"I don't know!" Stuart almost yelled, "Maybe he wanted some leverage with Fuller. I took them months ago, I don't know why he didn't use them."

"How do you know he didn't use them?" I said, looking at Gripper. My bouncer stepped off Stuarts hands and he yelped again. I watched with equanimity as he rolled away and struggled to his knees, shaking blood back into his hands and fingers. "I mean, pissing Paul Fuller off might well be fatal."

Stuart shook his head, still flexing his fingers,

"Paul was only interested in scaring him, said he wasn't worth more than a smacked arse...And anyway you've still got the pictures" he said reasonably.

"Well, you seem to have had a foot in both camps." I said.

"Safest place to be." Said Stuart, glaring at Gripper.

I thought about that. Pictures, pictures, pictures ...

"Why did you take these?" I said, waving a selection from the wall at him, "And ..." I focused on the top most picture in mid-semaphore, "...And – who the fuck is that?"

The photograph was taken outside my cottage and showed the cheerful frontage and the crumbling low wall that ran along the alley leading to it. It had been taken at night with a fast film and looked eerie with the backwash of orange ambience from the nearby street lighting. Almost out of shot and slightly blurred, a woman in a red dress was sitting on the end of the wall. The curve of an umbrella obscured her face and over the dress she wore a short, dark jacket with a high collar. Stuart sat up and looked at the picture.

"I don't know." He said sulkily. My Rottweiler prepared to strike again. "No! Really! I don't know," Stuart protested, getting breathlessly to his feet and backing off, "She was just there, the night Hammond went round to your place. She left just after he did."

I groaned. Perfect. It seemed I was being stalked by everyone.

"What's up?" said Gripper, craning his neck to look at the picture.

"Nothing." I said, "I've had enough. Let's go."

"Can I have my camera back?" Stuart was attempting to regain some composure.

"No you fucking can't!" I said and added for good measure, "You see, I was right. It would have been shit."

XVIII

THE MOON

This card signifies a period of chaos. At its best it can be inspiring and profoundly creative, at its worst it could indicate a period of intoxication, blackout, even madness.

CHAPTER EIGHT

When Gripper had eventually dropped me at the cottage and roared off into the night, I felt I'd had more than enough for one day. It was just a little after 10 o' clock and the drizzle had turned into a determined downpour that was whipped up by the wind and lashed around the house in fitful gusts. I could hear the steady roar of the sea below me as it frothed and boiled, and I stood, getting soaked, staring through the winking light of a single street lamp to the little low wall where my scarlet woman had perched while she spied on me. Spied on me being spied on by Stuart. They were all fucking bonkers.

I shifted my brain into neutral and took an early night, closing my eyes, listening to the wind and sea from the comfort of my bed and wiping the touch of Stuart's fingers from my memory. The thought of them crushed under Gripper's steel toe caps helped

Morning dawned not much brighter and the grim implications of my tete a tete with Stuart began to sink in. He had been paid by Ben to take photographs of Paul Fuller, for the purposes of blackmailing him, presumably should Fuller object to having his porn profits diverted elsewhere. An astonishing sleight of hand considering Fuller's reputation. From my own experience, I knew that Ben was not a man to be put off his objectives by anything as footling as other people's feelings. He was beginning to look as duplicitous as Stuart, who was himself playing a dangerous game with Fuller. And where the hell was Lois? Who's self-aggrandising on the situation was given more credence by a sudden streak of truth. What was the shiny pink business card I'd found? I'd forgotten about that in the face of Stuart's shenanigans. It was probably an appointment with her bloody hairdresser. But most importantly, what the hell had any of this got to do with ME?

I always came back to this, the crux of the matter. We are all conscious of how people regard us. Our friends, our family, work colleagues, husbands, wives, lovers. Whether we care or not is another matter, but most people are influenced to a greater or lesser extent by others' opinions. And most people would like to believe that others think well of us. There were plenty of people I'd met along life's leafy paths who might have been irritated by me or exasperated or slightly inconvenienced. It's difficult to live your life around people without occasionally rubbing them up the wrong way and the only way to completely avoid these occasional clashes is to live up a pole in a desert. But I'd always believed that any small annoyances that my personal trail had created were so slight that nobody could care enough, or could be hurt enough to harbour the kind of grudge that would manifest itself in this kind of spite. I'd already found more than one person lurking in the shadows – Stuart with his camera and my red lady, whoever the hell she was. Yesterday, I had no idea that I was being silently dogged by freaking weirdoes.

I pondered all this while I ate breakfast and began the fiddly process of lighting the fire in my small open hearth. Although it was October and dark days hadn't settled in, the season was beginning to throw up the odd chilly day. The answer phone was flashing and I ignored it. With comforting, flickering warmth on the way, I sat on the floor with a spliff and laid out Stuart's pictures in front of me. Despite the scrutiny for clues, apart from the scarlet sentinel, they were just one uninformative, obsessive shot after another, detailing my fairly unspectacular comings and goings. I also spent a fairly fruitless time rummaging in the bowels of Stuart's camera. It was a digital SLR Nikon that must have cost a pretty sum but I had the photos it contained, the indecent evidence of kidnap and torture, and I was sure he wouldn't press the point. Apart from the shots of me in grotesque bondage, there were others he'd obviously taken surreptitiously at the Pink Parrot on Saturday. Pictures taken while I talked to Nikki and Jane, shots of a few boozy pervs, pictures of Gina, various low-life luminaries – another of me talking to Miss Vixen. There was nothing illuminating in any of them. No red dress, no obviously crazed killer, unless, of course, that happened to be Stuart.

To avoid processing the crockery holocaust in the kitchen, I pressed the stereo into service (God, how that word ages me!) and listened to a little Gong while I puffed my way to obscurer thoughts. So. Was it Stuart who was responsible for sending me the pictures of Paul Fuller? Given the pile of pictures on the floor in front of me, it surely couldn't be beyond the bounds of possibility? But why? And if Stuart was telling the truth, one fact was unavoidable: just like the keys, these had been Ben Hammond's property. Bought and paid for. No, no , no. I was definitely not going to go down the whoddunit route. I drifted for a bit, allowing good old-fashioned stoner music to curl around inside my head and search for inspiration. Other than a niggling reminder that I would have to get hold of Tom at some point, answer came there none.

I leaned across and punched the button on the answer phone. There was a slightly hysterical but definitely ghoulish message from Gina, who had obviously seen the news about Ben. She wanted me to call her 'but now, babe, as soon as', presumably to gloat. There was a very polite message from one of my regular clients wanting to see me for a session and to my now infused and giggly satisfaction, Max had phoned to say 'Hi'. And Lucy had called to remind me about the exhibition by Bob 'The Balloon' Carlton. This afternoon. Fuck. I'd forgotten. I really didn't feel up to Bob. Then I remembered the plan I'd hatched to sneak up on Tom, the drag artist formerly known as Tamara. I called Lucy and confirmed our date.

"Do you think he's trying for a Turner prize?" Lucy asked.

"He's certainly trying for something." I said.

Bob Carlton was a rubber fetishist who had created his own unique artistic niche. He had mystified the London critics with several terrible shows and they had usefully converted their bafflement into appreciative insight, for those of the public less well-informed. Bob enjoyed a certain amount of naughty celebrity. He had featured prominently on Eurotrash and a few daytime chat shows keen to titillate their audiences by interviewing weirdoes. Unfortunately for them, Bob was irritatingly, overwhelmingly, boringly *normal*. He had a technique in patient conversational tyranny that could reduce even the most rabid interviewer to obloquy within minutes. He had very little to say and he said it slowly, at great length. For all these social shortcomings, Bob was actually a very nice man. And he was extremely generous with the booze.

We were standing in the airy Gothic interior of a redundant church. Deserted by the heathen masses, its stout sandstone worthiness had been converted, with literally no imagination and even less money, into a gallery and arts forum. The delicate watercolour blue-green wash of its unremarkable stained glass had been overwhelmed by powerful down-lighters strung carelessly from the lower fan vaulting in the nave. Other windows along the sides of the aisles had been blocked to accommodate a series of 'community' inspired murals that gave the new space the feel of a drop-in centre. The scattering of suppliants, now worshipping the beauty of mans creation, were enjoying free drinks and nibbles and nodding sagely at a series of screens advertising 'happenings' of various kinds. Lucy and I were standing in front of one such. It was titled 'Arousal' and featured Bob 'The Balloon', naked except for a rubber gimp mask. He was slowly inflating a latex balloon attached to his penis. I watched this process with all the trepidation you might expect.

I started on my fifth glass of champagne as Lucy and I moved on to the next feature. It displayed Bob propelling himself around a pool in a red inflatable suit to the strains of Handel and it was called 'Water Boatman'. The film had been ludicrously sped-up.

"Oh God, not red." I muttered as Bob whizzed around the screen.

"What's wrong with red?" said Lucy.

"I'm being haunted by a woman in red," I said, remembering the fuzzy picture and my even fuzzier memory, "She seems to dog my every move at the moment."

"What do you mean?"

I grabbed some passing nibbles and told her my woes.

"The whole thing's getting out of hand," I said, "I don't think Stuart's going to bother me again because he knows Gripper will kick the shit out of him and anyway, I can't see why he'd be involved in all this."

"But if he's been obsessing over you -?"

"I've been thinking about it," I said, "Stuart's a voyeur. He might be a mendacious little sod but I don't think he'd get mixed up in anything really hands- on."

"So you want to talk to Bob about Tom? But why would Tom be involved? I know you two didn't exactly end on a high note but, well…"

"You're right there," I said, "He's trying to work his way towards guilt free retirement in the sunny suburbs with Doris, or whatever her name is. But I can't think of who else might dislike me enough."

"Do you think he'd do something this drastic though?" Lucy said, wrinkling her nose, "And where would he get hold of the photographs and keys?"

"I need to know if he knew Ben," I said, watching Bob in endless motion in front of me, "And I don't know where this red dress comes in, if it does."

"You say you've got a picture of this woman?"

"Yes," I said, "I think so, if it *is* a woman. It's not very clear."

Lucy looked at me,

"You mean, you don't know?"

"Well," I thought about it, "It could be another trannie," I said, "And that would make sense if it was Tom, but I don't know. In any case," I added, "I've just got this awful feeling that I've met her – at that party I told you about – but I was too fucked to remember."

Lucy grinned at me.

"You're your own worst enemy, JJ," she said, "You should stick to what you know. This isn't 'The Maltese Falcon'."

"Yes, I know," I said, "I could never take anyone seriously who called themselves a private dick. I'm still going to talk to Bob though. I want to find out if Tom's got anything to do with this because if he has I'll probably kill him."

"Hang on," Lucy said, catching sight of something over my shoulder, "it's Eddie Meyer, *you* know," she added as I looked baffled, "Bob's American buyer. I'm going to go and sweet-talk him. You said you'd be nice. Go and talk to Bob. Be nice. Don't drink too much." This last exhortation as she hurried away was a little horse and stable door but I put on a smile and made my way over to Bob.

I cornered him in mid-soliloquy as he was explaining to a small knot of increasingly desperate onlookers the thinking behind a piece of artwork titled 'Re:Birth'.

"Well, I felt as if I ought to share some of the feelings, I mean, physical feeling, on the skin as well as those in the mind, the sense of immerging, a chrysalis, an imago – er – immerging into a butterfly through the skin, the second skin. When I was in Hamburg I was working with some people who were polymerizing latex but *not* with chloroprene, which as you know…" He droned on for a bit while a screen behind him showed Bob in stop-motion being clothed in layers of rubber, one after another, until the last layer applied was an inflatable sleep sack. The process was then reversed until Bob was naked, finally immobilised and happily priapic, shrink-wrapped in a vacuum bed. This cycle repeated endlessly at speed and was quite mesmerising.

"Bob!" I said with as much enthusiasm as I could muster, "How are you? Great show!"

"Hey JJ!" he moved towards me with his hand outstretched, freeing his grateful guests to flee towards the nearest drinks table, "Haven't seen you in a while. How're things going?"

"Oh, you know, chugging along." I said.

Bob was a tall, thin man with cadaverous features and an alarmingly generous smile, like Death enjoying a mini break. For today's presentation he was dressed from head to toe in a black latex body suit that made him look like an emaciated sea lion. This impression was given a surreal twist by the black top hat set on his head at a rakish angle and the rather deplorable Man at C & A sandals on his feet.

"Chugging, eh?" he said, "Well, I've had a call from the Saatchi Gallery, might be something good happening. Are you coming to the party afterwards at my place? Got a few friends coming over, should be good. Lots of pretty girls, handsome young studs. Are you looking for a stud, ha!ha!? You know, I was at a party in Miami where all the waitresses were dressed as puppies. I'm not into that furry stuff as a rule but – "

"Speaking of friends, " I interrupted. I could see Lucy steering a slightly startled, dark haired young man in our direction, "Have you seen Tom lately? I need to get in touch with him. Have you got his number?"

"Oh yes, oh yes," said Bob, "It's at home somewhere. I think. I'm pretty sure. Yes. But that's the thing, actually, in fact, he said he would be coming over to the party, I twisted his arm, said it would be fun. So, nothing to worry about, eh? Though, I mean – actually, you two aren't, um. I mean, Tom said…"

"No, Bob, it'll be fine." I hoped that was true. And a party would be an excellent icebreaker for a chit-chat between two gay divorcees. Lucy arrived with Eddie Meyer on her arm and handed him to me as if she was passing the baton in a relay. He was a lot taller than me, even in my heels, and I watched him take in my tattoos, my posh frock and my corset. A smile played about his lips and he began to look speculative. Oh. Good.

"Eddie! Eddie!" Bob trumpeted, "Let me introduce – another of our wonderful coast's wonderful artists. JJ Franklin, Eddie Meyer!"

"Pleased to meet you. Are you coming to Bob's party?" he had the slightly whiny vowel sounds of the Jewish Noo York intellectual, a little too Woody Allen for my taste. In every other way, though, he was the anti-Woody, a good 6'5" tall with large dark features and big hands and feet. His expensive cotton T-shirt was worn outside his carefully ironed jeans and he seemed to be wearing army boots. He moved surprisingly quickly for a big man but rather inelegantly, his upper torso strangely static, making his hands flap like giant gloves. One stopped flapping and made the mistake of resting on my bottom. In a heroic move designed to save my financial bacon, bless her, Lucy thrust herself between us, pointed at Re:Birth and said,

"How long did it take you to film that?" Bob didn't let us down.

"Ah, now that's an interesting question because obviously the continuity would be a problem in the context of ..."

I smiled and inched away from Mr. Happy Hands as Bob began to explain deadly technicalities. Lucy maintained her position between us nodding interestedly and occasionally flashing a radiant smile at Meyer but I could see the pain in her eyes.

Lucy cried off Bob's party that evening. I could hardly blame her. I wouldn't be going myself if the spectre of Tom, the ghost of Christmas past wasn't going to be at the feast. Especially since Meyer had telegraphed his intentions with all the subtlety of a frat boy at a hazing. It was going to be difficult enough to approach Tom as it was. He presented as almost psychotically normal, his soft underbelly now well hidden by sensible undies as he strove to kill off his previous incarnations in filth and kink. The notion that perhaps Tamara had resurfaced and was haunting the streets with her own agenda was going to be difficult to introduce tactfully into the conversation.

Bob the Balloon lived in a large Art Deco house perched amid its own huge rockery and some lush gardens on the cliffs above the seafront. Private steps led down to the pavement and the plebs below as they passed by on their way to amusement arcades and rock salmon lunches. Although its once proud concrete constructivism had been soured to dish cloth grey by the salt air, Rock House still retained a certain modish glamour, inside and out. The inside at the moment was crammed with glamorous people admiring one another and enjoying screenings of Bob's latest work. Bob's parties were an often diverse mix of high art and fetish indulgence. There was plenty of PVC and, of course, latex on show amidst the party frocks and well dressed connoisseurs. After the witching hour, any pretence usually deserted the denizens of Bob's eyrie on the cliff and the early hours would often turn into a sweaty, spanky humpfest. Bob on these occasions remained a cheerfully attentive host, breezily unfazed by even the grossest acts despoiling his soft furnishings. I even saw him maintain a characteristically tedious soliloquy whilst being blown by a spectacularly leggy blonde, only pausing to pat her head paternally and sip his Bacardi and Coke. Thankfully it was still early. I worked my way patiently through drinks and conversation around the downstairs, keeping an eye out for Tom, stopping occasionally to shriek and kiss the air beside the faces of various art groupies I mostly couldn't stand. Thankfully there was, as yet, no sign of Eddie Meyer so I sought out Bob.

I caught him in the kitchen, still rubbered up and mixing what looked to be an absolutely lethal punch.

"I've been looking for Tom," I said, watching him empty a bottle of vodka into a large green bucket.

"He said he was coming," Bob said, pulling various bottles from crates on the floor and scrutinizing them at arm's length, "I spoke to him this afternoon. He said he was going to finish work, go home, get changed and come over. Mary's gone on holiday with her mother apparently."

"OK," I said, "I wondered what he'd been up to lately. If he's sneaked back on the scene, you know. He used to dress a lot and I thought maybe…"

"Haven't a clue." Bob said, now pouring Crème De Cacao and raspberry liqueur together into the mixture, "I haven't seen him around, but then I've been in New York. Do you think I ought to put Absinthe in this?"

I looked at the bucket. It might have been my imagination but a heat haze seemed to be forming over it.

"Yes." I said, "Definitely."

People were still arriving an hour or so later and it was a bad sign when I started to dance. Dance to the light of the ever-changing screens of Bob's rubberised experiments and the rhythmic slap of a pretty young thing's impromptu over the knee spanking. I'd dropped a couple of Es and everyone was becoming a lot more lovely and a lot more witty. Certainly I was laughing a lot more. Bob's punch was deceptively damaging. Smooth and sweet, with odd unpleasant key notes, it seemed to contain the same kind of neurotoxins as rattlesnake venom. I took a large tumbler full on an extended tour of the house, now determined to meet everyone I'd spent the rest of the evening snubbing, even the egregious Eddie, should he present himself. My triumphal progress was brought to a sudden halt when I met Max in the conservatory. He was lounging with his usual relaxed vitality on one of the sofas dotted among the flora of Bob's expensive hot house exotics. He looked right at home. Tonight he had forsaken his usual colourful apparel for black and it made him look so much more dangerous. To my immense irritation, he was accompanied by his own hot house exotic, a pretty young red head. He smiled up at me

"Hey Jay! We have to stop meeting like this."

"Hi." I said, somewhat thrown off my stride. I noticed the red head move defensively closer to him and for some reason this irritated me even more, "I'm looking for someone." I added lamely.

"Aren't we all?" he said, "This is Charlie, by the way." I exchanged desultory greetings with red, her expression probably mirroring my own and I found myself getting cross with Max, in spite of the bliss pills. As I was about to exit, feeling slightly silly once again, salvation presented itself in the form of a lithe young man who had occasionally indulged himself in corporal favours at my hands.

"Patrick," I said smiling slightly more broadly than I would normally, "How are you?"

An oafish grin spread across his face like crazed china and I realised he was enjoying some form of stimulation not occasioned by meeting me.

"Fuck yeah!" he said. I looked at him seriously, aware of Max's amused scrutiny.

"OK Paddy," I said, turning him bodily to face me, "Tell mummy what you've done." Patrick looked suitably chastised and fished inexpertly in his pockets, eventually retrieving a goody bag that contained several small pink LSD blotters, some tabs of E and about a quarter of hash. He offered me the packet.

"Does mummy want some?" he asked. Oh, dear. Oscar Wilde said many beautiful things about the terrible nature of temptation and I knew I was about to demonstrate that there was indeed truth in beauty. If I was going to have to put up with an evening of Max leering at his girlfriend and Tom twittering on about his, I was going to need some assistance. Go on, say it – a pathetic excuse, but the sad fact is, I don't actually need one at all. I looked at Charlie. She was wearing a black leather sheath dress that buckled up under her bust. Like most red heads of the carroty kind she had fine, clear skin and her breasts were two perfect mounds of soft, pale ivory. Yes, it was perfectly understandable. I put one of the blotters on my tongue and washed it down with a little poison punch.

"Good boy." I said and patted Patrick on the head.

"Fuck, yeah!" he said.

I looked over to Max but the conservatory was filling up with party goers, a colourful melee of people babbling too much gibberish too loudly. I decided it was time to remove myself from the barbarian hordes to somewhere a little quieter and with any luck, Tom would become apparent. I tried to look for a way out through the bobbing heads. The swell eddied and parted and to my surprise, I spotted Angell Falls sitting in a leafy corner on a high stool talking to a large man in a turtle neck sweater. I dithered for a moment then went over to her.

"Angell!" I said, "I thought you'd gone back up to London."

She uncoiled her legs and leaned forward, trying to place me.

She was much more typically dressed tonight, in thigh-high red PVC stiletto boots and a matching military style red PVC jacket with black buttons and epaulettes. Her companion glared at me until her frown cleared.

"Oh, yes, I remember, you came to the hotel. Talking about Ben. Well I didn't have much choice. The police dragged me back down here again," she narrowed her eyes at me. Interpreting her look, I shook my head. "I haven't said a thing to them!" She didn't look convinced.

"Did you find out what you wanted?"

"Well," I said, "Not really. You don't know Lois, do you?" I added, "She was in that picture I showed you and something's come up – "

"Christ!" Angell got to her feet and sought the arm of her minder, "I'm not going to talk to you about anything else, OK? Fucking hell! Why is any of this your business? Stick it somewhere else, honey!"

She stalked off with security in tow, derriere swinging and I was left looking at a sea of interested faces. I spotted Max leaning down over his luscious redhead, whispering something. *Fuck*. I about faced a little too quickly and ran straight into Eddie Meyer. *Double fuck!*

"Hey!" He was wearing a patterned cashmere sweater and cord slacks and though he couldn't have been more than thirty, he looked as if he'd been stuck on a golf course 'til late middle age had set in. I wondered where he'd left his driving gloves and a sun visor. "Great party, huh? I was hoping I'd catch you. Your agent – Lindsay, is it? – said you're a painter," he began to edge me toward the lounge, cutting me off from the herd like a seasoned predator. "She said you do erotic studies. I'd love to see your etchings, ha!ha!"

"Ha!ha!" I said, "We'll have to do lunch some time."

"Yeah, lunch. Do you live far from here?" Oh, God, this man was a nuisance. "Just a little way up the seafront," I said vaguely.

"Well, maybe... "

"Come out! Come out! Dolly's here!"

Bob had suddenly appeared beside us and flung open the conservatory doors. He began waving his arms about and herding people towards his terrace garden, twirling his top hat round on the end of a cane like a demented ring master. Eddie and I were thrust forward in the surge as the party began to sprawl onto the lawns in the freshening Autumn night.

Bob was a stylish gardener and decking gave little stages to displays of elaborately trimmed box hedges and erotic statues, all carefully illuminated with solar lamps stuck into the ground. A thick stand of conifers screened the garden from all but the gentlest breeze and there were still scattered dabs of colour from late flowering shrubs. And in the midst of all this grace and taste there was Dolly. Hard metal filled the air with a crashing, throbbing fanfare. Seagulls incautious enough to roost nearby woke up and wheeled into the sky, shrieking with rage. A fitting tribute.

Dolly Mixture is a burlesque cabaret artiste who makes a living performing at various alternative fashion shoots and parties. I have no idea at all what she actually looks like. I have seen her in so many guises, shapes and sizes that it's impossible to even guess. Tonight she was wearing a white, one-piece latex catsuit, possibly a tribute to our host. Only one eye hole was cut in the hood and she peeped out beneath the fan of an enormous purple eyelash decorated with glitter. There were no nose or mouth holes in the hood either, a creature deliberately deaf and dumb, but a breathing tube snaked from her face to a hole cut in the crotch. The rear accommodated a butt plug with a trailing white pony tail. Her boots were incredible. White platforms a good 12" high, studded with blinking, winking lights of all colours. They probably played the Marseilles, they could probably make toast. She was a pleasure model android that Philip K Dick would have creamed himself over.

To some heavy industrial rock she performed a routine of wild contortions with a pair of large extending fans decorated with white plastic roses and more tiny white lights. They left glowing trails in the night sky and streaky marks on my retina.

"Oh wow!" said Eddie, transfixed, "I *so* want some of that!" I looked at him and wondered. He was such an unlikely fetish fan but you never can tell. Everyone was applauding and laughing. I scanned the crowd but I couldn't see Tom anywhere. Perhaps he'd got cold feet. Perhaps Mary had come back unexpectedly. I could see Max standing on his own beside one of Bob's statues and wondered what Charlie would think if I went over and made flirty conversation with him. But I wasn't really up for naughty high-jinx, even though I was starting to feel comfortably light-headed.

Dolly finished her routine and came forward to the plaudits of her audience. She was immediately engulfed by Mr. Meyer.

"You're so talented! Hey, How d'ya learn to dance like that? In those heels? The costume! Wow! I mean just blew me away…"

I tuned out a little as Eddie was almost coming in his pants and managed to ease myself away from the adoring crowd around the diva. There were still plenty of places in the house where Tom could be lurking and I hadn't properly investigated the upstairs yet. Music started again and it looked as though Dolly was up for an encore. If she could escape from Eddie. I heard him say distinctly,

"I'm here to do a bit of business. Do you know where I can get some business?"

Dolly's eye lash fluttered theatrically and she turned away, making an elaborate show with her fans. Everyone moved forward again as she began another dance, leaving Eddie a little crestfallen. He said.

"OK. Sorry. Only asking."

A curious onlooker asked:

"Business? What kind of business?"

Now I was intrigued. I understood it to be something in the area of fine art but his furtive eye brow waggling made me seriously doubt the purity of his intent. Then he dumbfounded me.

"C. Brown. Anything really." He said.

Eddie Meyer looked like an overgrown mummy's boy with a slightly graceless attitude. A putz, a schlep, a schmo. He didn't look much like a fine art buyer. But then he certainly didn't look like a speed-baller either. He caught my eye. Fuck. My eye made a valiant attempt to escape that failed as he lunged towards me.

"Do you know where I could score?" He yelled above the cacophony of Nine Inch Nails and cheering as Dolly began unzipping strategically placed circles of latex on her catsuit. Jesus Christ! How was this guy still on the street? I wheeled around,

"Sorry. No." I said and beat a hasty retreat back towards the house. I left him flitting round other guests in his quest for nectar like a giant, ungainly moth in a Pringles sweater. I caught up with Bob in the living room. He was fondling the business end of a Dayglo pink dildo with some calculation and judging from the way his jaw was working, I realised a certain amount of 'business' had favoured Bob rather than the luckless Eddie.

"I thought you said Tom was going to be here?" I knew that my grasp of things was going to get pretty tenuous in the near future and if my ex didn't very soon present himself, posh frock or not, I wasn't going to be able to do anything more sensible than point and laugh.

"That's what he said." Bob sparkled and sniffed massively, holding a finger to one nostril then the other. I leaned forward as he began to sway happily.

"Where did you find Eddie Meyer?"

"What?" Bob was now manhandling the dildo in a crudely suggestive fashion and eyeing up a slutty party girl in a school uniform and roll top hold ups.

"Eddie Meyer?" My peripheral vision was starting to get a little hazy.

"No idea." He said with a grin and made a successful dive for slutty girl as she hesitated too long by a bowl of Twiglets.

Hang on a second...I thought...

My mobile phone rang. The scrum behind me began to boogie and I found myself dancing involuntarily as I fumbled in my pocket. Bob upended his slutty girl on the sofa and brandished the dildo. Lube for God's sake! Need more MDMA...

"Babe! There you are! Why didn't you phone? I left a message ... Christ, where are you?" It was Gina.

"At a party," I said, keeping a wary eye on Eddie through the window, "Sorry. I was going to call, I've had a bit of a weird time. Is it about Ben?"

"Yes. I saw the news about him. A suspicious death – "

"Can I give you a bell back tomorrow, honey," I said, "It's getting a bit loud here." I noticed Patrick on the lawn dancing slowly around with his arms in the air, laughing at his outstretched finger tips. He looked like a man enjoying a startling revelation about the corporeal nature of his own anatomy. I heard Bob shouting "Can someone get me a wooden spoon. There's one in the kitchen!" Eddie seemed to be deep in conversation with Angell's minder on the terrace...

"Yeah, sure but that wasn't why I called," she said. I put my finger in my ear as jollity ebbed and flowed behind me. "It's Lois. She still hasn't turned up but you'll never guess who has! Her sister! She has a sister! Michael said he saw you yesterday and ..."

I looked down out of the windows of Bob's seafront seat and

tried to assimilate this startling information. As I did so, with Gina still prattling in my ear, I saw a figure walk out of the shadows below and stand with what seemed like deliberate theatricality beneath a street lamp on the promenade. Lily Marlene!

"Fuck me!" I yelped, "Jesus!" I snapped my phone shut, cutting Gina off in mid flow and pressed myself against the window like a hungry zombie. It was Miss Scarlet, without question, it was *her*. It seemed as if Hercule Poirot was assembling all the suspects in the library before a dramatic dénouement. She turned with the flourish of a model at the end of a catwalk and began to stride away from the house and up the street. I was suddenly galvanised into action.

"No. No. No. No." I caught the startled look on several faces as I started to fight my way through the clumps of now frankly superfluous humanity towards the door.

The steps that led down through the rocks from Bob's place were steep and tricky. I wasn't altogether co-ordinated and after a giddy arms and legs pantomime that courted vertigo and disaster, I landed in a bit of a wild rush on the street below. The fresh air hit me in a blast and I gazed around, slightly panic stricken. Then I thought I caught sight of her, walking quickly away from me on the other side of the road. I dived heedlessly across, to the loud annoyance in squealing tyres of a motorist, all badge and bull bars. Coming to a halt on the other side, I realised with frantic hilarity that the acid was finally kicking in. Just what I needed. I could see the glittering, gleaming reflections of the street lights in yesterday's rain puddles, organic and orange. The dark beast of the road coiled black and shiny with these glowing, winking scales and the buildings began to loom dangerously. I resisted the urge to scream with laughter at these phenomena and scanned the now hopelessly strange horizon for my speck of red. The real acid test is recognising what planet you are on and I knew that very soon I wouldn't have a clue. On one memorable occasion I had become lost in space the instant I'd set foot outside my own front door. My neighbours were robustly unimpressed by my comical cries for help as I stumbled around the front garden, dazzled by street lights, bushes, plants and the inexplicable serendipity of the night sky. Now, catching sight of what I hoped was my target, the only familiar thing, I plunged into Wonderland, chasing the white rabbit.

Coping with co-ordinated motor function in combination with sight and sound overload didn't prove that easy. Everything was large and I was recklessly aware of the space around me. Constant distractions from fascinating things like cars, the lighted windows in people's houses and the incursion of the occasional nocturnal seagull made keeping my eyes on the prize very difficult. Especially when I had to stop in panic every few minutes and wonder what the hell I was doing anyway. What the hell *was* I doing? After a absurdly frenetic interlude, I was finally sure I could see her about 100 yards in front of me, the red dress swinging along hypnotically, illuminating the night like a danger sign. I fixed on it and picked up speed. Time to unmask Zorro, I thought idiotically, or maybe Spiderman, or the Incredible Hulk, no that's just plain stupid. The Scarlet Pimpernel would be more appropriate, although as far as I could remember, a Pimpernel was a kind of flower and that didn't need a mask. Babble, babble, babble went my brain. And then suddenly, she vanished. She winked out of existence just as she drew level with the pier. Shock resolved itself into slight consequential thought: she has gone on to the pier. Obviously she would. Oh, bugger.

Like most grand Victorian constructions, the pier had lasted far longer than expected and far beyond its useful life. It jutted out into the sea, a gnarled and arthritic middle digit, pointing rudely at the French. Despite this defiance, its structure was decaying, its peeling paint, rotting timbers and broken windows all evidence that people's leisure habits had become more sophisticated than just sitting somewhere vaguely jolly eating ice cream. Several noble efforts had been made to jazz it up with bars and art events but it was finally closed, amid much acrimony, and declared unsafe, while an argument raged in council offices about plans for its restoration.

The main gates were locked and bolted but there were many gaps in the fencing surrounding them. Everywhere was festooned with official notices about the hazards in store for the unwary traveller but I followed the red dress through a gap in the fence, and officially into danger. It was dark, very dark and it suddenly seemed so much colder. I felt as if I was stepping off the land and into the sea and I could hear each foot fall echo dully on the wooden flooring as I tottered towards the arcade in front of me. The windows stared blankly back, their cataracts of dirt and neglect making it impossible to see inside. I listened. I could hear the sea below me, the wind and the vague creaking of old timber. I couldn't hear any footsteps. Concentrating my addled brain cells on the surround sound, I came alive to the subtleties of every moving thing and somewhere ahead of me, behind the grubby façade, I heard a door pull softly shut.

The arcade was open and I went inside, trying to make as little noise as possible. I was instantly engulfed by blackness. The stale air held the scent of soured candyfloss and cat's piss. The only light was from the moon as it rode fitfully through the clouds and the jaundiced glow from the seafront behind me. Shapes loomed up, slot machines in rows like dusty metal soldiers shouldering arms, the echo of dead pin ball machines played in my head, glass cabinets with horrible amusements, grabbing arms, laughing sailors, clowns' wide eyes and gaping mouths. I had walked into a cold tomb of silent, half-glimpsed nightmares. And I was tripping. I began to tread carefully past these laughing monsters, becoming convinced that I would wake them with each hollow footfall, every silhouette throwing up a new danger. Some people would pay for the kind of adrenalin rush I was experiencing but I was only conscious of how horribly fast my heart was beating and the unladylike sweat springing up on my forehead. The one-arm bandits were the worst, dotted round like sentinels, watching blindly, their grinning mouths waiting to be fed. I was conscious of how loud and fast my breathing sounded as I tried, with no success, to keep a grip, meandering round, hopelessly lost, only just resisting the urge to gibber.

I tried to make my way towards the end of the arcade, as I became more and more panicky and overwhelmed. The dark was making blue velvet flowers in my eyes, the only light and sense of space now were the moonlit windows to the right and left. They seemed to be getting brighter, shining like TV screens with hard, white static and I didn't want to look at them. I was walking in a surreal picture, De Chirico, Magritte, Grunwald, Bosch, jumping at shapes I could no longer identify that seemed to posses their own beating life force. One, step, at, a time. The air oppressed me, made up as it was of malevolent particles I could actually see if I concentrated hard enough. I tried not to concentrate and remembered to breath.

I finally reached a door. My whole body was shaking with the effort as the floor seemed to be slipping away from me in a dusty wooden spiral, disappearing into the bowels of the pier, the sea, the rabbit hole, the Styx. I desperately needed something to hang on to and I grabbed at the door handle. It was locked. It was fucking locked! I made an inarticulate noise of anguish.

"Please!" my voice sounded whiny and strange, "Oh, please!"

Then I heard laughter. A little ahead of me and to my right, a gentle mocking giggle that froze me in terror. It might have been real, it might have been spewed up from somewhere in my subconscious but I let go of the door handle as if it were electrified and hurled myself away from the sound. Back through the machines, back through all the monsters, bouncing off the dead amusements as if I were a pinball myself, they may have joined in the chase, I didn't care. After what seemed like a lifetime, I got to windows and a wall and after more back stage blundering about in dust and confusion, I found a door. I shot through it and out like a slug from a salad spinner. Straight into a blind collision with another body. I jumped back and screamed but someone held on and shook me upright, a large, soft, hard, black shape. I tried to focus on it through the terror. Fractured darkness whirled and settled suddenly. It was Max. God, it was Max! I recognised him with a swoop of relief and gratitude that was almost orgasmic and the shock dropped me to my knees. I put my hands flat against the reassuringly cold, real decking of the pier head.

"Oh fuck, fuck, fuck, fuck ..." I kept repeating it like a comforting mantra until my heart had stopped trying to escape my rib cage and leg it somewhere safer.

"Jay," he said, "What the fuck are you doing? Are you trying to get yourself killed? It's not safe here."

"She's here!" I babbled, "The red dress – she's here!"

"You're tripping," he said, stating the obvious.

"Yes, but she's here. I saw her and I heard her."

"Who?"

"The woman."

"What woman?"

"The red one. The woman in red," I sat back on my heels and pointed back towards the arcade, "She's *in there*!"

"Come on," Max said, gathering me up, "I'll take you home."

"But ..."

"Don't be silly. What are you going to do? I'll take you home."

He marshalled me patiently away from the arcade and off the

pier while I giggled and hiccoughed my way through attempts at explanation that, judging by Max's increasingly fixed expression, only seemed to make matters worse.

Once I was in the bastion of my own safe house, I felt much better. Max invited himself in and raided the fridge, bringing me a bottle of lager he'd opened in the kitchen. I subsided on to the sofa, in slightly shattered comfort and grappled with the concept of drinking.

"Right," he said, "Tell me what you were doing on an abandoned pier in the middle of the night. I saw you leave the party and go tearing off up the road."

I settled myself and let warmth and light filter back in. I took a moment or two to enjoy the sensation. I suppose I must have looked slightly deranged.

"Why did you come after me?" I said finally, adding with a sense of rash abandon, "You know you have amazing eyes!" He lowered them and smiled. I could see his dimples and the Goddess was back, whispering profanities in my ear. She and I were definitely going to have words later.

"You looked slightly mad", he said. "I didn't think it was a safe state to go running round town in. So what were you doing?"

"Mad," I repeated, "Yes, mad. I'm sorry, Max," I said, managing to digress from lunacy momentarily, "Paddy gave me some acid. It's this woman."

"So I gathered. On both counts."

"*This* woman," I said, retrieving Stuart's photograph from my desk drawer, "The woman in the red dress. A foxy lady." I got a little zing from the ecstasy and began to boogie, "You're a sweet little lurve maker – "

"Whoa! Whoa!" Max grabbed my hands and tried to still the dance. I carried on bouncing and grinned at him like an ape. "Why is she so important?"

"Because she's haunting my dreams." I said, lunacy was definitely taking hold again and just for a moment I looked at Max and allowed myself to wish profoundly. To wipe away all the disappointments, the learned behaviour, all the cynicism and look at him with a naivety and simple desire uncluttered by experience. It only lasted a poignant couple of seconds but that was enough. Quoth the raven 'Never More'. He was watching me. I switched the silly smile off.

"Well?" he said.

"I know I've seen her. I know she's something to do with the whole Ben mess. I was at a party. I'm never taking drugs again. Where's your girl Charlie?" I added with what seemed like complete pertinence. Max looked at me and sighed, putting down his beer bottle. He wagged a finger at me.

"I'm coming back tomorrow," he said. "And you can tell me then why I had to rescue you off a pier in the middle of the night."

I got up to show him out and we stood facing one another by the door. There was a moment of certain tension.

"You mustn't wag your finger." I said, breaking it the only way I knew how. He looked at me and grinned, his surprising eyes sparkled devilishly.

"I'll wag all I like," he said, "And you need your lovely round bottom smacking for being so bloody silly."

I started to laugh, astonished at his cheek. Generally speaking, men know their place with me and they enjoy it. Those that find the walls unassailable get bored and try elsewhere, if assailing is what they want. It's the nature of this particular beast and nature being nature, there's very little I can do about it. But Max may just be smart enough to find a weak spot. I would have to shore it up. I showed him out, still laughing,

"Thanks for bringing me home." I said, looking out at the still alien landscape of my surroundings.

"No problem. I'll come over first thing tomorrow," he said, hunching into his leather jacket. He turned to leave, then paused. "Oh, and Charlie's not my girlfriend." He said. I watched him walk back up the alley way, the ghost of his wry smile winking in my mind's eye. Then I retreated back inside to concoct some spells, define the divine and let what remained of the night lapse into the twilight zone created by a tiny piece of pink paper and my monumental lack of self-control.

V

THE HIEROPHANT

The Hierophant seeks to bring harmony through discipline and order.
It indicates a well meaning spiritual influence, reminds us we are
not alone and warns against being stubborn.

CHAPTER NINE

Even though I'd spent the rest of the night in the air, as witches say, I found there was too much conflict to see properly. I had cast the circle and called the quarters, set my mirror to receive but the guardians really weren't going to be fooled by me getting high and silly. Quite right too.

As it happened, I didn't see Max the following morning either. To be honest, I was glad. Acid wakes you up with a lovely clear head and I cringed at the memory of the giggling, dancing, grinning lunatic that had so obviously lusted after the man in black. I would have to regain my composure and set the record straight.

As for my nocturnal dash around the pier, well, that was just plain stupid and I wondered whether my scarlet woman had been some kind of lurid hallucination. It occurred to me that as far as I could recall, Tom had been conspicuous by his absence from Bob's happy throng. I made a quick phone call to a surprisingly chipper Bob, who confirmed that Tom hadn't shown at all. Had he been lurking in the dark, unsuitably dressed and giggling? I was sure there were probably quite a few people out there who weren't spending a drizzle filled afternoon asking themselves questions like these.

I had a session booked for the evening, although it was a client I wasn't particularly looking forward to seeing. I'm allowed to say that. These relationships are professional. Just as there are some stationery suppliers that the office manager doesn't much care for, there are also some painful little pervs a professional dominatrix has to meet. And Nigel was one of them. But it occurred to me, as I turned over the rubble of the last few days, that he might actually prove useful for once. The trans community in our neck of the woods isn't really that large – although everywhere it's larger than you may think – so there was a pretty good chance that he may actually know one or more of the players in my sordid little melodrama.

Come six that evening I was prepared to do battle with Nigel in something suitably forbidding. Nothing too radical though, as it was a house call and I'm too old to feel rebellious about being stared at on public transport. I don't drive, in case you're wondering. Not because I can't but because the last vehicle I owned (a Mini) had committed suicide on the impromptu cross-country stage of my return from a club. In other words, I'd driven it into a hedge. For some inscrutable reason, the insurance had sky-rocketed, possibly due to several other, er, similar incidents and I considered it safer and cheaper all round to leave cars to people who were less committed to drunken debauchery than me.

Nigel lived in that mandatory part of every townscape that had indulged in 1960's concrete communism. Anonymous, squat blocks of flats crouched in uneasy orange silence under the sodium glow cast down by rows of sentinel street lighting. There were hard metal railings and empty open spaces and the whole neighbourhood seemed to pause under its own nightly curfew. I always felt unnerved and solitary stepping off the bus into this wilderness, where feral youths roamed the shadows but after a tense five minute walk, I was welcomed into the tidy comfort of Nigel's flat.

I'd known him for about two years and he had contacted me

initially through my website. He was not really an ideal candidate but at the time I must have been seriously strapped for cash. He was a part-time postman and relief care worker whose busy schedule allowed only limited time for the beatings he so richly deserved. There were many not quite unpleasant things about Nigel. He was short and stocky with vigorous dark body hair that I suspect he dearly wished could be transplanted to the Homer Simpson comb over that graced the top of his head. Despite his broad shoulders and slight beer belly, he had preposterously thin legs and when this was all attired in the floral dresses, lace collars and pretty buckled shoes he preferred, he looked like a Barbary ape who'd been strategically shaved, then dressed by Laura Ashley. The other not quite unpleasant thing about Nigel was his dick.

Now, although my sexual orientation offers a breadth of largesse to all comers, I must admit a preference for men. I find them more dynamic and they come equipped with things that are generally much more satisfying than any number of carefully crafted plug and play accessories. I am talking about the beauty of the male genitalia.

As an artist I can appreciate the horror that accompanies the realisation that any honest depiction of a fine figure of manhood must necessarily include that strange collection of soft dangly bits that essays the male reproductive equipment. It disturbs with an embarrassed scribble the sweep of the thighs, the muscles of the stomach, the tight, taut buttocks. For a few short minutes of creation, the good Lord seems to have adopted Hans Bellmer as a stylist. Simply on aesthetic grounds I can almost applaud the Victorians' fig obsessed Bowdlerisation of Greek and Roman statuary. However the crux of the matter for me has never been that slightly self-conscious grimace that accompanies unexpected male nakedness. I tend to tackle a man's tackle much more holistically, so to speak. My study of the male genitive equipment has hardly been exhaustive but I have never come across a cock and its other accoutrements that I found repellent, or even mildly disconcerting, for that matter. I have always found something fascinating in the different shapes and sizes of men's bits, particularly pricks, most especially in slight tumescence. This is obviously where the holistic bit comes in. However, it's not entirely a question of what a hard-on can do for me, although I don't mind admitting the thought flits across my mind. A cock does actually have an appeal which is all its own. Even an erection, that ultimate outrage to bourgeois sensibility, is a thing of beauty and a joy forever as far as I'm concerned and the contemplation of a man in such extremis gives me an enormous amount of pleasure. I feel duty is due to Priapus, that potent little tutelary to eroticism, a favour that is very seldom acknowledged. The Greeks and Romans understood it, the Victorians did not. The cock comes (ho, ho) in all shapes and sizes, girth, length, straight, bent, foreskin – yes, no, pierced, tattooed… No two are the same and if you're a completist like me, the possibilities for pleasure are endless.

I have a particular fondness for Prince Albert piercings: not only do they make sex better but they look stunning, giving a garland to beauty, like dressing a statue to the gods. Having said all this, and coming right back down to earth with a thunderous crash, Nigel's tackle had something unpleasant attached to it. It was probably Nigel because he was blessed with an offering that would have shamed a buffalo. His enormity gave the lie to the oft prattled consolation that size doesn't matter. It does and in his case, the thought of that livid leviathan lurking under Little Miss Fauntleroy's frock always made me feel slightly queasy.

Nigel was a man who shopped almost exclusively at car boot sales and his house was littered with the evidence, everything from flights of Beswick ducks to lava lamps but at least it was neat and clean and warm. He knew the drill and greeted me with the appropriate servility and a glass of red wine. The latter was more important as I subsided into an over-stuffed sofa while he went off to get changed. Most of my clients like to greet me 'in role' but Nigel always took his own sweet time. It didn't bother me as the clock was ticking as soon as I stepped through the door. I sampled the vintage (not too shabby) and wondered how to introduce my dilemma into the conversation. As it was, Nigel spared me the trouble.

"So did you hear about Lois?" he called from his boudoir. "Nikki phoned me and she's full of it. Apparently her sister's turned up at the house and insists on staying there until the silly slut comes home."

"Yes," I raised my voice above the subdued twittering of the television, "I didn't know you knew her."

"Mike Taylor introduced us at the Parrot. Ages ago. She just sat around at 47 smoking and sponging off Nikki and Jane. The job centre tried to get her to work in an old peoples' home – you can imagine how that turned out! Can you believe she wanted to do film work?! That's probably where she's gone. She was always giving it "I'm an actweth," Nigel did a surprisingly good impersonation of Lois, "Cocksucker more like…" I realised Nigel meant literally rather than figuratively and took another sustaining gulp of La Belle Français. It was actually a rather lovely St Estephe and I was determined to drink as much of it as possible without falling over. It surprised me that Nigel might think Lois was actually off somewhere filming though. As far as I could tell, she'd always been bleating on about her starring role but no-one had taken up her option, or indeed even taken her seriously.

"Yes," I said, "She was always talking about auditions and filming. I heard something about The Bill." The response from the other room was muffled and I went on, "Why do you think she might be off filming?" The reply came,

"Sarah Williamson."

"Who?" This was a new one on me. There was a short hiatus from the next room and I stared at the grim cartoon domestic being enacted on the screen. I caught the phrase 'You dahnt nah nuffink…"

"And should I know Mike Taylor?" I asked, backtracking.

"I don't know," said Nigel, immerging in all his floral glory, looking anxiously at me for approval, "I think they were, you know, seeing each other. She said he lived next door. What's the matter?"

Michael! Gina's nice but dull friend. But surely…

"Is it my new dress?" Nigel looked worried, "Don't you like it?"

He had gone for lace and a rose printed crepe de chine billowed up with a froth of petticoats. There was a pink bow tied around his plaited wig and he wore red, buckled shoes and ankle socks. It was certainly spectacular.

"No, sorry," I said, "I mean, it's not that. Your dress is lovely. You look very good." I pulled myself together and stood up. Nigel glowed with pleasure and looked at the floor, being suitably demure. I decided it was time to get to the action and ushered him through to his bedroom.

"Who's this Sarah Williamson?" I asked casually.

Nigel pouted and stared at his shoes. He began to swing from side to side with his hands behind his back, one toe scuffing the floor in front of him. He was now in character so further sensible conversation would be impossible.

"Not telling…" he said, the pitch of his voice subtly adjusted to sulky schoolgirl. Oh, crap. Never mind. I picked up the slack.

"That's *very* naughty," I said sternly, "And very naughty girls get a good hard spanking round here." I put my hands on my hips and glared down at him. In my 4" heels I'm a good 6' and Nigel barely came up to my chin, "Well?" I demanded as Nigel pouted again, "I see. Bend over, young lady."

D.I.Y tools are very useful and I suspect many hardware retailers are secretly plagued by perverts. Where else can one purchase lengths of rope and chain, padlocks, cane, fixings and clamps without exciting comment. Using leather cuffs, I tied Nigel's floral alter ego over the folding builder's work bench he kept in his trim little bedroom for just such occasions. These easy store items are useful for having a robust and adjustable flat surface and many holes in the steel legs to use as fixing points. Once Nigel was suitably pinioned, I went to work. I let him settle for a moment, bent almost double over the hard surface, head down, bum up. Then I waited a little longer in silence just for spite.

"Has Violet been naughty?" I asked, referring to the apparition's ludicrous soubriquet, "Is she keeping secrets?" There was an engrossed whimpering from the other side of the work bench,

"You'll have to speak up, Violet, I can't hear you," I said and went over to him.

"Yes." He said.

"I *beg* your pardon, young lady?!"

"Yes, mistress!!"

"I think someone needs a lesson in manners. I think someone needs to learn it's rude not to speak when you're spoken to."

I pulled up his dress and pulled down his frilly white knickers, revealing the pasty white mounds of Violet's bum cheeks in all their splendour. I regarded this vision for a moment and then decided on something drastic, after all: neither of us was here for the good of our health. Certainly Nigel wasn't. From an assortment of interesting items on the chest of drawers I selected two short chains, each with a crocodile clip at one end. With a small smile, I then attached a pair of solid metal drop weights to the other. I leant heavily on Violet's back and rummaged briefly between her furry thighs.

"Mistress indeed." I said and held him down while I clipped the weights to his scrotum. There was a temporary interlude of unpleasant squealing while I stood back and watched the weights swing between his legs, pulling down pinched folds of skin from his balls. He eventually subsided, moaning, as he realised it was less painful to stay still than wriggle. I picked up a leather paddle and pressed it against his buttocks, setting the weights swinging again.

"Say 'Sorry, Miss'." I said and let him have it, a sharp, nicely ringing slap.

"Sorry, Miss." He gasped. I hit him again. And then again, evening up the strokes on each of his cheeks, nicely spaced, getting gradually harder, twelve on each, until he started to yelp, saying 'Sorry, Miss' after each smack. I finished up with one shot (thirteen for luck) right between his legs – the last place he wanted it. Without getting into grim technicalities, I should say that Nigel is a seasoned masochist. A gentle, sensual warm up, a nice hand spanking with lots of teasing and admonishment is infinitely preferable to cold start, brute force and much more satisfying for me. But Nigel knows what he likes and Violet gets it hard and heavy. He was groaning as I picked up a cane. It was a wickedly thin dragon bamboo and I knew it would deliver a sting like vitriol.

"Now Violet is going to take a deep breath and tell me what secrets she's keeping about her friend Lois." I tapped his reddened backside with my cane to let him know what was coming.

"Lois wasn't my friend." He mumbled. No change there then. I carried on tapping his bum.

"So why are you keeping secrets?"

"Not telling." Oh, well. I lifted my arm and heard the satisfying swish as the cane sliced through the air and the stinging whack as it landed. Predictably Violet squealed. I decided I wasn't really in the mood to play games so I gave him another, then another, three in quick succession. I listened without remorse to the anguish. I watched the weights swing.

"You *are* telling, young lady." I said.

"I don't know Sarah Williamson, Miss." He said, still managing to be sulky.

"Why would Lois be filming with her?" There was silence, so I set to again, landing the cane slightly lower in a more painful spot across the top of his thighs. There was something more like a shriek emitted from Violet at this and he began to squirm, despite the swing of the weights urging him not to. I moved forward and began pinching the red tramlines that were blossoming on his skin. He was breathing heavily.

"I don't know, Miss" he said, "We met Sarah at the club, she was handing out flyers."

"What sort of flyers?" I didn't wait for a response, this time I just hit him.

"I don't know!"

"*Violet* – "

"I don't know, Miss! Really I don't. Promise and cross my heart!"

"Good girl," I said, "So why would Lois go filming?"

There was an infuriating silence. The relationship between a submissive and a dominant is a symbiotic one, each has something the other needs and the careful balance struck between them depends very much on personality, like all relationships. The deplorable practice of deliberately behaving badly in order to be punished is called 'bratting' and Nigel had just demonstrated an even more blatant example than usual. It is best ignored, the worst punishment that any sub can endure. Unfortunately, much as I would have loved to, I couldn't ignore Nigel on this occasion. He was enjoying himself far too much so I decided it was time to push the envelope a little. Strangely enough, I'm not really that much of a Sadist. The power and the glory are more of a turn on for me than actually hurting anyone. For Nigel, though, I might actually make an exception.

"Insolence!" I said and stood back. If he could have seen how far I drew back my arm, I was sure he would be re-thinking his game plan. I brought the cane down with speed, a serious blow, bordering on the judicial. His response this time was more like a scream and he began to struggle, without hope of freeing himself, a testament to the sturdy versatility of home improvement aids. I waited just long enough for the searing follow through to set in and then let him have it again. I kept it up, varying the heat of the stroke and the length of the wait. I felt between his legs occasionally, telling him what a rude girl Violet was and how I was only thinking of her welfare while I punished her.

I indulged Nigel in all his favourites, taking my time and checking occasionally to make sure he hadn't zoned out and forgotten his safe word. Safe words are very important when you're having this kind of fun because half the turn-on for a lot of people is having their cries for mercy ruthlessly ignored. Most people use the traffic light system: green for OK, amber is hang on a second and red is stop *now*. But it's always as well to check they're not so spaced out that they can't respond at all. In scene jargon this is known as sub-space, a euphoric, eroticised high that can leave you as completely unaware of your surroundings as you are of any real physical damage being done. Nigel is just as much a pro as I am though and he got his money's worth without a problem. I finished off with six nicely measured cane strokes, possibly the hardest he had ever endured, until he'd stopped shrieking and had begun to sob and moan in what seemed like quite genuine contrition. I went over to him. I could smell the heat of his toasted little bottom. I dragged the session back to the subject in hand,

"Well, Violet? Why do you think Lois is off somewhere filming? And I won't ask you again" I said. His voice wasn't above a choked whisper.

"I don't really know if that's where she went." The words

came between gulps in a sort of wail, "I just heard them talking about auditions. I just assumed the flyers were for the auditions."

"Are you chastened, Violet?"

"Yes, Miss."

"Are you going to be a good girl?"

"Yes, Miss."

"Very well. Good girl, Violet." I said.

The screams he emitted as I unclamped the weights on his testicles and the blood rushed back were a happy reminder for masochists everywhere that all good things come to those who wait. I pulled up his knickers, noting with grim approval the ferocious red welts striping his backside. They looked wince inducing and I wondered how vindictive I might actually prove to be, if provoked enough.

I untied him and helped him off the bench and he collapsed to his knees in front of me. His face was streaked with tears but his eyes were shining and his whole body was trembling with an epic endorphin rush. His lap now looked like a floral tepee as he knelt, a small wet patch forming at the apex of the totem. So much for teaching him a lesson, I seemed to have shown him the road to Damascus instead.

"Please, Miss, please..." he said breathlessly.

I didn't really want to endure the coda but I'd already paid for the tune...

"Very well, Violet, as you've been especially good."

I folded my arms and waited while he completed his evening's entertainment by hand. I'd developed a technique of throwing my eyes slightly out of focus when dealing with these particular moments with Nigel.

On the bus ride home, I pondered the news about Lois and her possible bid for stardom. In the SM scene, there are many more submissives than there are dominants. The excitement of having control taken from you, of being used, possibly even abused, trusting someone else with your welfare and your satisfaction, seeing the response your submission creates, this is an extremely powerful lure. How many women out there, how many men, have fantasised about being forced, pinioned, slapped, insulted and aroused, oh so much against their will? I'm guessing it would definitely run into double figures. It is a very adult way of being needed. I am a dominant and I appreciate this. But where the ground becomes precipitous and slippery is in deciding where these desires spring from and how this should be 'dealt with'. Psychologists have regular field days with the projected neuroses of their subjects and, more alarmingly, governments attempt to legislate against what is basic human nature – the need to be loved on our own terms – in case we all turn into serial killers or paedophiles.

Yet the gruesome fact remains that most tabloid monsters are control freaks, dominants, for whom the demonstration of power without consent is the most important aphrodisiac. I am a dominant and I appreciate this. Significantly, though, none of these dangerous people have the outlet and company of the regular SM scene, where consent and the community would undermine and expose them. They are waiting in 'respectable' disguises cultivated by years of frustration and conservatism. Was Lois a submissive? Had her life taken her somewhere into dangerous respectability looking for love? In spite of the fact that Nigel will have a hell of a job sitting down for the next week, which of course is part of the pleasure for him, I have his trust and I will never abuse that, however much of a pain in *my* arse he is. On the other hand, it's much more likely Lois was just getting her rocks off in front of a camera to service a much more egotistical demand. So, we're back to the same question. Where the hell is she?

It was a little after nine when I got back home. It had stopped drizzling and a new moon was playing peek-a-boo with the straggling clouds. The air felt fresh and clear but it was still cold enough to get me crouched in front of the grate teasing a fire into life. I watched it smoke and snap, let the new born flames play tricks with my half closed eyes. Like the razor sharp private detective I was becoming, I was startled into wakefulness half an hour later by a loud hammering on my door. I'd fallen asleep. Well done, Jay, on the ball, as usual. I struggled to my feet in the half light, padded into the hall and peered out at the gloom. It was Lucy. She stood in the alley, her large grey raincoat flapping around her in a rising gale. She was holding a bottle in one hand and as I opened the door, I saw her stagger briefly against the wind. I felt a twitch, somewhere deep down in my psyche. Another doorstep. Another bottle. Another time...

"Sorry to burst in on you so late," she said breathlessly, discarding her coat and thrusting Chablis at me, "but I thought I'd better bring you a peace offering."

Lucy bearing gifts definitely meant she was after something. Lucy is a little like a not-quite-benign Mother Superior. Since she started to take responsibility for selling my pictures as well as filing my taxes, she's seen it as her duty to disapprove of anything that might interfere in what might loosely be termed 'my affairs'. Unfortunately, this pretty much seems to cover everything I do. Bringing coals to Newcastle in this way was a little like Mother Superior offering you a condom and some lube. I found an ashtray for her and opened the bottle.

"OK," I said, settling back down in an armchair and tucking my feet under me, "What do you want?"

"That's rude." She said, rummaging in her bag for cigarettes, playing for time, "Why should I want anything?"

"You said it was a peace offering. Why should I need appeasing?"
She smiled at me. We've known each other a fair few years

now and subterfuge is useless. She squirmed her shoulders back into her seat and kicked off her shoes in front of the fire, a favourite move on cold days. She looked at me through her curtain of hair and wiggled her toes against the warmth.

"OK," she said finally, "I think you're going to be cross with me." Oh, dear. After my exertions with Nigel and my impromptu nap, I'd started a slight headache. Wine was not the cure. Nor is news that will make me cross.

"How cross?" I asked, shading my eyes with one hand.

"We-e-ll…"

I waited.

"Right," she said at last, finally lighting a fag, "It's Eddie Meyer – "

"Oh, fuck him!" I subsided back into my chair and covered my eyes with *both* hands, "Can't you just deal with him. Say I've got small pox or something. No – say I've got genital warts, herpes – say anything- "

"Calm down, Jay. Just listen…I've said you'll go out with him."

I could feel myself almost rising above the chair on a cloud of anger.

"Lucy," I'd said dangerously, "You know that I love you. But what the FUCK ARE YOU THINKING?"

"Listen…Listen…Just Listen! After you left Bob's party last night Paul Fuller turned up with his entourage and got pally with Eddie! He must have smelled the money. He asked him over to his place for a party of his own. Now I know what you said about Fuller and those photographs and I thought…"

"You thought what?"

"That you could maybe return them."

"For fuck's sake, Lucy." I rubbed my temples and stared down at her fawn slacks as she stretched out her legs. I was a little surprised to see nail polish on her toes under the gauzy beige of her tights. She wasn't wearing any on her fingernails. My mind flashed back to Tom and one of the laughs we'd shared in the brief, happy few months before the rot set in. After a night out on the tiles for Tamara, an early morning call from the postman had him stumbling bleary eyed and unshaven to the door, mercifully make up free. Except for the shrieking scarlet polish on his toenails. There really was nothing he could say to the smirk of the postie as he signed for his new socket set and tried to look manly.

In truth, I was furious with Lucy. There had been other occasions where she'd made a point of voicing her concerns about my lifestyle or behaviour, even once going so far as to 'borrow' my car in an attempt to stop me attending a party the night before a gallery appointment. I'd indulged her because she had helped me out in so many ways. But she'd never done anything this stupid before.

On the other hand, there was a chance that a trip to Paul Fuller, the owner of Bare Faced Cheek and porn rival to the late Mr. Hammond, might prove enlightening. I let out a long sigh.

"Let me deal with it, Luce, OK?" I said and gave her a hard look, a painful effort against the tension in my scalp. At least she knew when to back off.

"Did you see Tom last night?" she asked, changing the subject with a hopeful smile and offering me the bottle.

"No." I said flatly, "I don't think so."

"You don't think so? What do you mean?"

I considered my silly trippy trip on to the pier and remembered that Max had promised to come round. He hadn't. Well, that's men for you. As reliable as – well, actually I can't think of anything less reliable than a man, so let's just leave it at that. I opened the draw to my desk and showed Lucy Stuart's photo of the Red Lady. She raised her eyebrows and squinted at it.

"Nice dress." She said evenly, "This the woman you told me about? You think this might be Tom?"

"Yes. She turned up last night."

"You spoke to her?" Lucy looked amused.

"Not exactly." I said.

"Sorry," she said, still smiling, "It's just that I can't imagine Tom lurking round in the dark like this. Stalking. What the hell for? I thought he'd cut and run."

"Husbands." I said, "Ex-husbands…"

Her smile faded.

"Point taken," she said, "There were a lot of things I wouldn't have put past Dave."

Lucy's ex-husband was legendary. An appalling tyrant in so many ways, I was never quite sure how serious some of her anecdotes about him were. I think she found it easier to make light of him by turning him into a baby-chewing ogre. There was no doubting her depth of feeling, though and it had kept her cheerfully single all the years I'd known her.

"How did you get to hear about Eddie, in the first place?" I asked, remembering his less than professional behaviour.

"Bob told me when I spoke to him about the exhibition." She said. "I think he works for some corporate brokerage firm. Bob said he was fixing deals for 'Cultural Investment' or something. I thought I'd just wing it. You've got to grab any action you can down here and if they're going to pay for Bob's rubbish…" She smiled and let her eyes roll up in her head.

"Right. I see." I thought about that. Cultural investment, eh? Well, he was certainly investing in a whole load of culture last night. He didn't look like a buyer. Maybe he was just an errand boy. I was fed up of thinking about Eddie.

"Well Bob certainly seemed confused on that subject last night." I said lightly. "And so was Eddie." Lucy laughed,

"Was he sober?" she asked, "Were you?" I conceded the point, closing my eyes. The headache wasn't going and I just needed some peace and quiet to sort things out again.

"Look," I said, "If I go out to Fuller's with him, will you do something for me?"

"What's that?" she stubbed out her cigarette and began to fish in her massive handbag for another. Lucy often lapsed into chain smoking. I found it absurdly irritating. Filling the government's coffers with an addiction to nicotine wasn't one of my vices, in spite of a myriad of others they could have happily taxed, if only they'd take the sensible course and legalise drugs. Think of the revenue, you idiots!

"Can you find Tom for me?" I asked

"Doesn't Bob know?"

"Fuck knows." I said. "I certainly don't have his number anymore and I lost track when he moved away."

"OK. Sure. If I can. Promise me one thing though, won't you?" I looked at her stern face and felt weary. "Take those pictures back to Paul Fuller and stop mucking around with dangerous people."

WHEEL OF FORTUNE

*This card is about changing fortunes, the purest luck,
some things that just happen. It signifies joy and abundance –
a change of luck, then, for the better.*

CHAPTER TEN

Made from the same geology that nourishes Epergne and my favourite wine, the Sussex Downs roll towards the sea in soft green folds that bare their teeth in a chalky grin at the Seven Sisters cliffs and Beachy Head, a beauty spot popular with depressives everywhere. 'Down' comes from the Saxon word for hill, another cheerful quirk of the English language and the countryside is so lovely that even the most forsaken shitholes are quaint and picturesque, and many expensive houses lord it over the views. Was it Kipling who said that Kent is the garden of England but Sussex is God's own county? Probably not, but Paul Fuller was by no means the only rich or famous person to align himself with the righteous and buy a beautiful house with a beautiful view here. The difference with Fuller, of course, was that he'd somehow acquired planning permission to build anew in an area of outstanding natural beauty.

To be fair, he hadn't actually done too much damage. The house, as we approached it, was a long, low ranch-style building that owed more to Dallas than it did to Watt Tyler. But it crouched unobtrusively in its pretty surroundings, inviting in the dark with large picture windows and fairy lights strung among well tended hedges.

"Cool huh?" Eddie said as he pulled in behind a Mercedes in the drive, "He knows how to spend a few." I didn't reply. The journey from Dean's Bay to Paul Fuller's hide out in the hills had been grim. Meyer had spent the trip experimentally clutching at my legs and saying, "Hey, sorry! Used to a stick shift!" with a chuckle. Yeah. Right. Like an automatic is a complete anathema to the Yanks.

So Lucy had thought a date with Eddie would be an ideal opportunity to hand back my nasty cache of photographs and rid myself of a dilemma? Well, I wasn't exactly going to do that, in spite of my promise. My imagination (yeah, that thing again) had conjured up plenty of unpleasant exchanges surrounding that scenario. But I had agreed to accompany Eddie on a fact finding mission of my own. For reasons I wasn't going to reveal to Lucy. I suspect stupidity was chief among them.

I planned to stay as little as possible in the company of Mister Meyer and hoped he'd be suitably impressed by our local mafia mogul and bugger off somewhere else. I was doing rock chick tonight, black leather lace up jeans, black vest top and silver bling, tattoos on show. There was no way I was going to tempt fate and overexcite Eddie by sticking on a corset again. But if this was going to be the kind of party I suspected then Eddie himself was woefully dressed. A hideous blouson wind cheater and slacks. His polo shirt was Ralph Lauren but he wore it like an army surplus tent. He was the accountant at an orgy.

There were quite a few other cars in front of the house. Music and the occasional shout of laughter greeted us from the grounds. As we crunched up the drive and approached the front door it was flung open unexpectedly and we were suddenly face to face with our host. I won't say Paul Fuller is larger than life because he's not. Probably not more than 5'6", tanned, well-muscled, relaxed. The first thing I was aware of was a deep voice, overtones of gruff Saahrf London fighting for control of the glottal stop with the received pronunciation of a lot of expensively purchased good company.

"Hey Eddie! Come in, mate! Great to see ya! Just gotta get something from the car. Make yourself at home. Trisha!" He wandered past me with a smirk and a look up and down, a comfortable saunter accentuated by the fine silk of his dark grey suit. I thought he looked a trifle overdressed for a party but all was soon revealed as he joined us again on the porch and held up a zipped black clothes bag,

"Haven't had time to change yet," he said, "Something for later." He grinned at us. His smile looked so mirthless because it was difficult to see his eyes behind the tinted shades. I knew that they were a Specsavers vanity project, though. He was, apparently, as blind as a bat.

"Don't stand on ceremony, come in! Trisha! TRISHA! Where the fuck *is* that girl…"

We followed him into the house. The entrance opened straight into a tiled lounge dotted with tribal rugs and trailing house plants. There were low, comfortable looking suede sofas and discreet up lighting. It had the subdued warm colouring, alcoves and arches of a Mediterranean villa and it was very much larger on the inside than it seemed from the front. And all surprisingly tasteful. As I took it in, a young girl scampered through one of the arches wearing nothing more concealing than a tiny red bikini. Her long blonde hair cascaded down her back in loose, looping curls, her breasts were small, apple ripe, her hips wide, her stomach flat and smooth. She had the tanned, long limbs of riotous good health and she wasn't more than about 18 or 19 years old. The Girl From Ipanema began playing in my head and I watched Eddie's jaw slacken.

"Ba-abe! We need anuvver ice bucket. I don't like *hot* champers!" The soundtrack was instantly snatched from tropical beaches and the illusion shattered. Her voice had the shrill nasal drone associated with ankle bracelets, tanning salons and vajazzle. You might be able to take the girl out of Essex but this lovely thing was a stick of rock that had Chigwell running all the way through it.

"For fuck's sake Trisha, just take our guests through," Fuller said, then to Eddie, "Take your jacket off, make yourself at home. I'll be down in a minute. Trish'll get you both a drink, won't you darlin' – and anything else you want..." His face screwed up and I guessed he was winking. Trisha gave us a breezy smile and said:

"Well, follow me then." She turned on her heel and led us through the arch, calling over her shoulder, "Baby wants her bucket!"

The party was at the rear of the house sprawling through a series of large rooms, linked with arches, all devoted to different amusements. Trisha took us through them, handing out perfunctory notes like a tour guide. There was a screening room where some intriguing Japanese porn was being enjoyed, a lads' games room with a full size snooker table and a massive wall mounted plasma TV, a larger lounge area with sofas, low tables and cushions on the floor. I noticed there was certain 'medication' available and bowls on the tables held condoms and other goodies. The piece de resistance beyond this last though, glimpsed through a series of open archways could best be described as a conservatory. If a conservatory can be said to house a half size Olympic swimming pool. Even the gardens beyond *that* were alive with lights and people and music. I was astonished at the scale of it and Eddie kept muttering "Oh, man!" in excited anticipation as he watched Trisha's jaunty red bum wiggling along ahead of us. By 'get us a drink' Fuller evidently meant 'show us the bar' and Trisha duly did so before disappearing with a cheery wave. The barman wore a waistcoat and a bow tie, together with the closed face of a professional paid to be blind beyond his dispensary. I perched myself on a stool with a glass of Dom Perignon and took in the scene.

"Don't say I can't show you a good time," Eddie said, settling beside me, "Jeez, this place is huge! Where'd you reckon this guy gets his money?"

"Property, I think." I said. I didn't say what kind but I guessed Eddie couldn't really be that naïve, not if he had any sense at all.

As if to confirm this he grinned and said, "Yeah, and the rest!"

There were certainly a good many guests enjoying Fuller's entertainments, still fairly sedately but I guessed the restraint wouldn't last all night. Some people had dressed up. High art fetishwear in shiny, colourful latex, surreal inflatables; tight corsets and ballet boots, punks in leather kilts and spikes, body art, tattoos and piercings as well as those more conventionally attired. There was a small scattering of TVs, the odd weirdo and a few who simply hadn't made the effort at all and lounged around in trackies and tee shirts. I was surprised at how many faces I recognised and a little alarmed too, given the reputation of our host. But the SM scene is like any group with similar interests – angling, Sunday cricket, stamp collecting – you tend to run into the same people and Fuller was certainly 'on the scene' in a good many ways. I wondered if he'd invited any of his cohorts from the party at the Pink Parrot.

"Shit! Who's *that*?" Eddie said far too loudly. I followed his gaze across the bar to the lounge area where an objet d'art was being offered a drink and a seat. To call her pneumatic would have been doing a massive disservice to Pirelli. Inflatable was more apposite. She seemed to be channelling the late Lolo Ferrari. Her tiny black mini dress was tortuously stretched over the most enormous pair of breasts I have ever seen and the rest of her seemed to consist mostly of platinum blonde hair and eyelashes.

"Let's go over and say hello." I said recklessly, keen to get rid of Eddie as soon as possible and mingle. I made a beeline straight for the boobs.

"What a fabulous dress!" I announced as a way of shoving Eddie forward, "I haven't got the legs to go for anything above the ground. My name's Jay and this is my – er – friend, Eddie. He's a great admirer of yours," I added, guessing that anyone with that much silicone must deploy it for the benefit of punters rather than family and friends. She looked understandably startled.

"Oh, yes – er – " Her companion was a stocky, well dressed man with a shaven head and he leaned forward and said,

"Nice ink. I'm Rick." He performed the introductions as we arranged ourselves by one of the low tables. It seemed Eddie's unerring instinct had led us to drinks among porn royalty in the form of the magnificently named Rick Turpin and Misty Licks. At the mention of Misty's name, I remembered Stuart and his pronouncements and the reason I was here. Misty Licks and Angell Falls, two of Fuller's leading ladies, whose sterling efforts in the cause of self-abuse everywhere were being renegotiated by the late Ben Hammond. I mustn't get distracted. I was then distracted by Rick offering me a plate, not of nibbles but of the villain's party requisite – white powder. Eddie was deep in meaningful conversation with Misty's breasts and I eyed Rick with misgivings.

"Have a toot," he said, pulling a silver coloured snorter from his jacket pocket, "I'm going to," he smiled, "it's going to be a *long* night!"

I dabbed my finger into the soft white substance and rubbed it into my gums. Cocaine. Great. Everywhere I turned. Please officer, it wasn't my fault, they forced it on me. But tonight, I wanted to keep a clear head.

"Maybe later." I said and watched Rick hoover up a quantity of Chas without bothering to chop a line. It's strange but cocaine has probably more street names than any other drug and you can tell a lot about someone from the slang they use. A lot of them seem to originate from the great jazz age, especially the Chinese references – Charlie, Chang, Ching, when frightened moralists believed all drugs were being supplied by fiendish, bald

Orientals with droopy moustaches and Fu Manchu henchmen. If it's Toot, then you're rock and roll, most likely a roadie, Frank and you're in the music business – but not Ozzie Osbourne, the bat out of Brum, who characteristically had his own word for it – Krell. Bugle – aging London hardman, Terry Farley – you sad old raver you, Gak and you're probably a friend of Lilly Allen, God help you. Sparkle, C, White Lady, Billie, Hunter, Zip, blah, blah. Believe it or not, I don't actually like it too much. "Do you know Angell Falls?" I was determined to pursue my course without resorting to stimulants. Again. Rick let out a snarl of chemical induced appreciation close to a money shot and widened his eyes,

"Yeah!" I waited. "Yeah." He said after a bit, "Yeah, I know Angell. Lovely girl, great ass." An enormous sniff, "Misty, you worked with Angell didn't you?"

Misty rested her permanently baffled gaze on me and said, "Yes. We did a couple of pictures for Paul."

"What about Ben Hammond?" I asked, "Someone told me you'd done some work for him as well." It was difficult to tell but she looked genuinely startled.

"Who told you that?"

"Someone who worked for him."

"Who?" she really did look alarmed.

"I don't really know him," I said, thinking that was probably true of Stuart after recent revelations, "I may have got it wrong." Her mouth formed a silent 'o' like a pink collagen tyre and Rick looked amused.

"Misty's a pretty name." Eddie leaned forward, picking up the slack, darting a stern glance in my direction.

She swivelled to face him and said, "Yeah. It's in a song apparently. My mum liked it." Fascinated by the notion that her name actually *was* Misty, I missed Eddie fishing in his pocket. He suddenly flourished a flat silver box and I expected him to offer round cigarettes, Sobrani Cocktail, perhaps, but instead he drew out a small coke spoon and leaned over the pile of goodies on the table, raising the spoon to his nostrils 2, 3, 4 times, shaking his head against the rush.

"I thought you were driving," I said.

"Didn't I say?" he said, "We're staying over. Paul and I have some business." I just stared at him. The look of wild amusement that danced in his eyes might have been something to do with the coke but I suspected he was just really enjoying his own sleight of hand. A very nasty thought occurred to me.

"I didn't know you and Paul were friends." I said lightly, hoping he'd deny it.

"You don't think I just came over here to look at pictures, do you? Or that guy's stupid videos?" he laughed rather wildly, which was definitely the coke, "Paul and I go way back!" Oh. Fuck.

I smiled tightly and reached for the plate.

VII

THE CHARIOT

Conflicting interests will be pulling in different directions
but victory will be won, even if it is hard fought, by playing
to strengths and reconciling opposites.

CHAPTER ELEVEN

Fortified with the extra zing of a toot (yeah, that's right I'm rock and roll), I managed to extract myself from Eddie's clutches. Doubtless he felt I would be returning later to consummate our union in one of Fuller's guest rooms. If that was right, he definitely had another think coming, along with a slap. It was disconcerting to know he might be on Paul Fuller's payroll, though, and I wondered if he knew about Ben Hammond, and how exactly he was involved with Fuller. Maybe he was just taking care of our friendly neighbour hood's stocks and shares, something nice and legitimate. It was a hope.

I left Eddie happily chatting to Misty Licks and took a tour round the pool. It was an impressive addition to the house in shining white marble with classical columns and plaster decorations of the leering grape dangling variety. The doors to the garden and the October night were open and a gentle steam rose from the water adding to the impression of a naughty Roman bath house. This was made sweaty flesh by a couple who were having sex in the Jacuzzi at one end of the pool. I hoped it was well chlorinated, especially as only a few people seemed to have bothered bringing bathing costumes. There were loungers dotted pool side and I wandered over to one where a doughty old party goer relaxed with her drink.

"Babs! What are you doing here?"

"Hello darling, sit down. I'm just watching, as always."

Babs was a former Press Association reporter who had been known, somewhat distantly now, as Terry. Like many transvestites, Terry had made the hopeful leap towards the goddess in his forties and in his case, the transformation was vigorously maintained at all costs. Babs was a pantomime dame liable to set fire to her bushel rather than hide under it. She made no effort to dress down, even when she was visiting her bookie. Her voice was gritty and camp, like a hooker on 60 a day and the only reason she had remained unmolested on the mean streets was that she was 6'4" and built like a brick shit house. Terry's wife had, very sensibly, moved to Australia. Tonight Babs looked magnificent in a bottle green ball gown that rustled with petticoats. She wore lace gloves and diamante studded shoes and the crown of all creation atop the cascade of polycurls was a sparkling tiara. An unlikely debutante, there was no messing with Babs. She must have been sweltering in the tropical surroundings of Fuller's heated pool but she showed no sign. I was rather surprised she was on the guest list.

"How do you know Paul Fuller?" I asked

"We were at school together." She said, which was even more surprising, "Mitcham Vale comprehensive, mmmm, class of '83."

I settled myself on a lounger and tried to imagine the young Paul and Terry – baggy trousers, maths lessons, bike sheds, detention...

"I know, it's hard isn't it, darling?" said Babs reading my thoughts, a rueful smile tugging the corners of her mouth, "We've all got so damn old. Anyway, Paul has a thing for TVs, as you may know," she sparkled wickedly, "It's a good job he doesn't have to try and hide the wrinkles like I do." She patted down her skirts and raised her glass to her lips.

The only really remarkable thing about many transvestites is how few of them look like ladies and how many of them actually look like ladies of the night. I'm not talking about gender dysmorphia here, I'm talking about heterosexual men and KINK. Employing an arsenal of fashion horrors that red-blooded males everywhere find attractive – high heels, fishnets, mini-skirts and suspenders, they do nothing more than reveal just how perceptive at marketing is the oldest profession. Of course, these predilections add nothing to the male physique and there are definitely no excuses for some. As I've been to many a trannie bash with Tom, in addition to disciplining quite a few, I've seen a fair number of disasters – a party where one strange individual seemed content to spend the entire evening distressing everyone by wearing literally nothing more than a filmy negligee. I remember another who wore a long elaborately patterned Kaftan, elbow length gloves and for some eccentric reason, a white, full face mask underneath an afro wig. She looked like a storm trooper dressed for Woodstock. But Babs was a creature apart. Completely confident, under no illusions, with no issues and, as far as I could tell, pretty happy with her lot.

"Did you know Ben Hammond?" I asked, feeling more confident I couldn't get into trouble with Babs.

"Hardly lamented here." She said raising a gloved finger to her lips, "I know Paulie was furious with him for some reason. I fancy this little shindig is something in the way of a celebratory wake."

"Oh." I said, looking around at the jollity. I spotted Trisha swaying to the music, clutching a glass and wondered where Fuller was, "Why was Paul cross with him?" Babs puffed her cheeks out and fitted a cigarette into a long ebony holder.

"All I know is he was asking round about Paul, you know, about his business, the sort of stuff he was in to. That kind of shit stirring isn't very wise."

"No." I said

I thought about the photographs again. With Stuart's double dealing help, Ben had obviously acquired some shit to stir. It was his insurance policy, his surety against interference in his plans. I had personal experience of how single-minded, how devious Ben could be when he wanted something.

"Did you know Lois has gone missing?" I tried to sound casual. Babs knew many things, she was wise in the ways of filth, like a deviant oracle. She blew out smoke extravagantly and widened her eyes at me in a shock of mascara.

"No I *didn't*." she said, "I expect Nikki and Jane are pleased." A squeal bounced off the lively echo of marble.

"Ba-abe!"

We looked up as Trisha went scampering over to Paul Fuller who had come into the pool room. He was dressed only in leather jeans, his pony tail limp in the close atmosphere, his glasses steamy. He seemed relaxed and happy. A wake for Ben Hammond, indeed.

"Someone told me she'd gone off to do some filming." I said to Babs, keeping one eye on Fuller as he greeted his lovely young squeeze with a hearty slap on the bottom. Babs made a noise that might have been spelled 'pswhofft'.

"You *are* joking aren't you, darling? Who in God's name would want to keep her for posterity?" I shrugged,

"Someone mentioned a Sarah Williamson – "

"Oh, *her*." Babs said and relaxed back into her seat.

"Do you know her then?"

"Why do you want to know?" She smiled at me like a shark overlooking a lost mackerel and took another long drag on her cigarette. She leaned over again and put a gloved hand on my knee, much as Audrey Hepburn might, had she been a raddled old journalist in need of a full body wax. I put my hand over hers and patted it, which is one way of answering a question.

"It's complicated." I said

"Isn't it always, darling?" She said, withdrawing the hand, "Actually, that's Sarah over there with her grim little friend." She made an excessive show of pointing and as I looked, I caught Paul Fuller turning his head to follow her gesture. Oops. "Come on, I have to find out now." She lurched to her feet in a flourish of petticoats and started purposefully round the pool. I followed in her wake, hoping Fuller was being distracted by his lovely girlfriend.

"Sarah's awful," Babs said in a stage whisper, "Paulie likes surrounding himself with freaks," she evidently didn't consider herself in this category, "I think it makes him feel less of an arsehole." As I trotted along behind Cinders, I could feel our host's eyes boring into my back.

Sarah was standing at the entrance to the pool room, a lumpy, twenty-something blonde wearing a figure hugging leopard print dress that was slightly too small and emphasised all the wrong bits of her cake and eat it figure. She was arm-in-arm with a short, stout, balding man who looked uncomfortable. He wore a decomposing beige linen suit and a shiny nylon shirt and stood beside her displaying all the vitality of a damp mushroom. A very odd couple.

"What's this about you hiring Lois Valentine?" she asked without preamble.

"Valentine?!" I looked aghast. Babs pulled a face,

"Yeah, that's her name." I thought about Brian, the hospital porter and how far he'd come.

"Lois what?" Sarah's mouth hung open a little, "Sorry, who?"

"Bloody awful girl, ginger hair, lisp." Babs managed an accurate character sketch in six words. Sarah frowned at me.

"Do I know you?" she asked but Babs ignored this,

"She's gone missing." She blurted. Captain Paranoia was

prodding me between the shoulder blades as I heard Trisha laughing close behind me.

"Let's go and sit down." I said.

"Er – " Sarah began but Babs propelled them both into the lounge and towards some vacant sofas. I cast a glance over my shoulder and was relieved to see Fuller fully involved undoing his girlie's bikini top.

"Lois Valentine – ?" Babs began,

"Yes. Yes, I know who you mean now. Yes, I hired her. So – ?" Babs made the 'pswhofft' noise again and threw her hands up in a 'what is the world coming to' gesture.

"But I don't know anything about her being missing." Sarah said.

"Sarah does a lot of Paul's scouting round the clubs," Babs said to me, "Like a sort of runner, aren't you dear?"

"I am *not* a runner," Sarah said, "I'm Mr. Fuller's assistant. I research talent, I deal with contracts, I – "

"Don't be silly, darling. And anyway I really didn't think Paulie would be desperate enough to want to sign Lois. I *mean*, she's *ghastly!*"

"I hired her as a *cleaner!*" Sarah said forcefully, "I'm not *that* stupid." There was a hilarious pause as we contemplated the dual strands of Lois as movie star / cleaner and the possible degree of Sarah's stupidity.

"Did *she* know that?"

Sarah shrugged her shoulders and I noticed her left breast had escaped its confinement and was oozing lopsidedly over the leopard print.

"I guess." She said.

"A cleaner where?" I asked.

"Priory Gardens," Sarah said, "We have a dungeon there we use for filming. I s'pose it's possible I might have given her the impression…"

"That she might get her break in the talkies." Finished Babs, greatly amused, "I see." She got to her feet like a dowager duchess rising gracefully above the hoi polloi, "Well, that's satisfied my curiosity, at least," she said, "It's bloody funny too." She winked at me before making her stately way back to her poolside perch and I was left staring at the most unattractive couple in the room. We regarded each other in silence for a moment.

"I haven't seen you before." Sarah said at last, cocking her head to one side.

"I came with – oh – well, I came with him." I pointed across the room to Eddie who was just now performing the rather inelegant feat of snorting cocaine from medicine ball mounds of Misty's breasts. They were so firm and so perfectly round that it was possible to do this while she remained standing.

"Oh, Eddie." Said Sarah and smirked. I didn't like that smirk one bit.

"A friend of Paul's, isn't he." I fished.

"*Oh* yes." I liked that even less.

"I didn't catch *your* name." I said to Sarah's companion, changing tack. He raised his head to speak.

"Gordon." Sarah said, to my surprise. And then to my astonishment, "Gordon used to be Mandy." She patted Gordon like a pet, took a gulp of her drink and proceeded to tell me the whole sad story, referring to Gordon in the third person throughout, as if he were completely invisible. Gordon had apparently become convinced that the world would be a better place if only Mandy, his own particular lady in waiting, could deal with it. First a transvestite, then a fully committed transsexual, his adventure had taken him through assessments, psychiatry and hormone treatment. He had endured the mandatory year of living as a woman and had been considering breast augmentation surgery. Then, in Sarah's dramatic account, something had happened. She turned to him for the first time,

"You changed your mind, didn't you?" she said as if it was some simple choice between coffee cream and walnut whip . I sat in slightly stunned silence at the end of this sensitive recital. "You've still got boobs, haven't you? He has to strap them down," she confided, nodding in wonder.

I looked at Gordon as he shifted in his seat clasping his podgy hands together. I looked at Sarah as she smiled brightly at me, thinking what I might possibly say to this incredible specimen.

"You making friends?"

I jumped a little. With a sinking heart and a smile that matched Sarah's for sickly sweetness I turned round to face Paul Fuller as he leaned along the back of my sofa, arms relaxed in front of him, pinky ring winking ludicrously.

"Yes," I said, hoping to keep the slight tremor from my voice, "Fantastic party."

"Yeah. Eddie said you're an artist, among other things..." he grinned. Did he actually sharpen those teeth?

"Yes, that's right." I was definitely uneasy now. I have never made a secret of my professions, either of them. I could hardly hope to pay the bills if I did. But I keep them strictly separate. I have a website under my own name advertising my credentials as a painter, all arranged in complimentary colours with nicely framed illustrations and glowing testimonials set down in controlled san serif. The triple X version under my nom de porn (don't laugh, it's 'Mistress May') is a shrieking, over-18 romp in Bodoni Bold with lots of caveats and glowing rear ends. If you're a casual enquirer, there is *no way* to connect the two. *If* you're a *casual* enquirer.

Fuller straightened himself up and put his hands on his hips. I couldn't help thinking of the horrible photographs, their graceless contortions and how much more of Fuller's body I'd seen than he realised.

"We need to have a chat later." He said, not at all dangerously and I felt unease turn to panic.

There's only one good way of dealing with panic in my book and I headed to the bar to relieve my feelings by ordering several elaborate, cheerfully coloured cocktails. What had I learned so far? Ben was known and disliked universally among Fuller's friends and colleagues. He'd also been noted prying into Fuller's business. It would be interesting to know who had pointed him in the direction of the party at the Pink Parrot. Maybe Stuart? That would certainly be in character. And Lois had been offered a minor role in all this scrubbing of the toilets. Was it a minor role? What about Eddie Meyer? There was obviously a lot more to his visit here than 'Cultural Investment'. How had that come about? I felt the exquisite lift of a very large French Martini wash round my gums and focussed on Eddie. He and Misty had been joined by a stringy young man in sweaty rubber pants whose intake of amphetamines had left his whole body jerking at the slightest sound as if he'd been dosed with strychnine. Eddie was looking at him with some amusement and Misty with undisguised distaste. I watched Paul approach them and speak to Eddie. A look passed between them and I put down my drink. Time to be nice again and see what else I could get myself involved in.

By the time I'd made my way back through the lounge and tangled briefly with pants boy, getting unpleasantly showered in perspiration, Eddie and Fuller were heading out of the noise and excitement into the main hallway, towards the reception room we'd entered at the start of the evening. I hovered around underneath an arch and watched them disappear into a room near the front of the house. The business Eddie had mentioned? Possibly. Maybe they were just going to go and smoke some crack somewhere more chilled? I was getting a little too pissed to make sensible decisions and decided to balance things up with the usual livener. Yeah, very sensible…

The evening was definitely warming up. Under the combined influence of a little too much of everything – Fuller had certainly refined his Columbian imports well – I hovered by the archway and gave some assistance in a little light punishment, waiting to see when Eddie and Fuller would immerge. Bare bottoms presented themselves and I took charge of a Sjambok while a gorgeously attired Goth Grande Dame in a black leather corset and Victorian riding hat took charge of a cane. My guess is the assembled rumpage would prefer the cane. The Sjambok, in the right hands, can deliver anything from a kiss to a decapitation. Unlike most traditional Western whips it's not plaited leather but thick carved hippo or rhino hide that's been rolled. There aren't many originals around these days – they're illegal in South Africa after riot police made the plastic and steel replicas notorious and it has to be said Rhino hide is also a little hard to come by. But this was 54" of glorious heavy leather and I used it judiciously, just as a warm up. I knew from personal experience that even when it's applied with restraint the Sjambok has a surprisingly unpleasant sting, like an electric shock. I gave them the gentlest of flicks, keeping my arm straight, standing well back and using the very end. There was soon a lot of attractive wriggling, shrieks and giggling going on along the line of two girls and two boys, bent like naughty school children over one of the long sofas. The lady in the titfer was an agreeably chatty sadist and while we took it in turns to whip up a storm, I kept up a scolding diatribe and a weather eye on the corridor.

After about ten minutes, to a ragged cheer and a scattering of laughter, the lights were dimmed and the music was turned up a few notches. A mad blue strobe started and I had to squint as people began to jerk in silent lightning to the break beat techno de rigueur in these situations. It looked like everyone was raving.

There was no way I could see Fuller and Co through this St Vitus dance and I was starting to feel dangerously euphoric. I could smell sex, sweet and musky and the perfume of warm skin. And hash and the antiseptic sting in my nostrils grazing the back of my throat. Just a little more toot, maybe..? I handed the Sjambok to my companion who stood looking elegant in stop motion, with whip and cane in one hand and a cigarette in the other, a circus ring leader with a panting, well-exercised four in hand. I was about to make my way unobtrusively along the corridor when I found myself face to face with Sarah's erstwhile companion, Gordon. He looked uncertain and a little frightened. His moon of a face a ghostly galleon in the erratic lighting. I took pity on him.

"Are you OK?" I asked. His gaze took a long time to settle and focus, he had been far, far away. He gave a little shuddering sigh.

"Yes. Yes, thank you, I'm fine."

"Look," I said, consciously adopting a gentle tone, "why did you come here? You don't look exactly comfortable."

"I don't know." He said, essaying an awkward twist of his shoulders for a shrug, "Sarah thought it would be a good idea to get out a bit."

In all seriousness this was a man whose choices in 'getting out' should have encompassed the laundrette, bingo or possibly a quiz night. Not here, with the children of Moloch.

"Really." I gritted my teeth, "She could maybe be a little more sensitive?" I suggested. Gordon looked stubbornly defensive.

"I was feeling pretty bad, you know," he said, "Sarah helped me a lot. I wouldn't have got through it without her." He smoothed down his shiny shirt with a peculiar kind of gesture, as if he was feeling for loose change.

"She's my best friend." He said and suddenly took my hand in both of his, pressing it into his chest with an odd and vaguely unsettling enthusiasm. I could feel the slight overabundance of flesh underneath the strapping and I looked down at the spread of his chubby fingers, completely non-plussed. He let go abruptly with a forlorn nod of his head and walked rapidly away, a hectic Dilbert in disco lights. Alas for my delicate sensibilities, not before I'd had time to notice the burgeoning erection in his pants. I shook my head and marvelled a little at how strange people could be. Poor, put upon Gordon, whose fetish turned out to be victimhood and humiliation. In Sarah he had certainly found the perfect foil. Who was using who, exactly? I'd wondered what the hell he was doing here but he was actually perfectly placed among this bunch of cheerfully practised and practising pervs. I seemed to be the only one on site with an agenda other than getting off my face and enjoying myself 'til it hurt. Odd. That was usually my *only* job.

Eddie and Fuller were still nowhere to be seen. As everyone was far too involved elsewhere, I ducked through the nearest arch. People were spilling into the hallways, their flesh made mortuary pale by the blue back lighting. I looked back at the Bacchanal and saw that a laser show was now in progress. Fuller had turned his enormous lounge into a nightclub. I made my way purposefully down a darker hallway, vaguely looking for a toilet but more deliberately wondering what Eddie was up to with Fuller. If Eddie was after 'business' then he'd certainly come to the fountainhead here. But why the hell come all the way from New York? He could just as easily get sorted for Es 'n' whiz in the Big Apple. That was the thing with drugs. They were a universal commodity.

A door opened suddenly in the hall in front of me and the object of my research backed out of it calling through the entrance,

"Great stuff! Thank you, sir!"

I darted back and flattened myself against the wall, shuffling behind an elaborate flower arrangement and hoping that the general gloom in the hall would do the rest. It helped that I was dressed like a cat burglar, although I'd have still looked bloody silly if he'd spotted me. Meyer did a little dance on the spot and grinned like a Cheshire cat. Very pleased with himself. He looked around, eyes passing over me, halting, moving on. For a second I thought I'd been made but he started off back towards Sodom with his strange flappy handed walk and I hesitated. Was Fuller on his way out? Was he alone? This little alcove was dark and secluded. I inched my way out and peered round at the door. Eddie might have been a Manhattan money man (or not – the jury was still out on that one) but he was born in a barn. It was open. I made a quick, furtive dash round to the other side and stood, slightly more exposed, leaning a little round the jamb, this time trying to conceal myself behind a jardinière of ferns. This was getting fucking silly. I glanced fearfully this way and that. Discovery would ask for no excuse before it smacked me in the face this time and I couldn't even think of a lame one. Although the thump of the music and the shouts from the party goers were still pretty intrusive, Eddie's woeful efforts at preserving Fuller's privacy rewarded me when I began to pick out the boss man's half of a shouted phone conversation. From the cadence of his voice, he sounded like he was pacing.

"…Like that. And she turned up at the fucking restaurant! That voice…God she's a shrieking nuisance. Dunno where the fuck she came from….No…Angell's not that bothered really but I had to get Danny to show the stupid tart out. Yeah…yeah, well she's certainly sticking her nose in. I'll talk to Sarah…Well *I* don't know! Find out! This cunt's more trouble dead than he was alive. I don't want it happening again, you understand? Yes, I fucking do!...Yes. Good…"

There was a sudden shriek of laughter and I jumped so much that I almost dislodged the ferns but it was only a couple of tarty party animals stumbling out of one of the other rooms. I eased myself out from behind the greenery and made a casual display of walking off down the hall towards the front of the house. The games room beckoned through another archway. There weren't too many takers for this lad's night out, just a couple of die hards drinking beer from cans and staring silently at the large football filled TV screen. I wondered briefly at the calibre of man who could come to a party offering unlimited sex and drugs and rock and roll, an all you can eat buffet of debauchery and still want to sit and swill beer and watch the footie.

I heard the soft thump of a door closing and I saw Fuller making his way quickly back towards the rear of the house. I couldn't see the couple anywhere. There was a desultory cheer from the lads as somebody or other scored a goal and I retraced my steps back towards the room Fuller had just left.

I half-expected it to be locked but the door swung silently open and I found myself in an intense, dark study, illuminated only by a small globular desk lamp on an enormous expanse of polished mahogany. I carefully closed the door behind me. In the shadows, beyond the pool of light, the room looked surprisingly untidy. There were unopened cardboard boxes along with books and CD jewel cases; some bookshelves were empty, while others were piled haphazardly with magazines. There were other boxes that looked as if they had been hastily torn open and the contents pulled out, papers scattered on the floor. The desk was relatively tidy with several neat piles of paper, strategically placed, a closed laptop, two empty glasses. I picked up one and sniffed. Whisky. I stood in the gloom and realised that the room was perfectly quiet. It had been sound proofed.

I picked up one of the sheets on the desk and stared at it. It was just a list of meaningless figures. Another seemed just the same. I opened the laptop, briefly. A password request winked at me insolently and I closed it again. I opened a couple of the desk drawers, wondering what I was looking for. The whole room looked as if it had only recently been unpacked and I didn't really have a hope of finding anything that might incriminate Fuller in Ben's death. What the hell would that be anyway? Memo to self: Must Bump Off Ben? This was just a slightly messy room with a desk in it as far as anything useful to me went.

I opened another drawer with no great hope and finally smiled. On the top of some envelopes along with a small tray of paper clips there was a set of house agent's keys. I grabbed them feeling senselessly triumphant. 124 Priory Gardens was hand written in tiny biro on the green plastic key fob. 124. Of course it was. I put them in my pocket and closed the drawer. The pretty pink card with the white crescent moon and 124 underlined three times just to make sure the card's silly recipient couldn't make a mistake. The moon in my tarot reading spelled changes out of my control, even mad moments. I was vaguely aware that the delusions of grandeur prompted by this evening's coke-fest might neatly account for this but it needed very careful handling in any event. More prosaically, the crescent moon on the shiny pink card had given me the address of Lois's cleaning job at the dungeon, although she could hardly have spent the best part of a week cleaning. No-one is that fastidious, least of all Lois Valentine. But…BUT… the overheard scrap of Fuller's conversation had all the characteristics of the Ginger One. 'That voice…shrieking…' No-one could shriek like Lois, I'd heard her. And what if it was *Lois* in the red dress? Michael said he'd seen them together but he'd already lied to me once about her. I knew Lois had seen Ben on that fateful Friday night, she'd told me so herself. It *had* to be Lois. As I stared into the shadows thinking, I was vaguely aware of the renewed thump of music. It took me a moment to realise why that was. The door to the study was open.

Paul Fuller and I just stared at each other.

VIII

STRENGTH

*Reminds us that strength comes from acknowledging our weaknesses,
overcoming them by recognising outstanding parts of our nature
and our outstanding friends.*

CHAPTER TWELVE

"You lost something?" He still didn't look dangerous, not really. He was smiling but the blanks where his eyes should be made him difficult to read. So even though I was wedged firmly in the top of the cookie jar with chocolate all over my face, I went on the attack.

"Where's Eddie?" I said, sounding peevish, "I thought he came in here with you."

He pushed the door wider with his foot, still leaning against the jamb,

"Let's go find him, shall we, darlin'?"

I followed him out into the hall. I had no idea what was going to happen next but I'd have to do some quick thinking. Paul Fuller may have been shorter than me, especially as my faithful old Cubans gave me an extra couple of inches but I only hurt people for a living. He seemed to do it for fun.

"Where's your toilet?" I asked casually, looking round me, "I've been over-indulging a bit."

He leaned across and took my upper arm in a startling grip. It was as if my circulation had been cut off below the grasp of his broad fingers. I gasped.

"We're going to find Eddie, though." He said reasonably, still smiling. Oh, fuck.

We walked briskly arm-in-arm back into the lounge. Fuller

seemed to know where Eddie was and guided me without pause through the pulsating throng, passed the bar and through a dark archway I hadn't noticed before. He bustled me down a short, narrow flight of stone steps between cold, bare brick, while I tried to look puzzled and offended, until we came to an abrupt halt in front of a theatrically heavy wooden door. It had iron hinges and a huge iron ring pull and he opened it slowly with a squeak and a clatter.

Paul Fuller had his own dungeon. Of course he did. This whole building was his pleasure dome in the Sussex countryside and what pleasure dome would be complete without one? Kipling would have been stunned. The only thing that really surprised *me* was the lack of imagination. Black and red. For every Domina's work room that is decked out in tasteful pastels, there are 10,000 others that are black and red. Have you ever been in a dungeon? I don't mean the Spanish Inquisition, Torquemada in the Home Counties kind, I mean the business-of-pleasure kind. Well, this one had all the usual trappings with the extra twist of no expense spared. There were tall cages and dog cages, hoists, chains and stocks. One wall accommodated a large, padded St Andrews cross that could be rotated to allow access to any part of the lucky subject's anatomy. Apart from the large equipment, the walls were festooned with whips and paddles, canes and floggers, hoods, cuffs, rope; implements and restraints of all kinds. There was nothing cheap and cheerful about any of it. Sturdy, well-finished wood and expensive German leather and chrome. Everything you would need, right at your finger tips, or indeed any other part of your anatomy, for an intense night in.

Eddie was enjoying himself, reclining in a soft leather sling suspended from the ceiling, watching Misty Licks and Rick Turpin fucking. Misty was tied over a flogging bench, doing stage orgasms while Rick grandstanded, smacking Misty's ample bottom occasionally and saying, "Yeah, that's right, oh yeah, baby…" without really looking at her. I noticed they were being filmed by a young man in an Iron Maiden tee shirt, crouched unobtrusively by a queening stool (don't ask). Never waste an opportunity, eh?

"Jay's been missing you." Fuller said to Eddie. Now, I don't remember mentioning my name to Mr. Fuller. Eddie looked up. His pupils were so widely dilated that I doubt he could have focussed on anything smaller than Norfolk and he beat a tattoo on his leg with an open palm, gently rocking the sling.

"Yeah, really? Aaah, honey…cute…"

"I don't want her to go wandering off," said Fuller, "I'd hate you two to get separated." Eddie smiled obscurely. He and Fuller seemed to be sharing a joke that I wasn't party to. Not a nice feeling.

"So I'll show her your room," Fuller said. He turned to me, "I'm sure you'll like it. It's very comfortable." And then to Eddie, "I might join you both later, eh? A ménage a trios?" He pronounced it 'troys'. Pedantry was no comfort under the circumstances. I didn't think pointing it out would have helped either.

I tried to protest but Fuller wasn't interested in debate. Without any further chit chat, he marched me out of the dungeon, back through the bar and the lounge. None of the occupants was in the least curious about my sudden extraction from the festivities. A beautiful black woman with swinging dreadlocks was dancing on one of the low tables to riotous cheering, her body piercings twinkling on the sheen of her ebony skin, a Nubian Goddess amongst Barbarians. The large scatter cushions on the floor were playing comfortable host to contortions of a less artistic kind. The whole thing looked, sounded and smelled like a Babylonian orgy. I searched round desperately for Babs but she was nowhere to be seen.

"I'm really not that tired," I objected, as we headed towards the stairs, "And I honestly don't know why you feel I've got to be sent to bed." I tried to pull my arm free but Fuller's grip was as ferocious as an alligator.

"I think you'll be safer in bed." Fuller said,

"Why, for fucks sake?"

"Language!" Fuller snapped, pausing briefly on the stairs to point into my face. He hauled me with surprising ease up the steps, mostly because I was trying to avoid having his hands all over me, "I'm not having people snooping!" he pretty much threw me in front of him as we got to the landing. I turned to face him angrily,

"I was *not* snooping!" I lied, "I told you, I was looking – "

"Yeah, I know what you said," he grabbed me again and frog marched me to a door at the furthest end of the corridor. He manhandled me through it and followed me in. "You must think I'm stupid," he stood in the doorway. "You're one of Hammond's tarts. He was a cunt!" he spat the word out.

"I was *not* one of his tarts –" I said, rubbing my arm. I was seriously fed up with people's assumptions about me and Ben.

"Christ you just don't get it, do you? I don't just invite *anyone* here. Eddie knows all about you. And Stuart Crouch – yeah that's right," he must have seen my expression turn from baffled to surprised. "He told me you've got your nose in my fucking business, so don't get on your high fucking horse. Gimme your phone." He pushed himself away from the door and I considered making a run for it. But he moved with such confidence, I was sure I wouldn't get very far. For the first time, I backed up.

"I don't want to smack you," he said easily, "But I will. Just give me your fucking phone."

I glared at him and fished it out of my back pocket.

He took it from me and said, "Blackberry. Nice. Business is

good then. I'll be back later. This is going to be a lesson. Be quite a change for you won't it?"

The door slammed and I heard the key turn in the lock.

Lovely. This was the second time in less than a week that I'd been locked in by a psychopath. Proof, if I needed it, that there were some things I was good at and others that I wasn't. Private detective would be somewhere at the bottom of my CV along with base jumping and ironing.

Fuller's guest room was large and beautifully appointed. A double sleigh bed in dark wood with inviting white sheets and bedding. There were sliding wardrobes in the same rich style with inset mirrors, a nightstand bearing flowers arranged in a tall vase, an easy chair in the same soft suede as those downstairs, TV and entertainment centre, everything any guest could require in fact. Except a key. I walked across the room and through a small arch to a door. The en suite – peach tiles and fresh towels. Nothing here I could use.

Back in the bedroom I noticed Eddie's ghastly jacket draped over the back of an easy chair. I rifled through his pockets and found a packet of breath mints, a receipt for the packet of breath mints from a garage and glory be, the keys to his hire car. Great. If only I could get out of here, at least I had a means of fleeing the scene entirely. And it was essential that I get out of here. Fast. I had absolutely no wish to become the meat in an unhealthy Eddie and Paul sandwich, breath mints or no. I pulled back the curtains. The room overlooked the side of the house. I could see the shrubbery below me shining with fairy lights. The windows weren't locked but the drop was some 20 feet or so. I hurried back into the en suite. The window there was only tiny, no use at all.

As the seconds ticked by and the door proved solid and unmoving, I realised that if I was going to avoid the party that was heading in my direction, I was going to have to jump out of the bedroom window. I craned my neck out again and attempted to reassure myself, not at all successfully, that it wasn't that far. What I really needed was a little more in the way of jazz powder and a little less in the way of gravity. As I looked down, trying not to get involved in the concept of vertigo, I heard laughter echo cheerfully from the gardens at the back of the house. Fuck this.

I could feel my heart pounding as I opened the window wider. The night air cleared my head a little and I could see that the bushes below came right to the side of the house in a dense and comfortable looking pillow. I hauled myself up and sat on the window ledge. If I could just turn around, then hang and drop, I could reduce the fall by more than 6'. I wriggled round in the opening, scraping my back and shoulders on the window, banging my head and bruising my knees. One leg outstretched, then the other. It was too late to change my mind now. My arms complained as I gripped as hard as I could, lowering myself down an inch at a time. I could feel the grit of the bricks against my cheek, hear my boots scraping below me. There was no way I should be doing this. No fucking way. I just kept repeating,

"Bless the Goddess, bless the Goddess, bless the Goddess," under my breath, in the hope that she would take pity and bless me.

"What the fuck – ?! You stupid fucking…" I looked up in panic. It was Eddie. His face in the window, white with surprise and anger, loomed over me like a puppet in a Punch and Judy show. It was the catalyst. My fingers lost their grip and I plummeted down. Everything was black and chaos.

The ground greeted me far quicker than I thought it would and thankfully too fast for me to worry about it. I landed awkwardly, half-upright, half-sprawled, winded in the prickly clutches of what turned out to be a privet hedge. Privet is surprisingly hardy and I rolled around for a moment as it buoyed me up, before tumbling to the ground on the far side. Landing on solid ground was almost harder than landing in the hedge in the first place but I managed to crawl to my feet, a little tattered and torn but basically in one piece. I knew I had to move quickly and in spite of outraged muscles, I forced myself to run round the side of the house. I could feel the scratches on my arms, the bruises on my legs, the air tearing at my lungs as I tried to cope with adrenalin and panic.

I saw Eddie's Lexus in the driveway and ran towards it. All I wanted to do was get away. Even if the whole evening hadn't been a disaster and I'd enjoyed Babylon and all its delights, I'd still want my own bed, as far away from Eddie Meyer's plans for the night as possible. I got as far as the verge next to the drive, eyes fixed on the shiny black limousine, when a hard blow in the small of my back sent me flying forward, the ground rising to meet me yet again. I landed heavily, smelling dirt and grass, tasting blood as I bit my lip. I twisted round as quickly as I could but Eddie was on top of me before I could think.

"You fucking stupid bitch!" he was yelling, "What the fuck do you think you're doing?!" He caught hold of one of my wrists and held it down. I could hear his heavy breathing, see his hair sticking up, his eyes looking wild.

"Let go of me you CUNT!" I yelled, not wishing to be at all mistaken. We struggled but he was a big man and heavy, in a way only a clumsy man can be. I suddenly saw the look on his face clearly in the back wash from the house lights. I saw absolutely what his intentions were. No fucking way! He might have been big but I was madder, much madder. With my free hand, the hand with the eye of Horus ring, Obsidian and silver, I punched him in the face with all the force I could muster. He fell sideways with a cry and I followed my momentum onto him and up. My hand hurt atrociously but it was worth it. Taking a leaf from Gripper's book, and just for *that* look, I aimed a kick somewhere sensitive. He curled into the foetal position with an anguished groan and I scrambled to let myself into the Lexus without bothering to look back at him. Fuck him.

Firmly locked in, juggling with the keys, out of Park, I managed to negotiate my way out of the drive without being further molested. In the rear view mirror I could see a diminishing Eddie struggling to his feet and staggering back towards the house. After that I concentrated on the road ahead. Now would not be the time to perform my usual drunken post party trick. It took a lot of concentration. A Lexus is a big car for someone used to driving a Mini but it has the advantage of intimidating other road users and I guess they all put my terrible driving down to the arrogance of the moneyed classes.

I worked it out on the way back to Dean's Bay. Both Paul Fuller and Eddie Meyer were likely to be very cross (no shit, Sherlock). Fuller had my mobile phone. Just going back home and sitting around waiting for them to come and get me wasn't really going to cut it. If Fuller had my mobile, he was presumably going to be calling my friends and contacts. How long before he realised I'd taken the keys to Priory Gardens? Why had that seemed like a good idea? In any event, I couldn't really go home and I couldn't go to Gina or Lucy or any of my usual stalwart standbys in times of crisis.

I parked the Lexus in a side street in the centre of town and left the keys in the glove box. I practically ran home. I had to assume that either Eddie or Fuller or some minion would be following me directly and I didn't know how much time I would have.

The alley outside my cottage was empty, which was as it should be at two in the morning. I gave a furtive glance each way before sprinting to the door. I went in and grabbed Ben's car keys and Fuller's photographs and a few other things, before leaving my lovely house cold and dark and hurrying down the steps at the end of the alley to the seafront.

I found a good old fashioned phone box opposite the dead, night time facade of a chip shop. All was still and quiet, the street lights shining down on strangely static space along the front. There was no traffic, no late night travellers not even a stray dog. Even the sea seemed silent. I wedged myself into the booth and rummaged in my jeans pocket for a scrap of paper I'd grabbed on my exit from home. I hoped to Christ he'd answer or I'd be spending the night walking the mean streets, freezing my bum off. I stuffed the machine with pound coins. It rang. It rang. It rang. And it rang. Please don't go to voice mail, just pick the fucking thing up you...

"Hello?" Sleepy voice. Thank the Goddess. Relief flooded through me for the first time that night and I almost collapsed in the phone box.

XIII

THE DEVIL

Is the card of temptation, an invitation to do as you would like,
especially with regard to material or sexual indulgence. It is also
a warning not to become addicted, a victim of excess.

CHAPTER THIRTEEN

Max rented a largish flat in a large house on one of the many roads that radiate out from the seafront. Impressively fronted with a toothsome keystone and manly pillars it was pompously Georgian, correctly proportioned and roofed in Welsh slate. Despite its butchery into flats, it was encouragingly well-tended on the outside, its imposing façade recently whitewashed, the woodwork of its doors and windows pristine. Even in the dark, I could see the front garden was neat and trimmed, a stark contrast to many of its neighbours, whose legacy of dusty hydrangeas and leggy shrub roses struggled through refuse sacks and builder's rubble. Max's apartment itself was a terrible betrayal of his landlord's high hopes. It displayed all the epic qualities exemplified by the term 'Bachelor Pad', before New Men started using exfoliants and worrying about their highlights.

There were piles of books and teetering stacks of magazines. Two, no, three guitars, an electric keyboard with more books on top of it. I stood in front of it while Max busied himself finding drinks and wondered what sort of noise it would make under the weight of literature if I plugged it in. There were plates, glasses, and bottles scattered all over the place. The computer seemed to be buried under Escher-like stacks of CD cases, the monitor plastered with yellow post-it notes and sporting a hat. And there was sheet music everywhere. Now I'm not the tidiest person in the world, in fact, when I'm working I can be pretty slovenly, but I felt a desperate desire to bring order to the chaos Max obviously lived in. This, ladies and gentlemen, is the mistake women often make. House-training a tornado would be a more effective exercise than tidying up after a single man. I moved a small heap of encouragingly kinky DVDs from the sofa and sat down as Max came in with alcohol. He was wearing a sweatshirt and jeans and handed me a glass of what looked like whisky and turned out to be Southern Comfort.

He had picked me up under the still arcs of the street lamps on the seafront in a slightly testy red BMW, rust and under seal the only things holding its rather battered chassis together. It was filled with litter and empty takeaway cartons, the back seat additionally boasting an itchy looking blue blanket, a stained pillow and a ladies PVC peephole bra. Once again he wasn't wearing shoes. Slumped silently in the passenger seat, I'd watched him change gear, accelerate and brake, all with his bare feet.

"Hey!" he recalled me as he settled himself amid the debris, "drink."

I nodded silently and took a sip of the liqueur. Things were beginning to catch up with me. I just wanted an open fire, a pizza and the comfort of my own bed – most of all my own bed. Then I could deal with things. But I wasn't going to be able to do that tonight. Tomorrow night? When? I took another larger gulp.

"Are you going to tell me why I had to rescue you again? If you keep it up I'm going to start thinking you have issues." Max looked quizzically at me. He was obviously concerned but amusement played around the corners of his eyes. Right. I told him and he stopped being amused.

"So I can't really go home," I finished, "And I can't really go anywhere they'd find me from my mobile. No-one's going to be looking here. That is – Christ Max! You're not some fucking friend of Paul Fuller's are you?"

"You jumped out of a two-storey bedroom?!" he repeated, incredulous. I stared at him, horrified at the easy assumption I'd made. Seeing my expression, he said quickly, "No. No, I'm not a pal of Paul Fuller's. I don't even know who he is. I just moved down here, remember? I haven't even properly unpacked yet." He looked round the room and shrugged, "Sorry about the mess."

I relaxed back into the chair and closed my eyes though I knew I wasn't going to be able to sleep yet. I was still too wired.

"What are you going to do?" Max asked.

"I don't know." I sighed, "I think I'm going to go to Priory Gardens tomorrow. I've gone through enough to get these keys."

"What do you think's there?"

I shrugged my shoulders.

"This is what I know," I said, "Ben Hammond was given an overdose. He wasn't a drug user – yes, I know there's a first time for everything," I added as Max opened his mouth to speak, "but I think not in his case. So someone vandalised his car, took his car keys, killed him..." I thought about that phrase and everything it signified, "...and brought the car keys and a set of bloody awful photographs of Paul Fuller getting his jollies round to *me*. Now I'm pretty sure Lois was one of the last people to see Ben at the Pink Parrot that Friday and she's disappeared. I find she's been employed as a cleaner by Fuller. At this place," I held up the keys to Priory Gardens. "And it also seems she's been harassing Angell Falls, 'poking her nose in' as Fuller put it. She might even be my lady in red." Max was bursting,

"Yes, but why involve you? And even if Fuller did kill Ben, why didn't he take his 'awful photos' as you call them away with him? Why post them through your letter box?"

"Yes, yes! I know. None of it makes sense. I thought it was

my ex-husband being spiteful. He's a TV, you know. I know he knew Angell Falls *and* Lois..."

"But what about what I said before. It has to be someone who knows you knew Ben and – "

"That could be any number of people." I said.

"But – "

"They're just queuing up outside the front of my house," I said and explained about Stuart and his photograph of my scarlet phantom.

"So that's what all that was about." said Max. "On the pier..."

I took another gulp of my drink and nodded.

"Jesus Christ, Jay!" Max was shaking his head, "I'd got not idea. Look, why don't you just go round to your ex and find out what he's been up to?" It was my turn to shake my head.

"He moved." I said, "I don't know where. I haven't got his number any more. Lucy's going to try and get hold of him for me. But I'll tell you the other thing I'm going to do tomorrow. That's send these fucking pictures back to Fuller. AND I'm going to tell him who took them. That nasty little sod Stuart had the cheek to go running to his daddy. I'm going to have his balls on a spike." I downed the last of my drink and suddenly felt like a wrung out dishcloth. I noticed the tears in my top and the mud on my jeans for the first time. I could only guess at the rest of it.

"Where can I sleep?" I asked.

The following morning, refreshed from a mercifully dreamless sleep on Max's couch and fortified with muesli and strong coffee I wrote a letter to Paul Fuller and sealed it into its brown envelope with the photographs. Not before Max had shuffled through them, though.

"These are nasty." He said with a frown, "Why don't you just burn them?"

"Because I don't know what Stuart's likely to say. I don't know how vindictive that psycho's feeling after the kicking Gripper gave him. I want to get mine in first. Play strength to strength." I'd written:

Dear Mr Fuller

I'm not going to mention last night. To anybody. These belong to you. I have no interest in them. They were taken by Stuart Crouch for Ben Hammond, who paid him. I am only interested in who posted them through my door.

Give my regards to Mr Meyer.
Jay Franklin

It had taken me quite a time to set the right tone, brusque without being rude, ending on a conciliatory note. I knew it was probably another stupid thing to be added to the list of stupid things I'd done lately, but I wanted rid of the photos and I was feeling bitchy enough to get my own back on Stuart. Max posted it before I could change my mind.

While Max went out shopping, I left a message for Lucy, letting her know I'd returned the photographs but leaving out the rest of the night's escapades. She'd find out soon enough and I didn't feel like getting another ticking off. I also phoned Gina, just to warn her about the irritating repercussions of leaving my mobile in the clutches of a vengeful gangster. I was too late.

"Honey, what the hell is going on?" She sounded stern, which is not like Gina at all.

I tried to give her a brief resume of my disastrous evening but it was difficult running a concise narrative through her fluent swearing.

"I'm really sorry," I said, "I hope you haven't been getting hassled. I'm not going into hiding indefinitely. I just want to let things cool down a bit."

"Hassled? I had some fat American creep wake me up at five this morning!"

"Oh, darling I'm so sorry. Just ignore calls from 'me' until I can get a new – "

"No, Jay. He came round. Banging on my door. He tried to barge his way in when I opened it – "

"Shit!"

"- demanding to know where I was hiding you – "

"Shit!"

"- It was lucky I had Phil with me."

"Oh, God. I'm *really* sorry, Gina." Thank heavens for another on the endless conveyor belt of Gina's boyfriends. I was horrified that Eddie had actually gone to the trouble of door stepping my contact list. What the hell was he hoping to achieve? Still, it could have been worse, at least it wasn't Paul Fuller.

"Just as long as you're OK." Gina said, "He looked like he wanted to do a bit of damage."

"Look, Gina," I asked, thinking of Lois, "How well do you know Michael?"

"What's he got to do with it?"

"Nothing, I hope. Did you know he and Lois had been – er – dating?" I tried to think of a more appropriate way of putting it and failed.

"What?! You're joking! He never said anything about it to me." Actually, thinking about it, I wasn't that surprised. How do you tell a beautiful, sexy young woman that you're dating an unhinged transsexual with an anger management problem? "We met a couple of years ago," she said, "Just after he'd got back from seeing his father. I think his parents split up when he was a kid and he'd just managed to track down his dad. Found him living with another man somewhere in Cambridge. I remember we had a lot of heart-to-hearts...But he's just too nice," she rallied, "I thought...but that awful trannie?! God, he kept that quiet." Quiet indeed. I apologised again to Gina and rang off, wondering what else Michael was keeping to himself.

Max came back and I indulged myself in a bubble bath while he practiced and watched the TV. I noticed the tunes he played and the general mood of the music altered depending on what programme was he watching and I relaxed in the hot water playing a game of trying to guess what he was looking at. The music would stop and he would flit to another channel, then it would start again, perhaps more serious, or maybe something light and frothy. Was he watching the lunchtime News or Loose Women? Maybe he'd found a Western, a cooking programme? There was something dangerously cosy about all this pleasant domesticity. How many times did he say he'd been married? Three? Perhaps they all started like this – smiling at the harmony. Maybe they'd ended screaming at the noise? How cynical am I? There was no getting away from the fact that I found him extremely attractive, though, and I was used to acting on urges like that. But Max the sax had 'serious' written all over him and that would lead to definite trust issues. Apart from anything else, I simply didn't trust *myself* any more.

I'd become so lost in thought, that I hadn't noticed the cessation of music from the other room. I was indulging in a little stress relieving fantasy (no, not *that* kind), the water was warm and I'd closed my eyes. I'd just moved on to how stunning I'd look at my third wedding when the bathroom door opened suddenly and Max stood on the threshold amid the steam.

"What the fuck are you doing?" I hoped the bubbles were covering what remained of my modesty, "I know this is your house but – "

Without lingering on my nakedness, he came over and sat

on the closed toilet seat. Having 'played' often in public and in clubs, not always fully clothed, I'm not at all bashful. But surely there are some places you can expect privacy? He looked rather solemn.

"Look," he said, "I know we've only just met but I can honestly say I've never met anyone quite like you."

It was a little odd coping with a conversation, in my bath, that coincided so ridiculously with my recent fantasy. And it *was* a fantasy. There are some points where I still make contact with the real world. Sensible expectations of my love life are one of them.

"Well, er, thank you." What should I say?

"I've been thinking," he said, shifting on the loo and looking earnest.

"Yes?" I'd almost prepared myself with some bashful girlish response – "Why, Mr. Darcy…" – when he said,

"I'm sorry but can you just tell me *why* you've got yourself involved in all this crap with Ben Hammond?"

I looked at him, completely thrown. Now he had me at a disadvantage and he knew it.

"I – "

"You went out a couple of times with a guy who died. Nothing to do with you. Someone posts his keys and some dirty pictures through your letter box. Nothing to do with you. Why didn't you just hand them over to the police? Jay, you've been running round in the dark, jumping out of buildings, getting involved with serious criminals. Why? You couldn't go home last night. Actions have consequences – "

"I told you! I don't like being victimized, Max. And I don't like being lectured, certainly not when I'm having a bath."

Max screwed up his face and made an impatient gesture,

"But this has nothing to do with *you*. You're just making more trouble for yourself," he hung his head briefly tired, then looked up, his beautiful eyes shocking me with their intensity. He said quietly, "I don't want to see you get hurt, Jay."

I shifted in the bath, deliberately sitting up, making a loud splash and held his gaze.

"Can I get dressed now?" I said after a short, silent tussle. He sighed and got to his feet.

"I'm serious." He said. Serious. 'Serious' written all over him. I watched him leave before subsiding back into the water with a groan. Why do I always have to fall for difficult men?

Max didn't mention the bathroom incident again but furnished me with his spare mobile phone and a clean sweatshirt and after a ham salad lunch, I took to the streets. The afternoon was warm with Autumn sunshine, in contrast to the drizzly days of the last week. Things are supposed to look cheerier in the daylight, but I wasn't feeling optimistic as I strode out. After Max's one man intervention, I'd started examining my motives for all of this. Was I just a lifelong control freak cultivated by a rudderless childhood? Was I really being victimised? No-one was going to sneak up to my front door in the dark and post anonymous filth, ho-no! Was that over reacting? And was I happy to visualise Tom tottering about in heels again so I could catch up with him and exact some revenge for that drunken punch? Unfinished business, all of it. God help me, maybe I was just bored!

Self-doubt crept in as I took a circuitous route towards Priory Gardens along the seafront. With a little warmth and clearing skies, the inhabitants of my pebble dashed utopia threw caution to the winds and bared themselves to October. Skinny chested youths, cheap tattoos, strappy tops, pierced belly buttons and muffin top hips all seemed to be heading in a slatternly pilgrimage along the promenade towards the suddenly attractive amusements beyond the pier. Fish and chips, candyfloss, sticks of rock, lager, Bacardi Breezers, shouting from the ferris wheel and the magic carpet ride, screaming, laughter, police sirens, vomit. All the things the seaside does so well. I watched these late season holiday makers relaxed and happy. Actions have consequences and now I couldn't just buy an ice cream and enjoy the sunshine. Like Max said, at the moment I couldn't even go home

The promenade runs along the seafront for almost two miles in a double stitched hem marking the boundary of civilisation before the plunge into the English channel. It is pinned to the foreshore at long intervals by ornate Victorian street lamps on the seaward side and dull concrete clumps of urban lighting on the other. It is wide enough to accommodate everyone and it was easy to fall into a promenader's amble, the sort of swinging, lazy stroll that begs for a walking cane and a silly hat. I didn't feel like wearing a silly hat, though. Just what would have happened, if I'd handed over Ben's keys and the photographs to the police as Max suggested? The photographs at least would have Ben's fingerprints on them, mine, possibly even Stuart's. Trying to pretend I'd got nothing to do with it when I'd had an 'association' with both of them would have been pointless. Then I remembered the laughter in the sinister dark of the empty pier. Someone was definitely taking the piss and I really wasn't being unreasonable wanting to find out who it was. I walked towards the pier, breathing in the salt fragrant breeze, working out a route to Priory Gardens and hoping that Eddie and Fuller weren't planning a visit there too.

On the beach, a little way from the pier, a large bonfire was being constructed. Made up of pallets and planks and bundles of thick kindling, it reached at least twenty feet into the sky and was cordoned off behind tape. A group of men in reflective jackets unloaded more wood from a van on the tackle way, passing it along, stacking it around the base of the construction, pointing, shouting instructions. In all the excitement, I'd forgotten that it was the beginning of the bonfire season.

Down in darkest Sussex the traditional bonfire night

celebrations have become seasoned with something more cheerfully sinister and pagan. Different bonfire societies around the county have their own banners and costumes. Some are mysterious monks, others sailors, yet others pirates and dandies and they are joined by pagans and Wiccans, Thelemites and, for all I know, Satanists. Green men, Morris in black face, wassailers, witches, warlocks and hobby horses cavort with skeletons in top hats, matelots, vicars and tarts in a flaming, torch lit parade that turns the streets into flickering rivers of fire. The music is loud and driven forward by shouts and whistles and drums, the whole boiling mess is punctuated with fire crackers and percussion caps and red flares melting the air.

Many towns and villages also have their own bonfire night, any time between the end of October and the end of November and Dean's Bay is traditionally the first of the season. The only town which always has its celebrations on November 5th is Lewes, near Brighton. Harking back to much earlier traditions and completely without rancour, they customarily burn the pope in effigy. Health and safety killjoys put a stop to their cheerful practice of rolling blazing tar barrels down the hill into the River Ouse but much of it still resembles a demilitarized zone. It is Samhain, it is Winter taking hold of Summer's faded crown, it is rimed with frost and clouding breath and it is bloody good fun.

The parade ends with the marchers throwing their torches into the blazing bonfire on the beach. The festivities finish up with an enormous firework display that climaxes with the destruction of a giant effigy – not the pope, poor bugger – usually some more topical grotesque. A few years ago Dean's Bay had blown up the Spice Girls. All that remained after the party ended and the revellers had tottered home waving their glow sticks, were Ginger Spice's eyes, peering in a startled fashion through the clearing smoke. I could see that this year's effigy was Simon Cowell and I was confident that nothing would remain of *him* after Dean's Bay Bonfire Society had finished with him. Good thing too. With any luck I'd be here, stress free, to see it.

I drew level with the pier and stared through the locked iron gates at the windows of the amusement arcade. Had I really gone staggering round there in the pitch dark? I stared at its unloved façade as if it might offer up some clue.

"What's up?"

I almost jumped out of my skin. I turned and was surprised to find myself looking at Gina's not so dull friend, Michael. He was huddled into a windcheater and his hair was sticking up in jaunty spikes. Ben and Jerry were waddling dourly round his feet, looking less than enthusiastic about their day trip.

"I thought it was you," he said. "You look kind of fed up." I looked at him and felt suddenly tired of subterfuge.

"Why did you lie to me about Lois?" I asked bluntly. He looked blankly at me and I held his gaze while the breeze caught my hair and flung it up around me. I smoothed it down and Michael dropped his eyes.

"I wasn't really lying," he said finally. "I just didn't want to mention it."

"Do the police know?" I asked. He shook his head.

"Christ, Michael," I boggled, "They'll find out and then it'll look really shitty."

"I was embarrassed!" he burst out, "It just started as a kind of friendship thing but then…and, well after that she wanted me to do things to her and I really wasn't up for it. Not at all," he emphasised, "And anyway, it was all over before, well … before this happened. We hardly spoke afterwards …"

"So you really don't know where she went?"

"No! And I really don't care either. The last time I saw her was with that woman in the Albert. Why does it matter to you anyway?"

"Because I think the same bloody woman's been hanging round

outside my house. You're sure you didn't see Lois on her own?" I emphasised the last three words slightly and gave him a hard look.

"Of course not. I told you. I told the police. Why would I make it up?"

"It doesn't matter." I gave a tired shrug in my over size sweat shirt and we both gazed for a moment past the barricades to the pier front while Ben and Jerry parked themselves on limp leads and yawned. Michael smiled suddenly.

"Do you fancy a run round the arcade?" he asked. I turned slowly and stared at him, watching his smile.

"That's not funny." I said. He backed away from me and made an elaborate conciliatory gesture with his hands, to the consternation of the dogs, who were still attached.

"What? What's the matter? Sorry," he said, seeing my face, "I'm only joking."

I left him standing by the pier head looking after me, a little confused. He probably *was* only joking but bumping into Michael had reminded me of all the reasons I needed to find that scarlet lady. Finding Lois was one of the ways I could do this. Lois either knew who she was, if Michael was to be believed, or she was actually the bloody creature herself. No-one else seemed to have got close to her. Apart from me, that is. I was certain that trapped somewhere in the murky landscape of my brain, she would be standing and waving and I'd have all the answers.

Priory Gardens was yet another tree lined street of impressive Victorian town houses gone somewhat to seed. 124 was probably the least impressive of the lot. Peeling grey paint, crumbling plaster, one of the downstairs windows was boarded up and bore the derelict stigmata of impenetrable graffiti. The front garden was a single slab of unlovely concrete and the only evidence that the house was actually occupied manifested in the uncollected piles of rubbish strewn like a messy obstacle course around the front. It stared dumbly at me with blank eyes and grubby indifference. I sauntered past, trying to assess whether there was anyone at home, looking around for cars, another Lexus perhaps? But there was nothing to tell. No-one hung round, no-one paid attention. I walked a little way up the street and sat on a low wall beside the squat grey buildings of the Priory Hill Medical Centre. I sat. I sat and waited and watched until my bottom went numb. People came and went from the medical centre, a few casting quizzical glances in my direction, but 124 Priory Gardens remained unmolested by interest of any kind.

In the cold light of day, gazing at the tatty frontage, I wondered again if pinching the keys had been an entirely good idea. The building didn't fit my notion of a film studio, a dungeon or even a private residence. It looked more like a crack house for transients. I sighed and took the keys out of my pocket. Enough procrastination! I jumped up and strode purposefully across the road hoping no-one would notice this speculative house call.

The front door had the soft, rippled look of wet wood and the green paint was peeling, revealing streaks of its pale flesh beneath. There were two keys, one I guessed for the front and one for the back. The Yale key turned and the door shuddered as I pushed it open, dislodging with a slither the pile of unopened letters and junk mail that littered the mat. Evidently the place hadn't been visited for some time. The entrance was wide and a large staircase rose vacantly from the centre of a grubby chequered floor to the rooms above, tatty carpet graced the treads and a dead pot plant sat forlornly on a table at the bottom. I could see a half-glazed door at the back of the hall which must have led to the kitchen. Apart from the pot plant the only ornament in a hall overwhelmed with magnolia woodchip was an insipid botanical print of daffodils. Next to the door, a hilarious certificate

202

of fire safety hung amidst the mould. One thing was certain. If Lois had been employed to clean the place, it was one date with destiny she had never kept.

The other thing I noticed as I shut the door behind me, like the prelude to a bad dream, was the smell. There was rising damp, un-regarded dirt and cold, musty plaster. But there was something else, a hint of foul, sickly colour, running like a ribbon through the grimy ambience of the whole building. I felt a dread rise in my chest as I walked further into the hall. There were doors to either side of the central staircase and as I moved towards the room on the right, the rank smell seemed to increase. I felt my heart beating hard, even though I knew no-one else was here. I knew why my heart was beating. I felt irresistibly drawn towards that door. It offered itself to me as if the pungency surrounding it were a visible lure, seeping out from beneath the sills, around the frame, through the keyhole. I knew why I was drawn. I put my hand over my nose and mouth and reached for the handle.

I opened the door on to shadows and the awful smell instantly became much stronger. I pressed my fingers harder into my face as my throat closed. The room itself was in turbid gloom, the day shut out by heavy curtains that fell to the floor. Specks of dust danced in hopeful chinks of light that lanced across the darkness from the window. I could make out shapes, some large and vaguely familiar. Without walking right in, I fumbled for the light switch inside. I could hear a humming sound. I found the light.

Technicolor suddenly leapt up and screamed like the slasher in a horror movie. The room was the mandatory dungeon colours of red and black. There was the usual equipment, a playroom set out for naughty games. But none of it mattered. In the centre of this centre for jolly japes there was a thing, a grotesque, bloody, black, grey… shiny and soft. Solid and liquid. A body. A body. Spread over a flogging bench. I could see three distinct arcs of dark cast off blood spatter against the wall at the head... I realised what the noise was. Flies. Humming. I couldn't speak and I couldn't scream and I couldn't cover my eyes. I felt the vision drop by bloody drop seeping far into my soul. Looking at a picture, at the television, at a computer game, filters reality, a lens between the viewer and the stink and sweat and heat. I found I couldn't move either. Reality cannot be coined with film or pixels, it just is. I started to shake. I was only peripherally conscious of my body and its monstrous need to vomit. I knew it also wanted scream.

I suddenly felt very cold and aware, aware of my fingers still on the light switch. Motor function returned from somewhere and I pressed the light switch down. Darkness fell and I managed to roll away from the door, leaning against the wall. I was again only faintly aware of sliding down into a crouch, my ears pounding. Inwardly the grand guinol made my eyes swim, the stench teasing at it like a sore spot. Fuck, fuck, fuck...

XI

JUSTICE

*Signifies the need for balance in all things, curb excesses,
be even handed. It also indicates there may be dealings with
the law and a fair outcome.*

CHAPTER FOURTEEN

Max had surprised me by appearing almost instantly. Or so it seemed. I'd managed to make it back outside and was sitting on the step when he arrived in a flourish of leather and rusty red BMW. I'd told him not to go in but he'd ignored me and we were both now sitting ashen faced in his car waiting for the police. It was stupid but I hadn't thought to call them. It was taking a while for my brain to function again. I'm an artist. My visual memory is something I reply on, when I'm not trying to impair it with booze and drugs. And I'd discovered a palette undreamt of by Bacon or Bosch, an account of death so vivid and alive that I knew I'd never get it out of my head, however much I wanted to. The magic tree dangling from the rear view mirror with its noisome mixture of happy odours wasn't helping my queasy stomach either.

"Are you OK?" Max asked.

"No." I said. He was turning to face me from the driver's seat, his black leather coat hunched up around his shoulders. It had started raining again, a dark shower cutting through the remains of a golden afternoon and the downpour was drumming insistently on the roof and windscreen. The deluge on the glass made it almost impossible to see out and the windows were starting to steam up. Through the grey I saw bright colours and flashing lights. "Help me." I said to Max. There was no time left for lectures about my motives and I didn't want to hear them.

"Of course." He said simply.

Max and I were interviewed separately at the police station. Although a positive identification of my corpse was pending, with the information I gave them Lois was obviously being pencilled in for the role. I told them honestly all I knew about her, which wasn't much. I told them about Ben's car keys and where I'd found them, there didn't seem to be any point in hanging on to the bloody things. There were a lot of things I didn't tell them, though. There was no sense in making things more complicated (ha ha) so I had to do a bit of creative recollection. I definitely didn't tell them about Fuller's party. It wasn't a question of protecting him: it was a question of protecting *me*. I'd seen how successful the police had been with Fuller in the past and I wanted to be able to go home. The questions seemed interminable. After a few hours, I was getting tired and angry and I could see they were treating my account with increasing scepticism.

The interview room smelled strangely of digestive biscuits, the walls were shiny and graffiti proof, the desk a ferocious faux mahogany. Everything was utilitarian, including the blank-faced policeman who sat opposite me. Eventually he was joined by the ginger moustache of my previous acquaintance and they embarked on the same questions for the tenth time, couched in slightly different terms, until my answers sounded guilt-laden, even to my own ears.

"I understand you've had a traumatic experience," said the moustache, who's name I now noted with grim hilarity was DS Holmes, "But this is a very serious situation, Miss Franklin and I'm not sure you're being entirely, well, frank." I noticed the slight smirk his companion gave and started,

"Oh, for God's sake – "

"Instead of coming to us with Mr. Hammond's car keys, which, let me remind you are evidence in a murder enquiry, you decided to do a spot of detective work off your own bat, probably destroying more evidence in the process. So ...let me get this straight. From some comments that Lois Valentine had made at a club, the – er – Pink Parrot," he checked his papers, "you thought it likely that she or someone she might know was responsible for putting the keys to Mr. Hammond's Astin Martin through your door. So you went to her home, rifled through her clothing," he narrowed his eyes, shaking his head "And found a set of house keys. And even though Ms Valentine would presumably need these keys if she were to go to the house, you assumed she was there and let yourself in. You can see why I find this a little difficult to swallow, can't you?"

"I didn't assume she was there," I said, "I told you, I was just curious."

"Do you take drugs, Jay?" he asked me unexpectedly,

"I'm sorry?" I said, the guilt of Cain descending on me.

"You said you passed out at a party. You can't tell us where. Was it drink or were you taking drugs?" DS Holmes looked bland.

"I was drinking a lot." I extemporised, without much hope. There really is nothing quite as inexorable as bland enquiry. "Look," I said feebly, "I had a lot to drink and I smoked one or two joints at the party. I passed out."

The detective leaned forward, his arms folded.

"So what did you talk about?" he asked. I sighed and leaned back. I knew they were doing it on purpose but I was coming to the end of my tether.

"Who?" I asked wearily.

"You and Ben Hammond. In your previous statement, you said he arrived at you house at four in the afternoon and left just before ten. You spent six hours chatting. What did you talk about?"

The silence invited sound, like a crooked finger teasing me out. There was nothing for it but to tell them the horrible truth.

It might at least buy me enough time to think of a way around admitting to the industrial pharmacopoeia that had sustained that evening's entertainment. I let them have the lot – the panties, stockings, stilettos, the ball gag...

"So you had sex." The unsmiling DS Holmes summarised my confession into four words that, under the circumstances, now seemed incredibly sordid.

"Yes." I stared at my fingers.

"Did you use a condom?"

"Yes! Why?"

"You still don't understand, do you, Miss Franklin? We are talking about a *murder* investigation. We are talking about *trace* evidence. You can't just tell us things *you* think are relevant. We'll have to take a DNA sample." He looked at his companion who made a note. "I've got to tell you, Jay, the only person looking suspicious in this whole business is you."

Finally, I snapped.

"Look! How do you think *I* feel?" I said, leaning dangerously across the table to the unmoving regard of the policeman, "I hardly know any of these people and yet someone has dragged me into this mess. And before you ask, no, I don't know who. I was trying to find out. For God's sake, do you think that if I knew who it was I wouldn't tell you?!"

"It might depend on who it was." Said DS Holmes inscrutably.

"What! Why?" Instead of answering me directly he said,

"I need to know that you're telling us everything. I don't think you are and I don't think you realise how important this is. Look, you're not under caution, you're not a suspect but I want you to think seriously about giving us the FULLEST account you can."

I closed my eyes. I could still see the colours of Lois's final resting place and I shuddered.

"I've told you everything..." I began. Holmes nodded and pushed himself away from the table with a scrape of his chair.

"OK," he said wearily, "We'll get you to come in tomorrow and sign a statement." He nodded at the uniformed constable who'd been dutifully taking notes and occasionally feeding me coffee. He gathered up his papers and I gathered up my wits in preparation to leave.

"Did you know your boyfriend's an ex-con?" DS Holmes was still relaxing in his chair, legs stretched out, arms loosely folded. I stared blankly at him, completely thrown. Gears crashed in my head. I saw the constable raise his eye brows at Holmes in amused disapproval before leaving us. I looked wistfully after him.

"Max Blackman? No," he said, "I didn't think he'd told you."

"He's not my boyfriend." I managed to say finally but the detective with the nasty ginger moustache had done some damage and he knew it. I could feel my head start to pound as the tension in my shoulders finally broke cover and began to blossom painfully behind my eyes. I put my fingers to my temples as he rose to his feet and stretched.

I got up, feeling confused and pursued. I tried not to look at him as I went out but he stopped me.

"Think about it," he said, "Naughty Max has done time for drug dealing..." He cocked his head to one side and raised one eyebrow theatrically "...and soliciting." He opened the door for me. "You should pick your friends more carefully, you know." He put his hand on my shoulder and checked my retreat once more, "Think about it. This is serious." He warned again.

I went home on my own. I didn't know where Max was and I didn't ask. Maybe I didn't want to know. There is always that self-deceiving blind spot between having a good time and paying for it yourself, playing safe and looking back with no regrets, and overstepping the mark into hardcore and the stark reality of corruption. I knew my morals would be fairly lacklustre when put to any standard test but I also knew that my extravagances were pretty petty compared to the kind of behaviour that could land you in prison. The beige detective had planted a poisonous seed that was germinating in thoughts of Max and some scarlet accomplice. *Ridiculous*. Had he really been so concerned for my welfare that he'd followed me on to the pier that night, or was he just having a good laugh at my expense? *Ridiculous*? Max seemed to be an unlikely Good Samaritan, he was so self-contained. I was overloaded with questions and I had no sensible answers. And I didn't want to think of the other thing, the thing in the room, in the house, on a street I knew.

Thankfully there was no-one lurking on my doorstep when I got home and I gratefully closed the door on everything the day had thrown at me.

I lay on my sofa in the dark and the quiet. The only light came from my open fire and it made the shapes and shadows of my familiars leap and twist. But it was friendly fire, warming and soft and my headache passed while I practised relaxing every muscle I possessed along with a good few others I probably didn't. I stared at the three card spread that I'd left on the table. Moon madness. The star – rest, recuperation, hope. The main problem, apart from murder, torture and mayhem, obviously, was that I still liked Max. Out of everything that had happened on this very trying day, Max rose to the top like trash floating on water. His allure remained undiminished, even though he now seemed to make more sense, at least as far as my personal attraction to him went. I was trying hard not to fall for the bad boy again and I was angry at him for actually being as bad as I thought.

In spite of the black and yellow tape in my mind surrounding the final resting place of Lois Valentine, I had to acknowledge that I couldn't have got it more wrong. Lois wasn't any mysterious lady in red, she wasn't any kind of conspirator or mastermind, she was a cleaner and she was dead. Why? In spite of her toxic personality, or even because of it, I couldn't imagine her having anyone intimate enough to generate such a brutal crime passionnel. Had she seen something? What had she known? For some reason I couldn't imagine Paul Fuller bothering to be so … so *enthusiastic* about beating her to death. I don't know much about this sort of thing but it looked to me like she'd been dead a while. No. I wasn't going to think about that again. Back under the rock.

My unhappy ruminations were cut short by a knock at my window followed by a knock on my door. I hauled myself reluctantly to my feet. Right – oh, I thought, whatever, whoever and if it's the police, or Fuller, or Eddie, well, I don't give a shit. It wasn't the police. It was Max. For some reason this took me by surprise. Even more surprising was the fact that he'd shaved and changed. He was now wearing a slate blue linen suit which clashed vigorously with a green candy stripe shirt. He also was carrying a bottle of wine, the sins of my father appearing on my doorstep again. Why did everyone assume alcohol was the only way to gain access to my home? I stared balefully at him and tried to imagine this picturesque creature in the drab romper suits so beloved of Her Majesty's prisons.

"Can I come in?" he said, holding up the bottle, as if I'd fall for that old trick.

"Sure." I said. It was a Cotes Du Rhône.

I didn't turn on any lights and after the wine had been opened we sat facing each other in silence and shadows. I couldn't think of a thing to say and I was conscious of Max looking steadily at me, so I kept my eyes on the floor, the fire, the light dancing round in the scarlet, ruby brown of my wine, anywhere but on his face. It startled me a little when he began to speak, in a quiet, even tone as if he was reading a bedtime story. My fire crackled and popped, adding to the sleepy-time atmosphere.

"I used to work in London," he said. "After my last divorce I lost the house so I was renting a flat in Hackney. I had a serious drug problem by then and regular work, session work, got really difficult to hold down. And, well, the gigs weren't that great either. I don't think modern jazz has ever really been a best seller."

"So you decided to deal drugs to stave off poverty?" I said, feeling fatigued.

"No." he said calmly, "I'm telling you what happened and you can believe me or not, it's up to you." He reached over and took the bottle from me with a sigh. "I know the fetish scene in London pretty well and I made contacts in clubs, and I'd use personal ads too. Men who want the whole girly experience and some fun punishment, you know, *you're* on the scene. They pay me, I play with them." He took a large gulp of his drink and topped up his glass. I did know, as the record has established, but I was growing fond of my indignation, it made me feel more in control.

"The odd client kept me in coke and occasional groceries. The problem occurred when I started doing favours for my dealer in exchange for freebies. Look," he leaned over to me, his odd eyes open and earnest, "He dumped on me and pissed off to Venezuela with his lady boyfriend. It should have been funny. They'd been watching us for six months and he left in the middle of the night, three hours before they broke the door down. Yeah, it was funny alright. I was the only one too stupid and too fucked to move quickly. They got me with four ounces – the rest of his fucking stash – and did me for possession with intent. And because they were pissed off they threw in soliciting as well. I spent a fucking horrible time de-toxing at Her Majesty's."

I felt light headed and warm in the wake of my headache and the wine was making me a little tipsy. Much better. Normal service was being resumed.

"If it's any consolation, I had absolutely no 'intent' of sharing my windfall at all. I was going to snuffle it all up myself."

I was enjoying a moment of exorcism. In the half-light, as

these things should be. Out, demon, out and here he was sitting opposite me on my sofa. I had realised, at the bleak tail end of one of the most stressful days of my life, that I had found my inner devil, my bête noir, clothed in flesh and bone and a candy stripe shirt. Imagine that, yourself – your own worst enemy, made a friend, an object of desire, a lover. It made me want to laugh for merrie olde Englande, although I confess that may have been some form of post traumatic hysteria. There is something about forcing a man of such obvious sexual charisma on to the back foot, making the man of mystery explain himself, that sets all things right with the world. This is one of the petty tyrannies women enjoy, certainly women sharing my particular predilections. Of course, misogynists might argue that women always behave like this, devising games that follow rules only they understand, altered periodically and randomly so that only they can prevail. Being a woman, I know that we have to develop inclusive strategies – the only games that really matter are constructed so that only men can win. It wasn't a question of winning with Max, though. After all, you can't beat yourself at chess. I was just happy that it wasn't always me who ended up behaving like a twat.

"As for soliciting," he began, "Do you know how hard it is to make a living as a musician? If I – where are you going?"

I'd got up and gone into the kitchen. I found the pile of old newspapers by the rubbish bin and returned with the Exchange and Mart.

"What's that?"

I found the ad I was looking for and stabbed a finger at it. Max squinted at it in the gloom and read out,

"Have you been wicked? Do you need to be taught a lesson? Discipline in very *strict confidence."* My mobile number was attached.

"Being a musician can't be any worse than being an artist." I said, relaxing back into my chair and trying not to smirk. I was suddenly enjoying this, I knew it wouldn't last. I watched various emotions flicker across his face – surprise, recognition and finally amusement.

"Well that showed me, didn't it?" he said.

THE EMPRESS

She is the defining card of creativity, mothering and fertility.
A benign and nurturing womanly influence or impulse.
Be wary of jealousy or over protectiveness.

CHAPTER FIFTEEN

It was one of those semi-erotic, confusing dreams that seem to make perfect sense as you wade through them, eyelids twitching, sleep walking confined to the occasional spasm. I was on the pier, amongst the dark amusements, my arms were tied behind my back and I knew that if I moved out of the circle drawn in the dust around me something terrible would happen. An Athame sat on my lap, blood and dust on its tip. Max came out of the gloom and untied my hands, then he put his arms around me. A wave of profound, pornographic arousal invaded my body and I could feel his fingers press into the small of my back, as he pushed his hips against me. I kissed his neck, then bit him gently, playfully, he dropped a hand and fondled my breast, squeezing the nipple, oh God! I looked up at him wanting his lips but Max had gone and Stuart was standing in front of me smiling. Why does my mind enjoy doing things like this to me? My dream crashed through a barrier of confusion and flight and I ran, or had the impression of running. Someone was laughing. It was a leafy country lane and I wrenched open the car door as it stopped, jumping inside, shouting "Go! Go!" It was agonisingly slow and the chassis was too close to the ground. I could have gone faster walking. Gripper drew alongside looking enormous and violent, his tattoos moving on his corded forearms.

"What's up, love?" he said.

"Help me," I said, "I'm going to be late!" But he just grinned and sat back, all chrome easy rider petrol head and disappeared into the dust. I looked at the clock on the dashboard. It was ten past two and beside it one scarlet nailed finger pushed the play button on the CD. 'Foxy Lady' burst out of the speakers in my head and I awoke suddenly with a cry that echoed in my ears like several exclamation marks. The bedclothes were screwed up in a frightened pile in a corner of the bed not occupied by me and I could feel the sweat cooling in a prickle on my skin. The car! The fucking car I'd got into on my lost weekend. The conviction that I knew this red queen, that I'd somehow brought my fate upon myself insinuated itself even more firmly and a shiver passed over me. I redistributed the duvet and settled back down, hugging it round me like a cocoon. The more I pressed the replay button in the memory banks, the more scrambled the tape became and as the dream faded, so did my certainty about its lucidity. When I fell asleep again, this time into comfortable dark, the only thing I was sure of was that I needed a holiday. Preferably somewhere warm, undemanding and liberally supplied with decent plonk.

I slept late, discouraged from venturing out from under the bedclothes by the gloom and the return of the rain outside my window. I listened to it hissing and buffeting, trying to find a way in beneath the sashes, while I clung to warmth and the lunatic notion that nothing bad could happen if I stayed in bed, a sentiment I doubt Mary Kelly would have shared.

I crawled out a little after twelve, feeling restored by clearing skies. I remembered that I ought to phone Lucy, having charged her with finding Tom, though, to be honest, I didn't know how much stomach I still had for R and D in that department. The answer phone was winking and I tuned in briefly to listen to various angry and puzzled messages from my friends wondering who the hell 'this American bloke' was. Lucy was there as well.

"Where the fuck are you? Oh, gawd, darling. I've had Eddie

phone me saying you assaulted him. What the hell happened last night? Look, just give me a ring will you…"

I was about to pick up the phone and do just that when a discrete knock on the door had me peeking round the curtain. Oh, God's bollocks! It was Paul Fuller. Actions have consequences…But it was a measure of just how well I'd recovered my composure that instead of cowering behind the door, I wrenched it open to face him. Nothing could barge its way through the trauma of yesterday, not even Paul Fuller.

He turned, hands in his pockets, the serious expression on his face transforming to a tight smile as I glared at him.

"Can we talk in private?" He glanced back down the alley watchfully, "I'd rather not stand on ceremony, love, especially not right now."

I looked at him in his fine silk suit and his silly shades and wondered if he wore elevators in his shoes.

"Sure," I said, "Why not. But I've said all I wanted to in the letter."

He sauntered into my front room and stood looking round and nodding, as if he approved of the comfortable shambles I live in.

"Your letter, yeah. Things have changed since then."

We stood facing each other, I wasn't about to offer him a drink and a sit down.

"So?"

He sighed, "I understand you've had some trouble with a cleaner," he said, "a *former* employee of mine told me she'd hired this…person." Former employee? Poor old Sarah. I wish I'd been present at that interview. "Given your position, your current position that is, I thought I'd better make a few things crystal."

"Right."

"I don't even know who this fucking cleaner is, was, and what she was doing at the set in Priory Road…"

"Cleaning, presumably." I said.

"...I couldn't give a fuck," Fuller gazed out of the window, "look, about Hammond. I personally thought he was an annoying little cunt. But I think it's important we both know I'm not in the habit of offing people for being annoying little cunts. I didn't think much of his motor, though," he added. "Flash fucker." I nodded, understanding.

"You probably picked the wrong night to register your distaste." He responded with a nod of his own and pulled my mobile phone from his jacket, handing it back to me.

"You left this." He said without inflection.

"Thanks." I looked at it, wondering what sort of damage Eddie had done.

"But you took something from my house. I'm not happy about that." He looked grave.

"Look," I said, dragging the conversation to the point, "I didn't mention where I got the keys. I said I'd found them in her jacket. OK? Your name has not been mentioned. I'm not interested in your business. I'm sorry I took the keys but I thought Lois – your cleaner – was the one who's been messing me about. I was wrong."

"Well, thanks to someone playing silly fuckers, it *is* my business now. I've got plod all over my property and they're a suspicious bunch. Has this... Lois got anything to do with Hammond?"

"I don't know." I said honestly, "She might have. I think she saw – "

"Actually, darling I don't want to know." Fuller drew himself up as far as he could go and turned to leave. "That stupid cunt is more trouble dead than he ever was alive. I had some posh tart come screaming at me in a restaurant how she was going to make me pay for messing with her darling. 'Daddy's a QC' – mad bitch."

Amanda! How had I forgotten about her? And why had I assumed it was Lois? God knows. Fuller moved out into the hall and opened the front door,

"So we're clear aren't we? My business, none of your business and I've got no fucking idea about Hammond. I've got enough on my plate as it is, I don't want any rumours starting."

Turning my mobile phone over in my hand, a thought struck me.

"Where's Eddie?" I asked, "He's been going round annoying all my friends."

"He's a twat," Fuller looked amused, "I told him not to be so fucking stupid but you gave him a black eye! He's seriously pissed off with you!" He grinned. I saw his shoulders shake as he stepped into the street and I realised he was silently laughing. "Thanks for the photos." He added, returning to serious, "That's something else I'm gonna have to sort out..."

I shrugged.

"None of my business," I said. He briefly held out a hand in a flourish of white cuffs and shining cufflinks, an offer I couldn't refuse. My fingers felt limp in his, remembering his grip, a feeling of bizarre complicity creeping over me.

"But you wouldn't be shocked, would you? Not in your line of work?" He didn't wait for me to reply but turned and looked seawards where a small scattering of trawlers were plying their nets at intervals in the fitful glitter of the horizon. He seemed reluctant to leave. Was there more he wanted to say? A small boy threw a stick for his dog on the beach below and it ran into the breaking waves, barking. The sound of the boy's laughter drifted back up the cliff towards us.

"Nice view." Fuller commented. He looked at me again, unsmiling this time, before he finally turned away and walked back up the alley with the easy stride of a man who hasn't been seriously baulked in anything since his mother died. I watched him turn the corner before slamming the door. With any luck that would be the last I'd see of Paul Fucking Fuller.

Picking up where I left off, before I'd been so rudely, I called Lucy and had to put up with the usual five minutes of swearing before she'd finally share anything with me.

"Eddie said you thumped him, Jay," she sounded almost as aggrieved as he must have been, "You just don't get clients by hitting them." This was, in my case at least, demonstrably untrue, but I couldn't be bothered to argue with her,

"Did you get Tom's number?" I asked. It was time to lay this particular ghost once and for all.

"Bob couldn't find it." She said and my heart sank, "He went round looking everywhere while I stayed on the phone. I don't know who his agent is but they must be on the verge of a breakdown dealing with him."

"Shit." I said.

"It's OK," Lucy said, "Bob knows where he lives. He's back in Dean's Bay." After all that! And how suddenly very convenient...

"Oh, for God's sake. OK. Well it's Saturday," I said, "I'll just have to take a chance of finding him in. What's the address?"

Conscious that Tom's rather more conventional cohabiter might be in residence, I dressed carefully, covering my tatts, making my hair nice, putting on makeup. Dressing up for make believe, bringing out my Clark Kent persona. Except that 'respectable' is my secret identity, mental is what I do every day.

I made my way up the alley wondering what on Earth I was going to say to Tom once I finally had him cornered. I didn't see the shape that loomed out of the long shadows at the entrance to the street until it was too late. I'd forgotten about the native New Yorker.

Eddie took me by surprise, jumping forward from his hiding

place, he shoved me hard in the chest, pushing me up against the alley wall, back into the shadows.

"I've been waiting for you," he hissed, screwing up the front of my jacket in one big, meaty hand. My stomach lurched for a moment, more from the shock of his approach than any real fear of Eddie himself. I knew this might be unwise but I still had the comfort of the light of day and people nearby. He thrust his face close to mine and I could see a cut where my ring had made contact, the bruise flowering under his left eye, across his cheek. I balled my fist at my side, feeling the reassuring lump of hard metal on my middle finger. "Unlike certain other assholes I could mention, I'm not prone to violence." He looked like a man about to compromise his own high standards. I didn't move. I learned very early on in life that a man on the edge of his temper will accept *any* verbal or physical reaction as provocation enough. "You have pushed me right to the limit, you stupid whore. You've got no fucking idea what's going on here, do you?"

When I didn't respond, he pushed his face even closer and said,

"Do you?"

I shook my head. He was certainly right about that, anyway.

"You think Fuller's hard? He's a joke! Fucking 'gangsters' playing Jimmy Cagney," he shook me briefly, "Fancy cars, jewellery – they aren't even yesterday's men. Your cops are all over him, he spends most of his money on fucking lawyers."

I stared at him. He might just be right about that. For all his frightening reputation, there often seemed more of the 'gangsta' with an 'a' about him than hardcore criminal, another cartoon villain to go with the rest. Mad Frankie Fraser, laurels so flattened by resting on his reputation as the Richardson gang's enforcer, he's become a criminal parody, conducting 'gangland' tours around London. Still, he probably has more problems with piles than pliers these days, being about 100. Dave Courtney OBE (One Big Ego) seems to have more 'acting' credits than bona fides as a crook. His tasteless website is full of video links, songs, merchandising and much self congratulation. John Bindon's connections to the underworld are murkier but he was still a dangerous diamond geezer with a 12" dick who supposedly fucked Princess Margaret, lucky girl. Legends surrounding his prowess with an erection still abound. Vinnie Jones' shotgun-toting film icon is apparently based on Bindon. But then Courtney claims it's based on him. Maybe Fraser and Fuller make similar claims. Apparently it's not enough to be a notorious criminal, now you can aspire to be a celebrity gangster and take a red carpet hard man as your role model.

"What are you trying to say?" I'd thought Eddie and Fuller had a BFF thing going and I wondered at this apparent volte face.

He stepped back, letting go of my jacket and wiping his hands together as if he'd got dirt on them. He pointed at me.

"Just butt out. You got no idea what you're getting involved in, OK?"

"I've got no idea what you're talking about," I said, "And truthfully, Eddie, I couldn't give a shit."

I really couldn't be bothered to loiter either, being aggressively yet enigmatically threatened. I barged passed him and into the street but he grabbed my arm.

"I'm fucking serious," he said, someone else who was serious. I began to wonder if everyone else thought I was joking, "Whatever you're doing, you're in waaay over your head," he pointed suddenly to his bruised face and leaned towards me again, "I might not be a violent person, " he said, "But I know some people with fewer scruples than me. And they are way more dangerous than that pussy in the purple shades." He let go of my arm and turned away. I watched him walk in his ungainly fashion across the street to the Lexus. I noticed today he had teamed baggy, mustard coloured cords, Dr. Pepper T-shirt and a red baseball cap with huge, white tennis shoes. In some ways Eddie Meyer was just a giant geek. Whether he was 'fucking serious' or not, was another thing and I didn't have the time or the head space to deal with him. Frankly, I didn't care what agenda Eddie may or may not have had going on, the less I had to do with him the chirpier I'd be. I had to see Tom. It seemed that I'd finally reached him, almost literally, by a process of elimination. The sooner I could confront this, the better.

Afternoon was bleeding into a chilly evening, the lights on the promenade flickering into dutiful life, the tide seething out through the pebbles, the cosy orange glow of local pubs inviting passersby to bide a while in comfort. It was bonfire night and people were starting to throng through the town. Street vendors had set up selling glow sticks, deely boppers, burgers and hotdogs. Buskers and street entertainers made life irritating in their immediate vicinity, spontaneous jollity was breaking out. I made my way resolutely past them all and across town towards the Pleasant Valley Saturday of Tom's new home.

Tom lived on the outskirts of the town on a pristine modern estate of sprawling red brick fashionableness, the neatly clipped aprons of each fastidious lawn were edged with hardy perennials and each pea shingle drive sported last years' must- buy saloon car. As I walked up the path and past Tom's Audi, the two-fingered salute to my continuing poverty, I hoped fervently that Mary was still with her mother. I had only met his new girlfriend once and her tight-lipped disapproval of me had hung over the occasion like a radiation cloud.

I rang the front door bell, feeling curiously exposed on the step, watched by all the other little boxes on the hillside. The cheerful ding-dong echoed loudly behind the closed door. I waited. I noticed Tom, or perhaps Mary, had planted a pot of Winter

Primulas on the step. The top contained several twisted cigarette butts amidst the mulch. Tom had always been a fairly heavy smoker and I imagined Mary sending him into the garden with a tut-tut. I tried the door bell again. The net curtains in front gave the house a lacy air of prudish respectability, like petticoats on a spinster. Still nothing. I hoped to God he hadn't gone out. Perhaps he and Mary were at the bonfire celebrations? I stepped back and followed a path round the side of the garage to the back of the house.

An enormous stand of Leylandii hedges next door over shadowed a neat little square of green bordered by shrub roses and Rhododendrons. A damp grey shed was covered in Russian ivy. The path broadened into a mossy patio where a few more cigarette butts were scattered next to a small concrete bird bath like a trail of unhealthy breadcrumbs. I looked through the windows but I couldn't see anything. I tried the kitchen door and found it was open.

A premonition seized me. Tom/Tamara was hidden in the drawing room, the hallway, the kitchen, the blade glinting as she turned it. It was a teen slasher flick where the cheerleader inexplicably searches the dark house without turning on any of the lights: "Brad! Stop foolin', Brad!" – her final screams gurgle into silence as she's creamed by the eponymous hero in his umpteenth resurrection with an unlikely piece of kitchen equipment. Hmmmmm. I pushed open the door and peaked gingerly inside.

"Tom?" I called out. The evening gloom was settling on the house like dust and just like Chelsea or Cindy or Casey I found myself strangely reluctant to turn on the lights.

"Tom?" The stillness was absolute. Empty. Nothing. He really must have gone out.

The kitchen was spacious country pine and looked clean to the point of being unused. The only odd note was an open bottle of red wine on a scrubbed deal table next to the window. There was a half full glass standing invitingly next to it. It had been carelessly poured and a little puddle of wine was leaching into the woodwork round the bottle. Following an epicurean urge more primitive than I could control, I picked up the glass and took a sip. Wow! A rich, fruity, full pinot noir that was way beyond the league of any casual drinker. I turned the bottle towards me and found it was a Corton Grand Cru 2003. This was a £100 bottle of wine. Left open. On a kitchen table in an apparently empty house. Alarm bells began to ring in earnest. This wasn't just something you opened and left. It was a bottle that toasted and celebrated, that you savoured with friends and loved ones. A frightening sense of déjà vu was overtaking me.

"Tom!" More urgently. I made my way slowly up the hall and pushed open the living room door. The room was furnished with comfortable looking sofas and clean, boring furniture. I noticed with an acute pang of recognition, the pictures of birds of prey that he collected, a familiar coffee mug, the awful gilt china mantel clock that had been our wedding gift from his parents. It looked strange in its new surroundings. Why the hell had he kept it?

"Tom!" Empty. I looked around again and pushed open the door from the living room through to the dining room.

"Tom ..." Empty. Nothing. Stillness. Tom sat in front of me at a large oval dining table. I say sat. He was slumped forward, his head and his arms on the table. The blood spread around his hands and fingers in a sticky pool that gleamed viciously in the twilight.

"Tom." Anguish poured into me as I whispered his name. Even if all the love between us had been lost in a relationship that had turned into an emotional potboiler both of us had hated, this was no ending at all. There will always be moments that we cherish in any of those contests of wills that pass for a marriage.

Shared inspiration that makes us laugh or cry or cling to one another, even if it's only a momentary lapse of all the helpless things that keep the contestants apart. I stood and was wounded by silence. It seemed hours before I could rouse myself enough to move, though it was probably only a minute or two. I walked up to the table. My heart was in my mouth and the taste of the wine was like vomit.

Tom had been shot once in the head, his dark curls slick with drying blood. I could see no gun. Beside his right hand was a cordless telephone, its surface smeared with gore.

It was too much. I was overwhelmed with grief and anger and fear. The only thing I wanted to do was run. Like the dream I'd had the previous night, I couldn't move fast enough. With a bubble building in my chest, I blundered out of Tom's nice suburban home into the darkness.

XX

JUDGEMENT

It is time to let go of the past and draw to a close prejudices that have defined us. There should be forgiveness, old wounds healed. Perhaps recovery from an illness.

CHAPTER SIXTEEN

I was on a spaceship. I could see the stars shifting and shining, twinkling different colours through the windows and there were planets turning below me. The bridge of the ship was curiously antique, like a Victorian study – a creation of Jules Verne in plum coloured mahogany, leather and brass. I wasn't afraid but I wondered vaguely if I was dead. I didn't seem to own any limbs and while a spaceship would be as good a place as any for weightless eternity, it would be nice to know. As I watched, the scene transformed and I was looking at a long table, smooth and curving, set for a banquet. There were no roof or walls and the stars were now lanterns haloed with twisting fractals. I watched them for a while, fascinated. After a lifetime, the sky caved in and settled and the room seemed to acquire some proper space. With a confusing jerk, the star-lanterns turned, rather prosaically, into bottles. Panic flowered momentarily in my chest as I struggled to find which reality was the right one until I realised with a shock that I was sitting at a bar. A bar? OK. A bar.

I waited for the schism in my head to clear and stared at the optics in front of me. My initial panic was wearing off and there was a cosy familiarity to the tune my head was playing. Drugs. I'd been drugged. Placing my hands firmly on the bar, I overcame a slight wave of vertigo and staggered to my feet. I was in the

Pink Parrot. Alone. It seemed that for one night only, I was to be its sole guest. Now why the hell would that be?

The club was eerie in its unmanned state and although it was dimly lit and empty inside, outside, in the darkness, lights moved and flickered and I could hear distant, rhythmic drumming. It was as if I were in some Stygian anteroom looking through frosted windows onto the flames and dancing figures of hell's shop floor. Still feeling a little high, I shook my head. Then I remembered.

I remembered the pool of blood gleaming obscenely around Tom's head as it rested on the polished surface of his dining table. I remembered running from his house in a blind panic. And in the street, the solid, concerned looking policemen in their yellow jackets, walkie talkies chattering and squeaking.

"Are you alright, Miss?"

I must have looked deranged, psychotic, guilty...

"Yes! Er – yes. Of course. I – er – I, I'm late." My voice sounded far away, my heart thumping, "I'm meeting a friend. I'm a bit late. Is there something the matter?" Jesus! The matter?!

"No. We're closing the road. Is your car here?"

"Closing..?" I couldn't think straight, "I haven't got a car."

"The bonfire parade starts at 7 o' clock..."

The kind policeman had told me the route, pointing out the blue public notices. I'd forgotten about the parade. My sigh of relief must have sounded like an impending asthma attack.

I looked again at the weaving torchlight outside the Pink Parrot. The parade. The first of the season. There would be spectacular fireworks and much drunken merriment and the Pink Parrot was dark and empty. It was right on the route and should be filled to bursting. Where the hell was Tony?

I'd left the policemen man-handling traffic cones and fled to the only person I knew in that part of town – Lucy.

She has a small house in the old town area of Dean's Bay, in the tangle of little streets below the castle. This part of the town had been the nucleus of the original fishing village and there were many half timbered buildings crouched together round the old tackleways and fish huts. In the fullness of time these fishermen's cottages had blossomed on estate agents boards from cramped fixer – up opportunities with outside toilets and dry rot to fashionably charming residences and the old town had the feel of an exclusive village trapped within an otherwise uncivilised estate.

I was always a little surprised that Lucy chose to live amongst such clutter. It was an old house with many overstuffed bookcases and much worn, dark wood. It had small windows and low ceilings and the street level was slightly higher than the ground floor, giving passers by the opportunity to look directly down into her living room. But people passed by quickly and it gave the place a bustling, lively feel that went with the urgent tick tick of the bracket clock near the door. Everything seemed brown and happily gloomy, with the same interesting nooks and crannies as an old fashioned antiques shop, a cosy little nest that smelled of pot pourri and furniture polish.

I stood in her bijou living room endangering the nick-nacks with waving arms and incoherent shouting,

"What the fuck am I going to do, Lucy!? Some fucking lunatic has shot Tom! I just…I just…Oh Jesus fucking Christ!"

Lucy made a stiff, palms-down gesture as if trying to put the lid back on my hysteria.

"Call the police." She said sternly, "I'm deadly serious, Jay. This has gone far enough. Call the fucking police. *Now!*" I noticed that for some reason she was wearing slippers and a bathrobe. I'd probably dragged her out of a bath.

"What the hell do I say? Listen, officer, I've found another body – ha ha! – and…and…you've gotta believe me, I've got nothing to do with this one either. Yes, well, he *was* my ex-husband but honestly, that's just another *weird* coincidence!"

"You're hysterical."

"You think?"

I looked at the windows of the Pink Parrot. Someone had lit a flare. It cast its fierce, mysterious light around the gloomy interior. Distant drums.

"Sit down." Lucy had pushed me back into an armchair and brought over a cordless phone, "and call the police."

I made a desperate, defeated gesture.

"How?"

She'd looked down at me and sighed, an expression of extreme weariness had shuttered her face.

"Have a drink." She'd said. A drink...

"So you've finally come back down to Earth?"

I spun round a little unsteadily and gawped. I wasn't really that surprised, not inside, not any more. But it was still a shock. The voice was right – rich and throaty, Capstan alto, same old Lucy Pellow. But the rest was all wrong. She was so familiar and so strange, my junk addled brain had kept this surprise for me like a treat. The red lady had always been here, this was just a reminder of the commonplace.

Her red dress was actually a vintage bias cut halter-neck that fell below her knees in swinging pleats. It reminded me of Hollywood and the golden age, glamorous premiers and Picture Post. Her stupidly high stilettos were patent scarlet and she wore a long black wig that curled around her bare shoulders. It was a preposterous image, so far removed from her usual colourless attire that she looked like a female Bird of Paradise that had spontaneously changed sex. Or maybe in the back glow of dancing torchlight, she was a model devised by the Vatican to warm the unwary against sin. This was particularly apt as she was also carrying a gun. I didn't know what type it was but it looked black and ugly and she was pointing it straight at me. I noticed with unease that she was also wearing latex gloves. We circled each other in silence for a moment.

"What did you drug me with?" I said finally. There were a lot of questions I wanted answers to but this one bubbled to the surface first.

"Yes. You would ask that, wouldn't you?" she smiled, "Ketamine. Don't tell me you've never tried it. You seem to have run through everything else." Ketamine is a powerful hallucinogen, a disassociative anaesthetic used on the battlefield and as a horse tranquilizer. It has been used as a date rape drug in its liquid form. She was wrong, as it happens, but I wasn't interested in banter.

"You killed Tom." I said flatly. Her smile faded and she looked sad.

"I'm sorry." She said.

"Sorry?!!"

Lucy held her hands up, still gripping the gun.

"None of this was meant to happen," she said earnestly, "None of it."

I stared at her. There was no way anyone could pretend that killing three people was somehow a tragic accident, a bit of a fumble, an unfortunate hiccough in the smooth running of your day. I looked at the weapon in her hand and she followed my gaze. With care, she brought it back down to level at my midriff.

"I really like you, Jay," she said, "I always have. I think you're a waster. But I've always liked you."

"Thanks." I said, trying to keep the sarcasm out of my voice. She walked round the bar. It was astonishing how the change of clothes had affected her whole bearing. She swung her hips and pointed her toes, head held high, her shoulders back. She filled the role of cartoon femme fatale to perfection, a sexy temptress whistling for Bogey. She picked up a glass and filled it from one of the Brandy optics, sliding it across the bar towards me with a clunk.

"Have a drink." She said gesturing with the gun like a psychotic dinner hostess. I didn't feel like it but I picked up the glass anyway.

"When did you start channelling Betty Bacall?"

She twisted a smile and a shy look down at her dress but she didn't answer. I watched the smile fade.

"I didn't mean to kill Ben Hammond," she said, "It was an accident. You know, it was your fault really." I just stared at her, completely incredulous. "If he hadn't started sniffing round you, I'd never have met him. Christ, he was persistent. He came to me pretending to want some pictures. He didn't of course." She looked a little wistful, "He *was* very attractive, I'll give him that, but he just seemed to have a nose for dirt, so then he wanted to know all about *me*."

I looked at her, considering my options but none of them seemed too promising. She had poured herself a ghastly looking mixture in a half pint glass from several of the optics behind the bar and was sipping it, gazing at me levelly, a half smile on her face. I could hear the drumming of the marchers as they wound their way round the town. It occurred to me that for someone who just wanted a shag, Ben's attention to detail had been fanatical. Perhaps he'd been lining me up for some further use in his porn enterprise and I'd had a lucky escape. Or perhaps it was just pathological, I'd never know now. And, in any case, my escape hadn't really been all that lucky. I finally took a sip of the Brandy.

"What happened?" I asked. She put her glass down carefully.

"I'm afraid there are some things that'll have to remain a mystery." She said, "He tried to blackmail me, is all you need to know." I choked slightly on the Brandy.

"How? Why?!" I couldn't imagine any circumstances under which Lucy might be blackmailed. I'd watched her shopping at Mark and Sparks. She ground her own coffee. She kept African violets and was allergic to cats. She was my fucking accountant, for God's sake! What..?

"I'm sorry," she said again, shaking her head, "He tried to involve me in his stupid trannie troll. You know what he was going to call his film company? Dixzar! Like Pixzar! God almighty! I'm not like Lois," she said angrily, "I never wanted to be a fucking movie star." She slammed her glass down on the bar so hard that some of the mixed liqueurs slopped over onto the surface.

"But – "

"Anyway. Two can play at that game. OK. Now I'm telling you. I followed him when he left your house. I was going to follow him home but he left again almost straight away in a taxi and came here." She said, "So I followed him here," she looked around, "and picked him up," she laughed and I remembered Janice's fury, "I lent him the last of my cash for a taxi, then he pissed off with some other bird …"

"You know he didn't even recognise me!" Lucy said holding up the skirt of her dress and letting it drop with a swish, "He'd only had a couple but he was stinking drunk… "

"He didn't normally drink." I said, still staring at her in disbelief.

"Yes, well. I had to let us into his flat 'cos he kept dropping the keys." She walked back round the bar to face me. "He pretty much passed out," she said, "I think he'd forgotten I was there," she looked rueful for a moment. Then she went on, "I shot him up with smack and took photographs. Him and the needles, the powder, the whole works. Him with his dick out. A bit of lipstick. I was going show him. Basically, fuck off or your fiancée and your family and all your straight friends are going to get this. I looked up the doses on the internet. I was very careful." She finished.

"You fucking idiot." I said succinctly. She narrowed her eyes at me. "And Lois? I suppose she saw you at the Parrot? But why bother with an idiot like Lois?" I was hard pressed to think of anyone simultaneously more annoying yet more harmless than Lois.

"I've known Lois a lot longer than you have." Lucy said, "And I've told you, I'm not going to talk about it. Do you know she called me the very next day? I thought she wanted money but she just wanted to talk. Talk and talk and fucking talk," she swirled the horrible cocktail round in her glass, "She took me to that place in Priory Gardens and that tacky dungeon where they were going to film her. She was so pleased with herself – "

"They hired her as a cleaner." I interrupted. Lucy just stared at me. And then she laughed. Too long and a little too hard. I could see now how desperate she looked. And angry.

"Well," she said, gurgling to a halt, "I suppose that's more like it. She was always blah, blah, blah," she made a yapping motion with her hand. "I had to stop her talking." She frowned and downed another gulp of her drink. Perhaps I could end this with a drinking contest. If I could keep her talking long enough.

"And Tom? There can't be any earthly reason why you had to hurt a blameless idiot like him." I tried to keep my voice light but I could feel a rising, dangerous anger that I knew would be hard to control. Lucy gave me a calculating look and put down her glass with a thump.

" Come on," she said, "this is going to end. Now." She gestured me ahead of her with the gun. So much for a booze-off.

We moved past the sofas by the dance floor to the only part of the Pink Parrot that was lit with its usual splendour – the dungeon (you guessed it – red and black). I stopped in front of the cage, another shock mixing uneasily with the drink and drugs already in my system. There, naked behind the bars, was Max, his wrists manacled above his head. His clothes were next to him in a pile with his green DMs and, in spite of the circumstances, I couldn't help being diverted by this visual revelation, a payback for the bubble bath incident. I noted with artistic satisfaction that

Max's tattoos extended down his thighs and calves and that he had an enormous…well, piercing, actually. He looked unamused in the extreme.

"Max!" I said, pushing my way into the cage," Are you alright?" he favoured me with a look of crushing irony.

"Super. Thank you."

I turned on Lucy as she came in behind me,

"What the fuck are you doing? Have you lost your mind? Tom? Now Max? And, yes, actually, why the fuck involve me anyway?"

"I forgot I had Ben's keys," she said, leaning back on the bars of the cage, pointing her gun towards us both.

"You forgot?"

"When I realised I went back but there were men outside his house. One of them was pouring paint on his car so I left. That's when I saw you…" I could feel memory cells shuffling, poised to present me with the storyboard of my lost Friday night. "You were about 100 yards down the road, falling about on the pavement. You were laughing and waving and I don't know whether you saw me, so I parked and followed you in."

"You were wearing that dress." I said

"So you *do* remember." She said, "I thought you would eventually."

I remembered effusive and embarrassing meetings and greetings, attempts at falling over thwarted by other people, music, laughter, gibberish. I remembered the amused slip fielding of my companions as I tottered round the kitchen, the sticky letters on the fridge that unexpectedly slurred the word 'clitoris' across my field of vision in a candy bright shock, Foxy Lady playing somewhere out back, hands helping me firmly into a chair. And after the explosion that had carried me, in the arms of other guests, from the kitchen to the living room, just one curtain call from never land gifted me a hazy recollection that left black humour threading through my sub conscious like a hangman's rope. Lucy's cold smile, her face dancing in front of me, a mask of a thousand unfamiliar pieces.

"You don't know who I am, do you?" she had said. I didn't reply. I couldn't. The operational parameters weren't set for recognition and speech. I guess I'd just grinned oafishly before passing out again. But I could now recall the look on her face as clearly as a favourite holiday snap. And I wondered seriously how much bullshit she was handing me about her motives for all of this.

"No. I don't remember." I said.

"I was going to put the keys in your bag. And you could get them back to Ben. Why the fuck don't you carry a bag?"

"I'd lose it," I said simply, "And the photographs?"

"They were right there in his bedroom. Along with some other stuff – of mine. It looked like your thing. I thought you'd know what to do with them and the keys." I'd been watching her carefully as she explained herself and now I just couldn't help it.

"What utter bullshit!" I said. She straightened herself up dangerously and dangerously I carried on, "You were just happy to drop me in it because I slept with him. That's what this is really about, isn't it? Wasn't he interested?" Bingo! I'd struck a nerve. It probably wasn't wise to take on Lucy as her gun toting alter ego but the notion that she had dragged me into the plot through some kind of misguided altruism defied intelligence. I saw the swish of her red dress as she pushed herself away from the bars and steadied herself, both hands gripping the gun, L.A Confidential style.

"None of this would be happening if you'd just taken them to the police like I kept telling you," she said. I moved defensively in front of Max. Light was beginning to dawn feebly over the distant horizon as several pertinent things occurred to me.

"Why are you wearing those gloves?"

"Your finger prints are on the gun," she said with a shrug, "I gave it to you to hold while you were off in la-la land just now. I should think your prints are all over Tom's house, as well as the wine I left for you. Did you like it?" I closed my eyes briefly and she laughed, "Christ, Jay, you're just too predictable for your own good. And you're right about one thing: the police are never going to believe you didn't kill Tom. And when they find you and Max here," she glanced up at Max, who was looking like a man who's been married three times too many, "There's going to be a trail of men you've slept with and I'm sorry, but I can't let you talk your way out of it either."

I marvelled briefly at the absence of what might be termed an appropriate response. It seemed that my life had been a series of strategies designed for coping with unexpected turns for the worse and I'd just become weary of it now. There would be no-one to seriously miss me, to weep and wail at my graveside, just a parade of ne'er-do-wells who would remember me from various parties or clients who found alternatives less accommodating. A gaggle of trusty pervs and pirates who would drink to oblivion at my wake. But then that's all anybody can expect, unless you're Ghandi or JFK. Let not a monument give you or me hopes – that's Byron and a lot of good it did him. Now was not the time for Romantic Poets.

"OK." Lucy raised the gun. Someone outside shouted loudly. The drums were getting much closer. A sudden fusillade of fire crackers made me jump. I looked up at Max and his eyes were riveted on Lucy. He was gripping the chains above his head tightly and I saw his shoulders flex. The drums got louder still as the head of the parade finally reached the Pink Parrot. I knew that Lucy was waiting for as much noise as possible to cover the sound of the shots. Another round of firecrackers would do it. I looked quickly around me. Having demonstrated my lacklustre flair for common sense in situations that plainly cry out for it, it has to be said that in surroundings packed with instruments of torture and dungeon equipment I am perfectly at home. I know the effect each implement has on the human body, the marks it leaves on the skin and the effect each has on the mind. The difference between a crop and a cane, a tawse and a paddle, a quirt and a flogger. In this environment at least, I am the difference between a Diva and a Dompteuse and it was bloody silly of her to expect me to react otherwise.

Without stopping to think about it, I grabbed the nearest thing to hand – a short thick riding crop – and several things happened at once. As if on cue, Max took his weight on his shoulders and levelled a kick at Lucy, catching her a glancing blow across one shoulder, just as I lunged, bringing the riding crop down hard on her wrist. She wasn't expecting a two-pronged attack and I heard her cry as the gun flew out of the cage with a clatter. Then almost at the same time, a gun shot from somewhere else, a squealing ricochet and dust bouncing out of the brickwork.

I dived for cover in the confusion behind a flogging bench. Was that her gun? Or a firecracker? I had no idea. I saw Lucy dive out of the cage and grab her weapon as another shot rang out. Max was struggling behind me and after a brief tussle, he managed, very impressively, to pull the fixings of his shackles bodily from the wall in a shower of plaster and flatten himself on the floor. Inside an edgy silence ensued, filled with peoples breathing and the echo of gunfire. Outside drums beat and torches flamed. Cautiously, I leaned around the bench. Lucy was pressed against the wall of the dungeon, concealed by pot plants. And standing by the bar, clipping rounds into the magazine of a pistol, was Stuart.

I didn't bother wondering how the hell he'd got in. He was wearing combat fatigues and was armed to the teeth. Lucy briefly leaned round the corner and fired a shot wildly towards the bar.

I couldn't see Stuart move but he must have picked up some kind of semi-automatic because the air was suddenly alive with rapid bursts of deafening gunfire. I retreated behind the bench and covered my ears as the area around me was turned into a cauldron of splintering wood, breaking glass and shattering plaster. Max had joined me behind the flogging bench and was trying to struggle into his jeans. The noise finally died down in a pitter patter of falling debris and I could hear him swearing,

"Fuck! Fuck! Fuck! Fuck!"

The lull didn't last that long. Lucy fired three rapid shots in succession and disappeared in a scarlet flourish round the corner into the main area of the club. Max was still swearing helpfully as I saw Stuart gather up his arsenal and begin to fire two assault rifles from the hip, across the dance floor towards her retreat.

"No, no, no." I said under the noise. I am stuck in a fetish club, with a half- naked ex-con, a woman who wants to frame me for murder and my stalker, who has evidently prepared himself to defend Waco. I was not going to sit in a cage and hope someone would feed me a banana. I made a desperate grab for the only weapon I could see in the dungeon that might keep me out of harm's way – the dark, gleaming coils of a bullwhip. In the dim and distant past, when I had fancied myself the Indiana Jones of the club scene, I'd frightened many sweet young things with the crack of leather and a teasing sting. But the bullwhip can be a dangerous toy and needs practice and wide open spaces and like the lazy bastard I am, I soon downsized to something less labour intensive. I seriously doubted I could take the end off a cigarette but no-one seemed about to light up and with any luck I might at least be able to maim from a safe distance.

I scrambled out from behind the bench and through the door to the cage carrying the bullwhip. I gained Lucy's former position by the wall and the now- tattered plastic fronds of Tony's cheap window dressing, just in time to have my senses assaulted again.

Stuart was casually strolling in our direction, shooting randomly across the dancefloor, at the bar and even into the ceiling. He appeared to be whistling through his teeth. Max was beside me.

"We've got to get out!" I shouted through the gaps in the gunfire.

"No shit! Where's that fucking maniac gone?" He meant Lucy.

"I don't know. I think there's a fire exit." I pointed to a door at the far end of the dancefloor with the usual signs above it. Rambo there was a direct obstruction. Lucy was somewhere hidden amid the sofas. On the principal that she had fewer guns that he did, I ducked round the corner just as Stuart released another pointless volley into the ceiling. A large chunk of plaster fell with a dusty splat and broke its back on a chair, releasing a cloud of powder into the club, momentarily obscuring everything.

"Come out of there you bitch!"

With Max behind me, I worked my way cautiously through the furniture, on hands and knees, keeping a look out for the red dress.

"I want my camera back!"

I could see the comforting green glow of the emergency exit sign appear through the haze. If ever there were an emergency…

"You were a fucking lousy shag!"

Given Stuart's response to said shag – to my recollection the kind of victorious hooting demonstrated by howler monkeys – this was a blatant lie. Just so you know, I'm not in the habit of reacting when rabid ex-boyfriends impugn my abilities as a Goddess but it occurred to me that all the while Stuart stopped shooting to shout insults, Lucy would have a perfect target as he grand standed in the centre of the dancefloor.

"I can't help it if you've got a small dick!" I yelled and was rewarded by thunderous gunfire ripping into the walls behind us.

"...fuck...say...for?" I caught Max shouting but I was crawling frantically towards the door. I'd got to within a suicidal sprint of it when I caught a glimpse of red stiletto peaking beneath the curtain that covered the stairway to the first floor. She was directly between us and the exit. Fuck. I was just about to relay this to Max above the furious staccato din of Stuart's insulted manhood when a sudden louder explosion rocked everything into peremptory silence. I looked into the haze of the club and saw Stuart sitting on the floor not 10 feet away, a surprised expression on his face and a dark red patch spreading through the shreds of khaki at his shoulder. I could smell cordite and looked up. Astonishingly, Tony was hobbling along behind the bar, breathless with effort, his face streaked with blood. He was carrying a 12-gauge shotgun and he had eyes only for Stuart. As Max and I crouched together, we saw the curtains move and part. Max said,

"Oh, no..."

""NO!!" I stood up and yelled but it was too late. A single shot from Lucy spun Tony in a tortuous pirouette and he collapsed behind the bar with a crash, taking a display of liqueurs and novelty beer glasses with him. He must also have hit the switch to the club's sound system on his way down as Donna Summer's 'Love To Love You' suddenly blared into life at a toe-curling volume. It was a scene from hell. Wrecked furniture, ragged bullet holes, bodies, plaster and dust lit up in the disco inferno of a glitter ball and torchlight. The noise of the drums outside was a grotesque counterpoint to the empty invitation to dance.

Lucy was still shockingly poised as she stepped purposefully towards Stuart.

"Just drop it and stay the fuck where you are!"

He entered with a bang of the fire exit doors and strode rapidly across the room, a surprising turn of foot for a man his size. Max and I froze. Lucy froze. Stuart was struggling to his feet. He was tall and black and heavy set with a bouncer's neck and shoulders stretching his leather jacket. He had tribal scrolls shaved into his tight cropped hair and he had twin gold eyebrow piercings; expressionless, he was a cliché of a man – 'this is Tyson, he's security'. I felt as if we'd been interrupted in some childish game by a grown up. He was carrying an automatic pistol that was bigger and shinier than everyone else's and in some uncanny way this *was* turning into a contest. The big man disarmed Lucy without a fight and kicked the other firearms from Stuart's reach.

The other two men who followed him in were so depressingly familiar I should have predicted it. Paul Fuller, unnervingly relaxed as usual and Eddie Meyer, wary and ill at ease. We all stood about like a bizarre face off in a spaghetti Western. Three gangsters, a Hollywood movie star, two tattooed perverts and a psychopath. There was no doubt who was in charge, though. Fuller turned to me.

"Turn that fucking racket off!"

I hesitated and glanced at Max, who was looking encouragingly protective, then hurried to the bar. Tony was lifeless in a pile of shattered glass. I could smell alcohol; an eclectic cocktail of spirits soaked into the carpet and dripped from broken shelves. I leaned across and managed to hit the 'off' button on the consol, trying not to look at him. Even with the jollity outside, the sudden silence in the Pink Parrot now seemed deafening.

"Right, back you go, darlin'." Fuller crooked a finger and I rejoined Max by the sofas, hoping no-one would notice if we inched towards the door. Fuller addressed himself to the assembled company.

"I'm not going to ask what's going on here 'cos I don't fucking care... "

"Mr Fuller..." Stuart began. Having got to his feet, he was

holding a hand to his shoulder and I could see blood oozing through his fingers, snaking down his wrist into his cuffs.

"Don't interrupt me!" Fuller jabbed rings at him, "I've been watching you, you two timing little cunt!" Even through his pain, or perhaps because of it, Stuart looked venomously at me. Fuller went on.

"So when Gerard here sees you unloading armour from your Fiat Punto out back, he gives me a call. How much did Hammond pay you?"

"Please, Mr Fuller – Paul…"

Only mildly distracted by the news that security was actually called Gerard, I was gently moving myself and Max towards the door, making as much space as I could between Stuart and whatever was coming next. Eddie looked at me and I stopped.

"How much?"

"It wasn't like that!"

"So you did it for nothing? Out of the goodness of your heart? Because that fucking trannie magnet was such a lovely human being?"

"No!"

"Then how much?"

Stuart looked as if his knees would buckle. He leaned forward like a runner finishing a long, hard race and took a deep breath. I didn't hold out much hope, frankly.

"Five thousand." He said finally. Fuller nodded.

"Right. Good." He kept nodding. My stomach lurched as he reached inside his charcoal grey, Jermyn Street jacket and withdrew…

"Please, Mr Fuller. Look…"

The explosion as Gerard pulled the trigger of his big, shiny gun took us all by surprise. We watched Stuart fall, his head jerking back, his feet lifting a little from the ground, his body twisting as if it would escape the shot. Then he was still. Max was gripping my hand hard as Fuller applied a lighter to the cigarette he'd taken from his pocket.

"There are some things that are fucking unforgivable." He said. I was horrified. I felt icy cold. This was my fault. Never mind that Fuller might well have guessed who took those pictures anyway– there would only have been a finite number of suspects at that particular party. Never mind that Stuart had actually tried to kill me. And never mind that it was Lucy's madness that had hauled me into this mess in the first place. If I'd just burned those fucking photographs… I was suddenly aware of Eddie Meyer twitching and shifting to my left,

"Paul," he said, "There was no need for that. There was *really* no need for that." Fuller turned on him.

"Well, sweetheart, you're right in it now aren't you?" He inhaled deeply, then let the smoke drift idly from his nose and mouth. "Right." He said and turned on his heel. We all watched in silence as they left, Fuller first, then Eddie following along uncomfortably with many backward glances. Gerard conscientiously closed the fire escape behind them. It struck me that Paul Fuller had reached the same kind of relaxed critical mass as Ronnie Kray when he'd swept into the Blind Beggar for a spot of butchery. It hadn't worked for him and I hoped it wouldn't work for Fuller either.

Lucy blinked once then turned to face us. Plan A for her was dead in the water. I could hear a growing roar outside. The parade had almost passed and a rear guard of iron troughs used to collect spent torches and carry new ones were drawing level with the Parrot. Their metal wheels made a thunderous noise on the tarmac, a fitting tribute to the day's carnage. I could feel a bubble in my chest reaching up and closing my throat.

"What's in a name, what's in a name?" Lucy repeated, shaking her head, "Do you know what her name is?" she said to Max. "J.J? You know her mum was some kind of sad old hippy," She gave the sign with two fingers, "Peace and love, man. Hasn't she told you yet? Oh well. J.J – It's bloody funny." The bubble burst and white hot rage flowed through me. None of this *was* actually my fault. The only thing I am responsible for is the here and the now of my actions. I cannot second guess criminals and lunatics. I dropped the business end of the bullwhip to the floor in a soft, shiny coil. Max said:

"You really are confusing me with someone who gives a shit about anything you have to say."

Stuart gave a grotesque twitch on the ground between us, blood spraying from his mouth as his chest suddenly heaved.

Lucy dipped quickly down, aiming for one of the weapons at Stuart's feet. As she rose, I pulled the whip back and stepped into it, throwing the plaited leather ahead of me, aiming with all my feelings at her face.

Revenge may very well be a dish best served cold but I myself think it ought to be hot and peppery, like a good chilli – marinated, left to fester a while, then delivered scalding to the lucky recipient. Ben and Lois might have been loves lost to someone else and a problem I frankly didn't give a shit about for Lucy, but silly, stupid, selfish Tom was an act of individual spite directed against me. His hopes and dreams for a decent future, bird-watching and reading the Sunday papers had been ended simply because I'd known him and this was payback time. I directed every drop of anger I had in me towards the hot tip of the bullwhip.

I missed, of course. After all I'm *not* Indiana Jones, and when did you ever gain the impression I was good at focussing? But it was a good enough shot all the same. The end of the whip snapped loudly, at speed, close enough to her face to make her stagger backwards in shock. Then to my surprise, she reeled and fell, hitting the floor hard, the gun flying from her hand for the second time. Unbelievably, there was Tony, the undead, his shoulder a pulped and bloody mess hanging on grimly to her ankle with his one good arm. He'd lunged at her from the floor around the corner of the bar but he couldn't hold on for long. I ran forward.

"Get someone!" I yelled at Max, "Get the police!" I glanced at Stuart, a gory froth bubbling from his mouth, "Get an ambulance!"

Max vaulted the bar and began crashing about looking for a phone and I jumped on Lucy, sparing not an ounce of my occasional over-indulgence in chocolate. If I could just hold her down long enough…but she fought like an unmedicated psychotic. I was overwhelmed by this familiar's predilection for heavy, musky perfume, her scarlet talons, the towering shoes. She punched and kicked and scratched. We rolled over, then back as she tried to reach for the gun. I slammed my fist down hard into the back of her shoulder, hurting my hand. Tony, from a short distance, his grip lost, tried to help by kicking her.

"Can't find phone…" Max jumped back over the bar.

"Some help here..!" I gasped as the maniac beneath me kneed me in the stomach and managed to wriggle partly free, gouging lumps out of my calves with those bloody stilettos. As she made another desperate lunge, I grabbed her hair and pulled. There was a strange ripping sound and the entire hairpiece came off in my hands, tangling in my fingers like bindweed. Lucy shuddered and let loose a terrible shriek. And then I saw why. Instead of her own hair beneath the lush black wig, Lucy Pellow was almost completely bald. There were just a few greying curls at the temples. The rest of her head was hairless and bizarrely sported strips of Velcro. I was completely dumbfounded. We looked into each other's eyes and for one terrible moment, I could see her utter despair. At times of heightened emotional connection a working Witch can become preternatural. Anyone can, actually, if you know how to channel it. Lucy, like Lucifer – the bringer of light. The star in my tarot deck, shiny, shiny. And then I *knew*. You've probably known for some time.

"Stella." I said. Lucy's lips parted and a single, plump tear spilled on to her cheek.

The dead bolts thudded back as Max wrestled the front door to the club open. The street outside was crowded and several people staggered back into the club with a surprised cheer. The moment between Lucy and me was broken and she scooped up the gun, barrel first. I heard someone scream as she flailed at me, one last effort, pistol-whipping the side of my head.

It was an explosively painful, deadening blow and I rolled over with a yell, holding on to my temple, feeling warmth beneath my fingers. Someone was screaming a lot now. I could hear Max shouting,

"Just give me your fucking phone! Call the police! Call a fucking ambulance!"

Lucy scrambled to her feet as I opened my eyes through a Wagnerian overture starting in my head. Chaos was clamouring. The death throws of the Pink Parrot saw people staggering round, craning for a look, not wanting to look, looking all the same. Lucy was running for the fire exit now, amid shouts and stares and yet more people piling in. I forced myself to my feet and set off after her.

"Jay! Please! For Chrissake, Jay!" I heard Max behind me but I carried on through the exit, towards the carpark behind the club.

The cold night air was a welcome shock, helping me to focus through the pain and through the darkness around the street lamps. The car park was full of cars cheerfully abandoned in defiance of the 'Patrons Only' signs as the streets were closed off for the parade. I heard the unmistakable click-click of high heels running and saw Lucy bolt into the street from the shadows at the entrance. I followed her.

The pavements outside were packed with people. The wardens were keeping the roads largely free for the parade which was winding its fiery way on to the seafront for the last leg of its journey. I was jostled by people wearing devil's horns and 'Scream' masks, witches hats, toppers, tails, skulls and crossbones everywhere. People were leaning from windows above the street and I could hear dance music competing with the dwindling sound of the drums. I stepped out of the throng and scanned the crowd ahead of me. The commotion at the Pink Parrot had spilled into the street. One young woman in her best party dress and cute pink rabbit ears was being led away with her hand covering her face. Those afflicted were horrified expressions in a sea of good cheer. I could hear the sound of distant sirens. They were going to have a job getting through this lot.

Just when I'd started thinking I was never going to spot Lucy in the hordes, I noticed people being pushed into the road a little further down the street and there were some angry shouts. Sure enough a scarlet figure with a strangely decorated pate was weaving her unsteady way towards the seafront a few hundred yards ahead of me. Ignoring the shouts from the marshals, I started off after her on the street side, just as she got free of the crowd at the promenade and ran down the steps onto the beach.

You don't run across a pebbled beach, you run through it, with much the same speed and grace as you'd run through phlegm. It would be a sure endurance test for anyone, perhaps they ought to make it an Olympic sport? The crowd waiting for the fireworks to begin thankfully weren't paying too much attention to a pair of less than youthful women careering along the beach, breasting the rises and loping wildly down the slopes, over reaching with every step. Or if they did, they just assumed the flailing arms and prat-falls were all part of the party spirit. I went as fast as I could, crunching and sliding, constantly thrown off balance by a sea of rolling stones. The wind had picked up and the surf was rising. My hair was being whipped up like the waves and I could feel the breath of the ocean on my right. I must have looked an unlikely Fury. My only consolation was that Lucy was having it much worse in those heels and taking them off would have meant she couldn't run at all.

I realised with a kind of agony that we were drawing close to the bonfire. I had almost caught up with her but she was clambering up onto the tackleway and would soon have the advantage of solid ground. The effigy of Simon Cowell smirking over the onlookers was lit up by spotlights on the foreshore and by the flames of the bonfire, giving him a demonic presence over his torch wielding acolytes, a figure risen from hell in a turtle neck sweater. Marchers from the parade were making their way down the tackleway and throwing their torches onto the fire to the cheers of the crowd. Lucy seemed drawn to the spectacle like a bald, red moth to a very big flame.

I could hear the waves crashing and seething as the sea made its way towards the high tide mark. Fire, water air and earth. Not good. All conjunctions of the elements are magickal but I could feel this one like a dark foreboding in the core of my being. The wind tore at my lungs as I finally reached solid ground near the blazing tower of the bonfire and I fought to catch my breath. The heat was ferocious. I saw Lucy ahead of me in a strange pirouetting silhouette. She seemed disorientated, as if she'd just come to her senses.

"Lucy!" I shouted. But my voice carried no distance. I was hoarse and the roar and crackle of the fire gleefully ate up the air between us. It ate up everything. I was vaguely aware of people beyond the barrier shouting as I clambered on to the platform close to where the flames were licked into dangerous prominences by the wind. Then it happened. The torches being thrown on to the bonfire were finding their target towards the far side but one stray brand, like a blazing hammer throw, transcribed a lazy arc towards her.

"LUCY!" I screamed. Time stood still as we all watched the comet fall to Earth in silence.

The torch hit her about waist high and her dress went up as if it had been doused in rocket fuel. She was ten yards away from me and perfectly still, an unreal thing, barricaded by fire, eerily reminiscent of the terrible, silent self immolation of Thich Quang Duc. Then I heard a thin, keening scream and she turned blindly into the flames behind her.

Pandemonium. In its truest sense, the centre of hell. I made for her first but the heat was too much and I couldn't get close enough. I was soon dragged away by marshals. And then there were firemen. I sat down on the hard slipway, hard earth, cold air, dancing fire, soothing water. I was faintly aware of someone crying behind me:

"Oh, God, she's burning, she's burning…"

Others were shouting. There was confusion and sirens. All too late, it seemed I heard the whoosh of a fire extinguisher. Looking down at my hands from what seemed like an enormous distance, I realised numbly that I was still carrying Lucy's black wig like a fetish.

"Are you hurt?" Paramedic.

"What?"

"Are you *hurt*? You're bleeding."

"Um…"

The face in front of me wobbled. Gratefully, I passed out.

THE LOVERS

This card signifies love in its most instinctive form.
A harmony on an intuitive level with a person, an idea, an object.
Head or heart choices will need to be made.

CHAPTER SEVENTEEN

Samhain had passed. Dark days were coming, light thickening. People who liked the dark were starting to look forward to Christmas and feel cosy about long evenings and warm fires. Shops were gearing up in earnest for the festive rush – Santas and elves, tinsel and trees were appearing in window displays like foot soldiers for the Brothers Grimm. Fake snow gilded everything. But I had lost much of my appetite for cosiness lately.

The aftermath of bonfire night was cataclysmic for Dean's Bay. Downtown LA we're not and, to be honest, I think even downtown LA would have raised a quizzical eyebrow when confronted with similar carnage. The local media, who'd been making do with the topical news equivalent of a tin of Spam were gifted a feeding frenzy the size of the Indianapolis crew. Not just the local media either. A tide of white vans bearing satellite links surged towards the coast from all points, despatching reporters for the main news channels to interview anyone who might have seen anything and a good few who hadn't.

Apart from several painful visits to the police, I barricaded myself into the cottage armed with enough booze to see me through a nuclear Winter. If I'd thought being stalked by Stuart had been bad, the constant coverage of my closed front door that 24 hour rolling news demanded was intolerable.

As for Stuart, the astonishing salve for my conscience was that he was alive. Alive and *conscious* after several touch and go weeks. When Gerard pulled the trigger, he was in the process of bowing down and it seems his inherent sycophancy had saved him from a death worse than fate. By lucky, lucky chance the bullet had lodged in his scalp. It was somehow unsurprising that Stuart could be shot in the head, at point blank range and still damage no vital organs.

Tony was recuperating from a broken collar bone and was enjoying his celebrity as an unlikely action man, giving lots of interviews about the evils of gun crime. The fate of the Pink Parrot was less certain. Supposedly closed for a re-fit, management were torn between closing it down in righteous indignation, or re-opening as quickly as possible to cash in on the notoriety. Reports are undecided but knowing Dean's Bay as I do, I suspect sleaze will win out in the end.

But even this was the least of it. Edwin Jacob Meyer, executive director of cultural investment for DWK International (New York, London, Stockholm) had been arrested in New York. *8 months ago*. Guess why? Yeah, that's right, his executive portfolio had been stuffed to bursting with his favourite party powder. As part of an arrangement between New York and London that had already plea-bargained him back to JFK in coach, Eddie had set up a sting operation to finally reel in Paul Fuller and cut off one end of a drugs distribution network that spanned two continents. Was this what lay behind his mysterious street corner threats? Presumably...maybe... In any case, this had all gone spectacularly tits up when Fuller and Gerard had dragged him into the Parrot and shot Stuart in front of him, but at least they could now charge Fuller with attempted murder. Oddly enough, the gun that Lucy had used to shoot Tony and Tom, the one with my finger prints all over it, never turned up. Fuller had taken it with him and I guess you could say he had returned a favour.

Embarrassing shockers revealing Ben's frilly escapades filtered through to the gluttonous masses. I suspect they had been leaked from the wreckage of his love life, keen for a small amount of payback, but I felt sorry for Amanda as her distraught features gazed out from these journalistic bombshells. The shrapnel fell far and wide and daddy's silk only added to the relish for those enjoying some class-based schadenfraude. If she's sensible, she'll marry some chinless stockbroker and retire to the country to terrorise the Pony Club with her thoroughbred offspring.

As for Lucy. Well. She died from the injuries she sustained in the fire and I know that her secret won't be safe with me for much longer. I've braced myself on a daily basis. It's too big and too juicy not to leak out now that scandal has its fingers picking over the remains.

It was some weeks after bonfire night that Max knocked on my door. I hadn't seen him since that night. Actually, I hadn't seen anyone. I hadn't been in the mood for company and I'd turned my phone off. My answer machine had filled up and the winking red light had so annoyed me that I'd pulled the plug on that too. He stood on the doorstep alone, for once breaking the decades old tradition and arriving without an offering of alcohol. He'd swapped his jaunty leather Summer hat for a fur trapper's with ear flaps that was somewhat at odds with the raw silk jacket that he wore in the teeth of the chill.

I hadn't really thought about Max. The police had been fairly desperate to find a place on the charge sheet for him but in the end they'd reluctantly admitted he'd been a victim rather than a perpetrator and released him. I hadn't thought about him because he belonged to that part of my psyche that concerned itself with pleasure and I'd spent the last few weeks thinking about other things. I reluctantly allowed him in.

"Have you heard the latest?" he said carefully, picking his way through the weeks of rubbish that had built up around my solitary confinement.

"No." I poured out two glasses and brought them through to the living room, picking up some takeaway cartons and vaguely throwing them at the bin. He'd removed his coat and his furry hat and was warming his hands in front of my fire.

"They've got Paul Fuller lined up for Ben Hammond's murder."

"Really?" I was finding it hard to summon up enough interest.

"And Lois, and Tom."

I sighed.

"I told them what Lucy had done."

"I know, but since Stuart's started talking, they seem to be really keen to get Fuller on as much as they can. They've got Gerard and his crew at Ben's place that night. Lois died at Fuller's house and I gather Lois knew Tom so…"

"Yeah."

"So they're trying to tie the whole lot together."

"That's just stupid."

"I think they're inclined to the belief," Max relaxed back on my sofa, "That Lucy was barking mad." He looked at me with his beautiful eyes and I felt my pleasure centres blinking awake and muttering sleepily. "She *was* bonkers, you know?"

"Oh, yes, definitely that. But not on purpose."

I looked at the table next to the fire. I'd left my three card spread on it – the ten of swords, the moon and the star. I'd lit three candles and placed one next to each card. It was a way of remembering but it's also a way of cleansing.

"I keep wondering, why did she pick on me?" Max asked, taking a sip of wine, following my gaze.

"She thought we'd slept together." I felt a smile twist my mouth.

"Where'd she get that idea?"

I shrugged, keen to move out of a jungle I didn't have the tools to hack through right now.

"Maybe she thought I sleep with all the men I meet."

"Do you?"

"Surprisingly few." I said flatly. There was a short silence and the fire spat. I let it lengthen.

"Jay," Max said finally, putting down his wine and leaning towards me, "I have to tell you…" I looked up to see him smiling and soft, "…you look terrible," he finished. "You can't do this. Shut yourself away and blame yourself. I know it's a horrible situation but it's not your fault. You can't legislate for a nutcase."

"Thanks for that flattering vote of confidence," I said, "Being told she looks awful is the fillip every girl needs."

"No – but – you know what I mean. You have to get back out there – "

"Has there been a post-mortem yet?"

"What?"

"A post-mortem on Lucy. There must have been. The inquest's next week." I stared glumly at the summons on my desk, another reason to stay grumpy.

Max covered his eyes briefly with his hands,

"There's no mystery about that, surely?" he pulled a face, "I think most of the town saw what happened…"

I took a large gulp of wine. I could feel the ghost of the Corton washing round my tongue.

"The thing is Max, I know something you don't."

He looked enquiring. I leaned over and picked up the Star tarot card from the coffee table and turned it over in my hand. I'd done a little research on the internet during my down time. I guessed Ben Hammond had too. Once you knew what the dirt was, it wasn't hard to figure out where to look.

"I've known Lucy for about six or seven years now," I flipped the card between my fingers, "Well, *knew*, I suppose. Thing is, I'm not sure now if I really knew her at all." ("You don't know who I am, do you?")

"I can understand that," Max said reasonably, "After everything that's happened. Who could really know what went on in her head? You thought she was your friend, it must be difficult... "

"I found out Lucy Pellow wasn't always her name," I said, "It used to be Stella. Stella Haskey."

"Oh." Max looked nonplussed.

"And before that is was David Haskey." Her 'ex-husband' Dave. How much can you hate yourself?

"*Oh.*"

"And if you're any fan of rubbish TV you'll remember a show called 'David to Davina'."

"Oh, fuck."

"The subject of which," I went on, still turning the card, "Was an occasional film extra, jobbing actor and generally unwary transsexual called David Haskey. I think they followed him over the course of a year or so. I can't really remember. It was pretty bloody awful."

The tone of the programme had not been sensitive and had come in for some criticism in the liberal media. Their subject hadn't really helped them. Earnest and confused, David had unwisely bared his soul. His hopes for the future, his bitterness at the past, his lacklustre talents as an actor, his rather camp obsession with the actresses of the great movie age. Even the show's title had been forced on him for the sake of a sound bite. David's femme name was 'Stella', not 'Davina', a tribute to the stars he admired and a positive reinforcement for his brave new world. But everything seemed to invite a comical spin. What had Stuart said? "Twenty stone of camp saddo squealing 'I want to look like Sophia Loren!' *I've* got more fucking chance." Yes, well. She'd certainly lost weight (not to mention her hair) and even my careful obsessing over photographs of David Haskey threw up few visual clues. She had transformed herself completely. Not into a movie star, not Stella, the sexy temptress with the flowing locks and S/M scarlet dress but Lucy, dressed by M and S, A

Study In Beige, an accountant. There can't be too many post-op transsexuals with a *female* alter ego.

The programme's conclusion was as trite as you might expect. The post-operative 'Davina' had 'been on a journey' and was looking forward to her new life, a fresh start in Sunnyville now that all her problems had been solved. The ultimate stupid makeover show, as if the gift of a celebrity designed kitchen/garden/wardrobe holds the key to future happiness; as if a sex change can make the problems of paying the mortgage, getting a job, finding love and peace of mind disappear. Participants wave at camera, fade, jaunty theme tune. The publicity the show generated was devastating for Stella and unhelpful for the transgendered community in general. She suffered a breakdown that was digested by the media with mournful relish, then she dropped out of sight. Sucked into the machine, chewed up, spat out again. And Ben Hammond had found out. How? He was certainly a first class tranniespotter. It hardly matters now. But he was probably the last person on the planet who should have been gifted the knowledge. And with the kind of indifference for other people's welfare that had become his trademark he'd tried to involve her in his stupid porn project. Dixzar? Godalmighty!

Did she really make a play for him? He was a charismatic and attractive beast, as I knew to my own cost. Maybe he'd used his charm to get her defences down. Did he ask questions about me or did he just concentrate on her? I'd gone through it a thousand times. Imagined her trepidation as he asks her out – was this her first tentative move into the dating arena? If so, she'd surely picked the wrong man in Ben. Had there been years of frustration? Loneliness? She's excited, he buys her drinks and flatters her but instead of the sexy assignation she hoped for he drops the bombshell: I know all about you. Does he call her Stella? Maybe even that name, the phantom ex husband, that term reserved for all abuse – David? Then he tries to blackmail her, makes his proposal. Be in my films, my company. I can make you famous. Again. Maybe he tells her about his plans, about Angell and Misty. All the horrors she thought she'd left behind. I didn't know how any of these scenarios were played out. Not for sure. But even if only some of it were true, you couldn't really blame Lucy for wanting to stop him.

"I think she just lost it, Max," I said, "And in her shoes I probably would have too."

"What about Lois?"

"Lois was a hospital porter. I don't know where she worked but I suspect they met when Lucy had her treatment. You can check. I don't care. Lois said that she was actually in the TV show but they cut her out. No one believed her. She seems to have been a lot more truthful than people gave her credit for."

"So the red dress was Stella." Max said, narrowing his eyes, "Yes. I mean I didn't know Lucy but that didn't seem quite real. You know, like dress-up."

"Yes," I said, "We all dress up to feel different about ourselves. Me more than most." Not that I'd done much of that lately. The wine was making me morose and I smiled at Max in his dress up of black jeans and purple shirt to show I was actually cheerful. I don't suppose he was fooled for a minute.

"I don't know what material Ben had on her," I said, "She said she'd taken it but it's all going to come out at the inquest, with the post mortem, you know…however things are cosmetically, I don't suppose it's that difficult to tell…" I trailed off.

People pretending to be other people, surrounding themselves with smoke and mirrors, camouflage and lies. Eddie Meyer, working undercover for the police. Was that all? I'd seen the incredible amounts of high grade Chas he'd been hovering up in the line of duty and remembered his threat about people he knew more violent than Fuller. Stuart, the closet maniac with his secret stash of weapons and photographs and God knows what going on in his head. Lois pretending to be a movie star with her mop and bucket. Then there was Ben Hammond, the consummate con artist, who almost made a smiling virtue of his vice. And Max here, who'd neglected to mention a criminal record, not that it mattered to me any more. Ironically, the only person who seemed to have remained genuine throughout was Lucy. The costume may have changed, sometimes spectacularly but she was, at least, an honest butterfly. All she had ever done was try to be herself – someone unremarkable. I wondered what she'd have said if I'd just straight out asked her if she'd killed Ben. She said she'd liked me and I believed her. But then there were those times when I remembered Tom and why she'd killed him. An unnecessary and spiteful thing to do and I remembered too the laughter in the dark on the pier and the look on her face, triumphant, mocking as she'd gazed down at me that lost Friday night. Maybe I was just kidding myself and she'd just straight up despised me. It was difficult to know how I could ever tell the difference again

Max interrupted the gloomy silence by getting to his feet and walking over to the table that held the candles. He leaned down and blew them out one by one and the lovely smell of hot wax filled the air.

"Hey!" You really don't mess about with my altar table and I prepared to launch into a serious ticking off. But he picked up the cards that were still on it and took the Star from my hand,

"Where's the rest of the pack?" he said. I changed my mind. Silently I offered him the velvet bag that held the others. He tipped them out and began to shuffle them, sliding the three stragglers back into the deck.

"The thing is, Jay," he said, "It actually doesn't matter in the end." His flat, broad fingers were as dextrous as a card sharp's and I watched intently as he cut and fanned. He suddenly stopped. "Oh, and by the way – Jay, JJ, what *is* your name?"

I smiled broadly, I couldn't help it. But I shook my head. Not in this lifetime, mate! Not for the dimples and the raised eyebrow, not for the eyes or the smile, or anything. It's not even going on my gravestone. He held my gaze for a moment then shrugged,

"OK. But it doesn't matter. It doesn't matter whether Lucy was your friend, or she wasn't, whether she was a girl or she wasn't, whether Ben was an arsehole or not, whether Fuller goes down for the lot or he doesn't. The only thing that matters is this." He spread the deck of cards out in one large hand, a world of infinite possibilities, each major arcana, each court card, each pip card a comfort, a counsel, an affirmation or a new idea. In many ways he was right.

"Pick a card." He said. Temptation is a wicked thing and I really shouldn't indulge Max. But then again…I put my 'yes, I'm indulging you face' on and slid one from the pack. I turned it over. It was The Lovers. Obviously it would be.

"OK." Max said and licked his lips. Those pleasure zones were fully awake now and prodding all the usual bits of me. I knew he was aware of this, damn him. I was not going to get pulled into moonlight and hand holding, hot, steamy, raunchy, yes I will she said yes… Oh, no. Not after everything. Not that dangling carrot. Not with Max Blackman.

"Marry me." He said suddenly.

Finally, after everything, shock settled on me with the shuddering air of an explosion. I looked at him for fully 10 seconds before I realised what he was up to. Then I burst out laughing and couldn't seem to stop. Max sat back in the chair with his arms folded across his chest looking offended. But I could see the twinkle in his eye. So it was game on again. And round one definitely goes to the sax man.

Oh and reader, you are fucking joking!

ACKNOWLEDGEMENTS

Thank you, one and all, I've done nothing without love. Thanks to mum for teaching me how to do this; thanks to Mark Ramsden for making life worthwhile and thanks to all the folk at Cutting Edge Press for liking weird stuff.

ABOUT THE AUTHOR

Ruth Ramsden lives and works on the South Coast, enjoying the bright sea views and penurious lifestyle she dreamed might be hers on becoming an artist. She is the illustrator and co-creator, with her partner Mark, of The Dark Tantra Tarot and has also collaborated with him on the book Radical Desire. She has been on the fetish scene for many years and continues to cultivate her collection of tattoos, along with many other deplorable habits.

Ruth likes Champagne, diamonds, Richart chocolates and Chanel No.5. Which is a pity really.